SCANDAL IN SKIBBEREEN

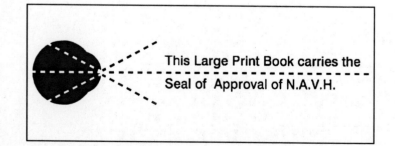

This Large Print Book carries the
Seal of Approval of N.A.V.H.

SCANDAL IN SKIBBEREEN

SHEILA CONNOLLY

WHEELER PUBLISHING
A part of Gale, Cengage Learning

GALE
CENGAGE Learning·

Farmington Hills, Mich • San Francisco • New York • Waterville, Maine
Meriden, Conn • Mason, Ohio • Chicago

GALE
CENGAGE Learning·

LIBRARY OF CONGRESS CATALOGING-IN-PUBLICATION DATA

Connolly, Sheila.
    Scandal in Skibbereen / by Sheila Connolly. — Large print edition.
        pages ; cm. — (A County Cork mystery) (Wheeler Publishing large print cozy mystery)
    ISBN 978-1-4104-7039-3 (softcover) — ISBN 1-4104-7039-3 (softcover)
    1. Americans—Ireland—Fiction. 2. Bars (Drinking establishments)—Fiction. 3. Lost works of art—Fiction. 4. Murder—Investigation—Fiction. 5. Cork (Ireland : County)—Fiction. 6. Large type books. I. Title.
    PS3601.T83S27 2014
    813'.6—dc23   2014016555

Published in 2014 by arrangement with The Berkley Publishing Group, a member of Penguin Group (USA) LLC, a Penguin Random House Company

Printed in the United States of America
1 2 3 4 5   18 17 16 15 14

ACKNOWLEDGMENTS

One of the challenges of writing about a real village in Ireland is deciding whether to invent characters or to borrow from the ones who actually exist. In this book there are some of each.

Thanks once again to Sergeant Tony McCarthy of the Skibbereen gardaí, who answered my questions about how the investigation of a crime that strongly resembles the one included here would proceed. Police matters in Ireland don't always resemble those in the United States, or what readers have come to expect in this age of *CSI* and digital evidence. You have to keep in mind the size of the places, which is reflected in the staffing of the garda stations. Skibbereen is a small town by American standards (with a population of about 2,700 people), and the garda station is small as well. When we met, I apologized to the sergeant for saddling the police force with a fictional crime wave, and I've given their fictional counterparts a lot of discretion in how they handle the events. If I've gotten it wrong, it is my error, and not due to the advice I was given.

Sheahan's Hotel in Leap has been operated by the same family for more than a century. The current proprietors were generous in sharing information about hiring regulations, food service restrictions, parking requirements, and so on — the nuts and bolts of running an Irish pub in a small village. I hope I have used those details well.

The Townsend family lived in the manor house overlooking the harbor in Leap from the seventeenth century until the later twentieth century, and the building is as I've described it. However, it is now a retreat house rather than a family home. I've tweaked a bit of the family's history for my purposes, although the founder of that family line, Richard Townsend, was a contemporary of the artist Anthony Van Dyck. I apologize to any Townsends who may read this book for muddling up their past.

If you're planning a trip to West Cork — and you should! — you'll find all the places mentioned, including Maura's cottage (now in ruins) and Bridget's just over the lane (still occupied), and the terrible road down the back of the hill. I have been thrilled by the warm responses from readers, who write to tell me that I've captured the spirit of Ireland and they're ready to get on a plane.

And of course, I have to thank my agent, Jessica Faust of Book-Ends, and my editor, Shannon Jamieson Vazquez (with whom I had many interesting discussions about Irish slang!), as well as the wonderful support network among mystery writers, including Sisters in Crime and the Guppies.

Is maith an scéalaí an aimsir.
Time is a good storyteller.

CHAPTER 1

Now that the high season had arrived, Sullivan's Pub was busier than Maura Donovan had ever seen it.

Of course, she'd only arrived from Boston about three months before, so she didn't have a lot to compare it to. Still, it was promising — it was the middle of the day, and she already had a nice crowd. It wasn't until later that the regulars would drift in and settle in their favorite spots, either at the bar or near the small peat fire, which Maura had found useful even in June. Plus, it seemed to please those tourists who wandered in: their eyes lit up at the sight of it. *Ah, a bit of Old Ireland,* she guessed they were thinking, and on a damp day like today they'd be glad of the warmth. There'd been quite a number of damp days lately.

But business was building. *Her* business. Maura still hadn't gotten used to the idea of owning a pub, though she'd worked in enough of them in her twenty-five years. She'd never owned anything of importance in her life. She and her gran had lived in a small apartment in South Boston as long as she could remember, and with Gran gone now, Maura had found that all their worldly possessions amounted to very little that she wanted to keep, except a few family photos and letters to and from her grandmother. Yet those had led her here to Leap, a tiny village on the south coast of Ireland, close to where her gran had been born, and landed her in the middle of a new and unexpected life.

Maura had to admit she was still worried that someone would find a reason to challenge Old Mick Sullivan's will, which had left her not only this ramshackle old pub and the building that housed it, but also his home a couple of miles away and the acreage that lay behind it. She'd gone from all but penniless to homeowner and publican practically overnight. It took getting used to. Not exactly what she'd planned for her life, but then, she hadn't really had a plan. Right now Maura was taking it slowly. She had no major changes mind, at least not yet. She'd cleaned the place up some — but not too much, as she was pretty sure the regulars came in because of the shabby, comfortable, and familiar setting. They didn't mind cobwebs in corners, the occasional puff of peat smoke when the wind blew down the chimney, or the dozens, if not hundreds, of postcards and newspaper clippings and posters and whatnot that decorated the walls.

"Gathering wool, are yeh, Maura?" Rose, her young employee, not yet seventeen, surprised Maura from her reverie.

"Maybe," Maura admitted. "I was just thinking — things *are* getting better, aren't they?"

"Bit by bit, they are. And it's not even full summer yet," Rose said. "With fairer weather, it'll pick up."

"I hope so." Maura silently counted the crowd. There was Old Billy Sheahan in his well-worn armchair next to the fire; two or three couples tucked into corners, looking happily settled there; and a few lone men who'd tipped a cap in greeting but seemed to prefer a quiet moment with their pint to conversation. She looked past the small clutch of patrons out the large windows facing the road and saw that it was raining again. Would it *ever* be sunny here? That usually didn't stop the regulars from dropping by, but it kept the tourists home, or maybe in Dublin where there was something else to do on a wet day, like visit museums, or so she'd heard. She hadn't seen anything of Dublin past the bus station. Maybe someday. Not so many museums in West Cork, although there was the Heritage Center in Skibbereen, not far away. But there was nothing she could do about the rain, except hope that it ended before she went broke.

Rose's father, Jimmy Sweeney, bustled in from the back of the building. Maura had more or less inherited him and his daughter as employees along with the pub. She'd quickly found that Rose was a lot more useful than Jimmy. "I'll be off to Skib for those supplies you wanted, eh, Maura?"

"Fine, Jimmy," Maura said. She'd worked with him long enough now to know that a journey to the nearest town, Skibbereen, often took him a couple of hours, even though it was less than ten minutes away, and half the time he returned without the supplies he'd promised but with a handful of excuses. Sometimes she wondered if Jimmy was doing it deliberately to punish her for inheriting the pub — she had a feeling that he'd had his hopes set on running it himself, although they'd never talked about it. But when she was feeling more kindly toward him, she just figured he was easily distracted. In this economy she didn't have the heart to let him go, and she was pretty sure he wouldn't push her far enough to fire him outright. At least Rose hadn't inherited her father's slipshod attitude: she was always eager to please and happy to take on more work.

So business had picked up a bit, on this wet afternoon, but it could still be better. Since she had some time on her hands, Maura was considering going over the pub's account books, something she had little liking or aptitude for, when the front door burst open and slammed against the wall. A blast of damp air preceded a woman who looked like a wet cat. Maura sized her up quickly: definitely not Irish. English maybe? American? Definitely urban. The thirty-something woman wore all black, including a fancy raincoat that seemed to be doing little to keep her dry. Her delicate shoes were soaked, and there was mud caked on one. "Goddamn lousy weather," the woman said, oblivious to anyone who might be listening — which was everyone in the place.

Oh, yeah, Maura thought. *Definitely American.* It wasn't uncommon to get American tourists in Leap, but they usually arrived wearing jeans and hiking boots, rather than what Maura suspected was a designer suit.

The woman spotted Maura behind the bar and stalked over to her. "Where am I?"

"Leap. In County Cork. Where did you want to be?" Maura said amiably.

"Thank God — you're American! Maybe I can get a straight answer from you. Everybody else around here has been giving me the most ridiculous directions. Like, 'Take the roundabout through the village and look for the old church,' like they can't tell I'm completely lost and barely know what a roundabout is, and I'm having enough trouble remembering to drive on the wrong side!" It was hard for Maura to tell whether the woman was spitting or just dripping.

"Why don't you sit down and dry off a bit, and maybe I can help you," Maura suggested.

"I need a drink," the woman said. "No, I don't. It's bad enough having to deal with that effing rental car, and the last thing I need is to get stopped by a cop now." Her eyes brightened when she spotted the espresso machine Maura had installed. "Please tell me that thing works."

"Sure does. What would you like?"

"Can you handle a grande cappuccino?"

"Of course."

"I'll do it," Rose volunteered. She seemed

16

fascinated by the stylishly dressed new-comer.

The woman shrugged off her wet coat and tossed it over a bar stool, then perched on the one next to it. "I must be insane . . ." she muttered, and Maura wasn't sure whether she was talking to Maura or to herself. "Why did I have to end up in the back of beyond rather than Nice or Venice?"

Rose slid the coffee across the bar and retreated a few steps. The woman grabbed it and swallowed, and a fleeting look of bliss crossed her face. "You may have just saved my life. Thank you. And I apologize for being so rude, but it's been a lousy few days. I think I'm in the right place, finally, though, so that's progress. So, tell me about this place. How big is it?"

"Leap?" Maura said. "What you see is about all there is. Population just over two hundred. A couple of paved roads, and a lot more that are sort of paved. You came in on the main highway. Were you on your way somewhere?"

"I really don't know." The woman looked around the room. Everybody quickly looked away, but it was obvious that they were interested. "Slow day around here, if I'm the best entertainment you've got. You know

17

this area well?"

"I've only been here a couple of months myself, so I wouldn't say I know it well," Maura told her. "But then, there's not a lot to know."

"What about the history of the place?"

Maura shook her head. "I don't know much, but I'm sure there are other people who'd be happy to help you with it. Are you looking for family history?"

The woman shook her head vehemently. "No way. I mean, more like who's who around here, who the property owners are or used to be, that kind of thing."

"Not my thing. Mick Nolan probably knows more. He works here, but he won't be in until later." Like Jimmy and Rose, Mick had come with the place, and more or less set his own schedule, although he always made sure to be around for the busiest times.

"Is he the owner?"

"No, I am," Maura said. She waited to see how the woman would react. Most people were surprised to see a twenty-something American woman running a pub in Ireland, and she was keeping an informal count of responses.

"You own this place?" The woman looked incredulous.

Chalk up one more in the "surprised" column. "I do." Maura tried not to sound defensive, but she knew how shabby the place must look to an outsider. She'd reacted the same way when she first saw it. Her first response had been along the lines of *What a dump,* but she'd been jet-lagged and sad and kind of lost. The jet-lagged part was long gone, and she was working on the rest.

"Oh. Well, good for you. You seem kind of young to be in charge, though. You're, what, twenty-five?"

"Yes," Maura said. "I inherited the place."

"Ah. Well, don't mind me — my mouth is running ahead of my brain right now. I'm just tired and frustrated and wet — and apparently caffeine deprived. Can I get another cup?"

"Sure. Rose, you want to do the honors again?"

"I'll be happy to." Rose set about making a second cappuccino.

Maura turned back to the woman. "I'm Maura Donovan, born and raised in South Boston, now living in Knockskagh, which is an even smaller townland up the hill a couple of miles from here. What's your story?"

"I'm really making a lousy first impression, aren't I?" The woman extended a hand. "I'm Althea Melville. From New York City."

Of course. Maura should've guessed New York, based on the clothes. "I take it you're not here to admire the scenery."

Althea shivered. "This is so not my kind of scenery. I hate the country; too . . . muddy. And there are cows."

Maura waited a moment for Althea to explain what she was doing in a place she clearly disliked, but the woman didn't add anything. And Maura didn't want to pry; she was learning that it was better to let people find their own way into saying what they wanted to say.

It wasn't long before Althea did just that. Her eyes darted around the room, and then her gaze returned to Maura. She leaned forward over the bar. "Can we talk?" she said in a low voice. "Privately? Maybe you can help me."

Maura glanced at Rose. "Think you can handle things?"

"Not to worry," Rose responded quickly. "You two go on, then."

Maura slid out from behind the bar and led Althea toward a table and chairs at the end of the room opposite the fireplace — it might be chilly but would definitely be more

20

private. "This way."

Althea gathered up her raincoat and bag and followed Maura. She looked at the chair with distaste, then spread her raincoat over the seat before sitting down.

Maura bristled at her rudeness, but she had to admit the chair had seen better days.

"How much do you know about the local gentry?" Althea began.

Maura stifled a laugh. If there was gentry around, she certainly didn't know them. "You mean rich people? The kind with yachts and stuff?"

Althea shook her head. "No, I mean the old Anglo-Irish families, the ones who owned everything and let the local peasants live on their land."

"Oh, *those* gentry. Sorry, still don't know any of 'em. If there are any around these days. Like I told you, I haven't been here very long. You should talk to Mick, since he grew up here. Or maybe Old Billy," Maura added.

"Old Billy?" Althea said.

"Yeah, the old guy by the fire." Maura nodded in his direction.

Althea glanced his way. "Why should I talk to him?"

"Because he's well past eighty and he's

lived here all his life and he knows every-body."

"Is he still, uh, all there?"

"Do you mean, is he senile? No way. His mind is sharp, even if he does spend a lot of time thinking about the past, if you know what I mean. But he loves to talk, especially to attractive young women, which in his case is pretty much anyone under seventy."

"I bet the tourists love him," Althea said drily.

Maura bit back a sharp remark: Billy was a local institution and on his way to being a friend, but Althea was right about his ap-peal. "They do, and he makes a point of entertaining them. Everybody leaves happy," she said shortly. "So, do you want to talk to him or not?"

"Okay, if you think he'll really be able to help. Would you ask him to come talk to us? But not here — somewhere where we won't be overheard."

"There's Sheahan's, the inn across the street. You could snag a corner table there, and you won't be bothered. But why all the secrecy? And why do you need me?" Maura asked.

"Because I have a feeling I'll need you as an interpreter," Althea answered. "You know, like a go-between or whatever you want to call it. I don't want to end up insulting someone, which I seem to keep doing. Please?"

Maura considered. It didn't seem right to leave the pub at the busiest time of day — but since "busiest" meant maybe ten people, Rose could handle it, especially if her father managed to find his way back from Skibbereen or Mick came in. Besides, Maura had to admit she was curious. What could have led this woefully unprepared city girl to the wilds of West Cork?

"Okay. I need to get something to eat anyway, and I'm sure Billy would appreciate a meal. You're buying."

"Of course. Thank you. Can we go now?"

"We can start. It may take a while to get Billy out of his chair and moving."

Althea stood up. "Then let's do it."

CHAPTER 2

Maura led the way back to the other end of the room. It looked like Rose had things well in hand. No sign of Jimmy, which didn't surprise her. No sign of Mick yet either, which was more surprising: he was usually fairly prompt, at least by Irish standards, which were more flexible than she was used to. She checked her watch: it was only five thirty. She had to admit that, after a dark spring, she was glad that the days had lengthened at last. At school she had never quite figured out how the changes of the sun's path translated to hours of daylight, but she enjoyed the results now. She made a beeline to Old Billy, who was holding forth from his favorite spot to a rapt audience of a tourist family of three. Maura couldn't be sure whether they were fascinated by his tales, however, or completely bewildered by his thick accent. Thank goodness she'd grown up with her gran's accent, but she knew it could be hard for outsiders to understand.

"Can I get you anything?" Maura asked the family, trying to be helpful.

They looked happy for the interruption. "No, no, thanks, we really should get back on the road . . . thank you so much, Mr. . . . uh. It was great to meet you. Come on, gang, time to get moving!" The father swept his small brood together and hustled them out of the pub, and Maura turned to Old Billy.

"Ah, Maura, if I'd had only a few more moments, sure and they would have bought me a pint." He smiled to soften his statement.

"I've got a better offer for you, Billy. This nice American lady here has offered to buy you dinner if you'll tell her some of your tales."

"At the inn, will it be?" he asked, eyeing Althea appreciatively.

"Sure, fine, at the inn," Althea said impatiently. Maura sent her a look, trying to tell her to slow down. Billy took his own time, and he'd earned that right after eighty-some years.

"Ah, that's grand," Billy said. "Give me a bit to get meself out of my chair here — my old bones don't work as fast as they once did."

"No hurry, Billy. I'll just tell Rose we're off," Maura assured him.

Leaving Althea pacing while Billy extricated himself from the depths of the sprung chair, Maura went back to the bar to have a word with Rose.

"What's that about, then?" Rose whispered.

"The lady in black, whose name, by the way, is Althea, wants to know something about the local gentry, and I figured Billy would be her best source, since I don't know anything. But she wants me along anyway, to help with Billy, so I'll be going too. Your father should be back soon, and Mick said he'd be in at six. If you have any problems just ring me on my mobile, all right?"

Rose smiled. "I think I can manage well enough. You'll be having supper at Sheahan's?"

"We will — Althea said she'd buy. I wonder if she has a place to stay yet. I hear Sheahan's rooms are all booked."

"Somehow I don't think the likes of her would feel at home upstairs there. Maybe you could send her over to Skib."

Good idea, Maura thought. Skibbereen,

population close to three thousand, might not be large by New York standards, but it was the biggest town around and had a decent hotel. Leap didn't have much to offer, beyond Sheahan's and a few bed-and-breakfasts. "I'll wait and see what she wants. Thanks, Rose. I'll be back after we eat."

Maura turned to find that Billy was now on his feet, if a bit unsteady — from age, not from drink. Billy could nurse a single pint longer than anyone she'd seen. Althea had taken a step back, probably because she'd gotten a whiff of Billy. He was a good and kind man, but Maura doubted if his clothes had been cleaned within the last year. Or longer.

"Are you ready, then, Billy?" Maura asked.

"That I am. And it will be my pleasure to escort two such lovely ladies across the way."

Now that it was summer, traffic on the main road had increased by a hundred percent, which meant a car passed about once every thirty seconds. Still, it took Billy some time to cross the wide road, and Maura and Althea flanked him to be sure no hurrying car came too close. It took another minute or so for Billy to make his slow way up the steps in front of Sheahan's door, and then he proudly led the way into the bar area there. He raised a hand to the woman behind the bar, who smiled at the sight of him.

"Well, if it isn't Cousin Billy! I thought you'd grown roots in your seat at Sullivan's!" she said. "Maura, your profits will drop like a stone in a well with him here."

"Don't worry, Ann, I'll be sure to take him back over again. Can we have some supper by the fire there?" Maura waved toward a cozy corner.

"Sure, till the lads start coming for the darts later."

"We'll be out of your way by then."

"Will you be needing menus?" the woman asked.

"Uh, please?" Althea said, looking none too thrilled at her shabby surroundings.

Maura made sure that Billy was settled in the seat nearest the fire. She let Althea take the corner seat, then settled in the one closer to the main room. Ann returned and handed out single-page laminated menus. Althea took one look and winced; Maura ignored her. When Ann returned, bringing a foaming pint for Billy without asking, she asked, "What can I bring yeh to eat?"

"I'll be having the lamb dinner," Billy said. Maura asked for the same.

Althea still looked pained. "Could I have just a salad, please? And a glass of water?"

"No problem. Maura, what'll you be drinking?"

"A glass of Murphy's, please." Maura had a secret preference for Guinness, but since Murphy's was brewed in nearby Cork city, she felt she had to show some regional loyalty, at least occasionally.

"Grand. And you, miss?" she asked Althea.

"Oh, just water for me. And could you put a slice of lemon in it?"

"Lemon it is. I'll bring you some bread while you wait for your meals." She left to go through a door behind the bar, where the sound of clanking pots emanated from the kitchen behind. Maura knew that Ann ran both the front of the house, when her husband wasn't around, and the kitchen, with the help of two young servers, although she had no clue how she managed it all. She returned quickly with a plate of brown bread and a small crock of butter.

"I'll bring yer drinks now," Ann said, returning a few minutes later to set the glasses down in front of Maura and Althea. "Half a moment with the food, then."

"No hurry," Maura said. There seldom *was* much hurry around Ireland, she'd found. Maybe things in Dublin moved a bit quicker. Maybe someday she'd find out, if she had the time and the money and was

29

sure that someone would keep an eye on Sullivan's while she was gone.

Billy raised his glass to his companions. "May your glass be ever full." He took a long swallow of his pint and looked very happy. Maura couldn't blame him: free drink, free food, and the company of two women a third his age — as far as Maura could tell, this was Billy's idea of heaven.

Althea leaned forward. "Look, can we . . ."

She was interrupted by Ann, returning with their plates. Ann set the more heavily laden ones in front of Billy and Maura: several slices of roast lamb, resting on a bed of mashed potatoes, the whole slathered with brown gravy. Then she set a plate heaped high with mixed greens in front of Althea, turned, and headed back to the kitchen.

"Did you know that your meal is called 'mixed leaves' over here?" Maura said with a straight face.

"It doesn't surprise me," Althea muttered. "Now, Billy, what I wanted . . ."

Ann reappeared bearing a bowl heaped with boiled potatoes and another overflowing with cooked carrots and kale. "All set?" she asked, then left without waiting for an answer. Billy reached for the bowl of potatoes.

Althea was staring with horror at the laden table. "You've got to be kidding. They serve potatoes with a side of potatoes here?"

"They do," Maura said, taking the bowl from Billy. "You know, they're good for you, unless you load on the butter — no cholesterol, good roughage, and plenty of vitamin C. A lot of Irish people survived on them for years, with not much else except a bit of milk and butter. Are you good, Billy?"

"I'm grand, thanks. It's always a treat to eat here at the inn. Although I'd be pleased if you'd start offering food at Sullivan's."

"What, so you wouldn't have to walk as far?" Maura laughed. "One step at a time, Billy. I'm still sorting out how the place works, and I haven't even seen full tourist season yet. But I'm thinking about it."

There was a minute of silence as all three dug into their meals. Maura forked up a piece of lamb. It wasn't gourmet, but it tasted good.

Not surprisingly, Althea finished her salad first. "Can we talk now? Before this place gets too noisy?"

Maura looked around the room: there were maybe ten people in it, mostly men, in twos and threes, all raptly watching some sports event on one of the two high-def televisions, tuned to different stations.

Nobody was paying their corner the slightest attention. "How about you start by telling us what you want to know."

Althea took a moment to gather her thoughts and looked back and forth between Billy, happily chewing his way through his generous portion of lamb, and Maura. "I've been trying to track down rich families in this area from way back, most of whom aren't even around anymore, which I probably should have guessed if I'd had any time to think about it, and I'm running out of time and this is the last place left on my list." She looked around and signaled to Ann at the bar, who walked over to their table. "I need a drink. You have Johnnie Walker?"

"I do."

"Make it a double."

Billy was still absorbed by his food, but Maura could tell that Althea was wound up tight about something or other. She forced herself to wait and let Althea tell her story her own way.

Ann approached, deposited a glass on a napkin in front of Althea, and retreated silently.

Althea picked up the glass and downed half of it, then sighed. "Better. All right, here goes. I work in a midsize museum in

New York" — she mentioned a name that Maura didn't recognize, even though Althea seemed to expect her to — "and over the past year or two I've worked on a team that's been putting together a major exhibition, called Portraiture and Social Class, which is supposed to open in October. It's a really interesting subject. We're juxtaposing commissioned portraits of the nobility with contemporaneous depictions of peasantry and following the evolution of each over a few centuries." Althea paused when she realized that both Billy and Maura were staring blankly at her. "Okay, I'll cut to the chase. Since it's already June, the exhibit is pretty much locked in now, and the catalog is ready to go to press. In fact, it's already late." Althea took a smaller swallow from her drink. "Then, about two weeks ago, I got a call from an appraiser friend of mine who works at an auction gallery in New Jersey."

"New Jersey? That's near Philadelphia, isn't it, now? I was there once," Billy said, unruffled.

Billy had been to the United States? That was news to Maura — she would have bet that he had never been more than fifty miles from where he was born. The man was full of surprises.

"So what was that about?" Maura said.

"Well, every so often they hold an open house, invite people to bring in their treasures and have an appraiser take a look at them. Kind of like *Antiques Roadshow,* on television?"

"I've seen it," Maura said. Usually a bunch of clueless people who brought in Aunt Minnie's chamber pot and wondered if it was worth thousands.

"I've seen it on the BBC here," Billy added proudly.

"So you get the general idea. Great," Althea resumed. "Anyway, my friend, Nate Reynolds, called me and said, 'There's something you should see.' And I said, 'Can it wait?' And he said, 'No, it can't.' So I went out to Jersey to take a look at what had him so excited, and I saw what he meant. A woman had brought in a small painting, wrapped up in a blanket, and said she'd inherited it from her great-aunt but had no clue what it was. Nate had a pretty good idea, but he wanted me to take a look at it to confirm it. It was a seventeenth-century oil sketch of a young man, probably around thirty, and I'd stake my life that it's an original Van Dyck!"

Althea looked expectantly at her audience, but Maura and Billy merely stared blankly back at her. Maura made a timeout sign. "Okay, I get it that you're excited, but my high school didn't teach art history, so you're going to have to tell us who this Van Dyck guy is and why he's important."

"Really? You don't know . . . ? Okay, fine. Here's the short course: Anthony Van Dyck was a Flemish painter in the early seventeenth century. In 1620 he went to London and worked for a couple of English kings, then he went to Italy." She paused. Billy was engrossed in using a chunk of potato to swab up the last of the gravy on his plate, and Maura still had no idea what she was talking about. "Basically, Van Dyck was a very popular portraitist who painted a whole lot of English nobility, including some of the Anglo-Irish nobility here. I talked to Dorothy Ryan, the woman who'd brought in the painting, and she said her grandmother and great-aunt were from Ireland and came to New York in the 1930s or 1940s. The thing is, the great-aunt never told anybody about the painting — Dorothy found it hidden in an old suitcase under her great-aunt's bed when she died. She'd had a simple will leaving everything she owned — which wasn't much — to her great-niece, and it didn't mention the painting. Luckily Dorothy opened the suitcase, rather than just throwing it out, and found the painting. She took it home then more or less forgot about it until she saw the ad about this appraisal event and figured it might be fun to take it in and see what the experts had to say."

Maura was beginning to see where the woman was going with her explanation. "So you're trying to track down where the painting came from? Why did you figure it had to be Ireland?"

"Well, the old lady had lived a very dull life once she got to New York, and I couldn't see any way she could have laid her hands on a painting like this, or even why she would want it, much less keep it for years. I checked to see if it was stolen, but nothing came close in the registry for stolen artworks. So I figured the best way to find out was to look in Ireland. I know Van Dyck worked here in this part of Ireland, so that fit."

"But if this Dorothy's got the painting, why are you *here*? In Leap, I mean."

Althea leaned forward and lowered her voice. "Because I think what Dorothy has is just a preliminary sketch for a full portrait, one that's been out of sight for years, maybe even centuries. A lost Van Dyck would be *huge* news in the art world. And I want to find it." She sat back triumphantly and drained her glass.

CHAPTER 3

Maura glanced at Billy, who was beaming, but whether it was because his belly was full with a good meal and a free pint or because he was following Althea's story was not clear. "Okay, let's see if I've got this right," Maura said. "You think this little painting you saw in New Jersey might be connected to a bigger one by the same important artist, and that one might be in Ireland, if it exists at all. In fact, you think it's somewhere near here, which is why you're here. Why do you care?" Maura asked.

"Because finding a long-lost painting by a master would be a really big deal, and because frankly, my job's on the line. You know what the economy's like. I've been at the museum for eight years now, ever since I got my master's degree, but once the grant funding for this exhibit runs out, I'm out of a job. And believe me, there aren't a whole lot of jobs for art historians specializing in seventeenth-century European paintings these days. So I figured if I could find the original painting and talk the owners into lending it to the museum for the show, and if I publicized it right, the museum would have to keep me on. Or at least I'd have a better chance of getting another job, with something big like that on my résumé."

Ann came over to the table. "Everything all right?" she asked.

"You haven't lost yer touch, Ann Sheahan — it was grand," Billy said, his hands folded over his belly.

"Sweet, anybody?" Ann asked. "Billy, I know you like the apple crumble."

"That I do. Will you join me, ladies?"

"Sure, why not?" Maura said, as Althea shook her head. "And bring Althea some coffee, will you?" Maura added. When Althea started to protest, Maura said, "The drunk driving laws around here are pretty serious, and you've still got to find a place to stay tonight."

"Oh. Right," Althea grumbled.

"Straightaway," Ann said and turned to head for the kitchen.

When she was out of earshot, Maura turned back to Althea. "So that's why you wanted to talk to Billy here about the local gentry."

"Exactly. I was hoping that whoever they are, assuming there are any and they're still alive, they might still own the painting. If it exists."

"Why here?" Maura repeated.

"This wasn't my first stop. Look, the woman who originally had the painting didn't leave much information behind, and Dorothy wasn't much help. She said her grandmother had been tight-lipped about just about everything, especially her life back in Ireland, and she didn't even remember the great-aunt."

Funny, Maura thought, *Gran was the same way — didn't talk about where she had come from, which was why I wasn't ready for what I found in Leap.*

Althea was still talking. "I did ask a friend to check censuses for the sisters and he found them in New York, but all the records said about where they came from was 'County Cork,' which as you know is kind of vague. Same with the ship's records. At least I knew I had the right family, but there's a lot of County Cork. Both Jane — that's the great-aunt I mentioned — and her sister identified themselves as 'servant' in the records, so I'm guessing they must have worked in the big house wherever the painting was, or at least that's what I've assumed. I've already visited a couple of dead ends. This place is my last hope, and I thought it was so out of the way that it was conceivable that a family could have had a major painting and nobody would have noticed. I know it's an incredible long shot, but I figured it could be worth it. Yours was the first pub I came to in Leap, and I hoped somebody might know something about any manor houses around here that might fit the bill."

Billy finally focused on the conversation. "Ah, you've come to the right place, young lady," he said, rubbing his hands together in anticipation.

Althea turned to Billy. "I have?" She was interrupted by Ann depositing dishes of apple crumble drenched in heavy cream in front of Billy and Maura. Althea all but shuddered at the sight. "My God, is that cream?"

"It is. This is a dairy region," Maura said, picking up her spoon.

"What's the heart attack rate around here?"

"Don't know," Maura said, digging in. She used the time spent chewing to try to figure out the angles. Althea said this was about

41

her job, and uncovering a lost artwork, but there had to be money involved. If this painter was such hot stuff, a new old painting would be worth a lot of money. Maybe Althea worked for a gallery that had its eye on selling the painting somewhere down the road. Maybe she was setting up an art heist. Maybe she was just plain crazy or obsessed. Who knew? Maura wondered what Billy's take on Althea was — from what she'd seen in the pub, he seemed to be a fair judge of character, even if he did usually give strangers the benefit of the doubt.

Billy took his time scraping the last of the cream from his bowl. Then he looked squarely at Althea. "Tell me, will any money change hands?"

Maura cheered silently, glad he'd come up with the same question she had.

Althea looked at him for a couple of seconds, as if trying to decide which story to pitch. Finally she answered, "Not for me. But maybe, possibly, for the painting's owners. I promise you, though, this isn't about the money. I'm looking for the attention I'll get if I bring home the painting, not the cash. But that said, yes, *if* I find the painting, and *if* the owners want to part with it, then it's possible that they could do very well, even in the current market for artworks, and they might be grateful to me for making it happen. But I'm not counting on it."

"And what would you be meaning by 'very well'?" Billy pressed.

Althea looked down at the table, avoiding their eyes. "The last known Van Dyck to come to auction was a small self-portrait, a few years ago. It sold for over thirteen million dollars."

Billy didn't seem surprised. "But whatever such a sale might bring, it would go to the owners, not to yourself?"

"Like I said, I might get something like a finder's fee, but I'm not working under contract to find it, or anything like that. I'm running around Ireland — and paying out of my own pocket, I might add — to save my career, because I really like what I do, even when it brings me to godforsaken places like this. Is that enough for you?"

Billy looked at Maura, and she could swear his eyes twinkled. "Then I'd be happy to help a fine young lady like yourself. You'd be wanting to take a look at the Townsends."

"The Townsends?" Althea repeated.

"The line goes back to the Townsends of Castletownsend, not far from here, in the seventeenth century — just about the time you're after," Billy said proudly.

43

"Hang on — let me get something to write on." Althea rummaged through her large and expensive-looking handbag and pulled out a leather-bound notebook. "Townsends of Castletownsend, you said?"

Billy continued, "The founder, Colonel Richard, served as a soldier under Oliver Cromwell and handed him the keys to Cork city when they won the battle of Knockoness. He bought quite a bit of land over the years. In the end they held a good deal of land around here, more than three thousand acres, I hear tell, in the early days. That'd be Irish acres, not regular ones, so it's more like two-thirds again as big. And they kept adding to it. Good thing he did, for I'm told the colonel had nine sons. I could tell you about . . ."

Maura stared at Billy. She'd had no idea he had information like this stored in his head, or what half of it meant. "Billy, how do you know all this?"

He winked at her. "I wasn't there for the ceremony, if that's what yer thinking. But we learned a bit about it in school. And the Townsends were well-known hereabouts. Yer gran worked at the big house, before she married and yer da came along."

Before Maura could follow up on this unexpected piece of information, Althea

44

interrupted. "Where would the biggest and best manor house have been?"

The glint in Billy's eyes took on a steely cast. When he spoke, it was, if anything, more slowly than before. "Well, let me think . . . There'd be Derry House, near Clonakilty. The old house was damaged during the Troubles, but some of it still stands. Or Roury House, not far from there, but that's not very large. There's a few other homes scattered about, in Bunlahan, Brade, Union Hall, Ballincolla . . ."

Maura realized that Billy was toying with Althea, as payback for her insistence, and sat back to enjoy the show. Althea looked ready to burst, and finally Billy took pity on her. "Of course, the big house is Mycroft House."

"And where would that be?" Althea demanded.

"No more than half a mile from where we sit, just over the harbor there."

"I've never heard of it," Maura said. "But then, I'm still new here, and I don't hang around with those kinds of people."

"Is anybody living there now?" Althea said, ignoring Maura altogether.

"Ah, it's a bit of a sad story, it is. It might go down better with a bit of whiskey . . ." He looked hopefully at Althea.

Althea gestured to Ann. "Can you give this guy whatever he wants to drink?"

Ann gave Althea a hard look, and Maura guessed she wasn't used to being ordered around under her own roof. "Billy, what's your pleasure?" Ann asked.

"A drop of whiskey, with the hot water, if you don't mind."

"No problem. Maura, you want anything else?" Ann pointedly ignored Althea, not that the woman seemed to notice.

"No, I'm set. I need to be getting back to Sullivan's anyway."

"So it's a whiskey for you, Billy. Won't be a moment."

"Are there still Townsends at Mycroft House that I could talk to?" Althea asked eagerly.

"There are, in a way. The family lived there the year round until the Great War, and only on holidays after that. But the one — William, it was — he came back to stay. He was a good landlord and a fair man. His daughter lives there still. Eveline, that is. She must be near ninety now, rattling around in that big old house."

"Is she the owner now?"

"And how would I be knowing that?" Billy asked. "She has a nephew, great-nephew, something like that, who looks after her affairs, but I can't say who holds the deed."

"Does he live there too?"

"Nah, he's a Dublin man now, comes down from time to time to see to things."

"Do you know how I can reach him?"

Ann set the glass of hot whiskey in front of Billy — and set the bill for dinner in front of Althea.

Billy took a long sip of his drink. "How would I come to have his number? I'm only a poor man from the village."

"Did this Eveline marry?" Althea pushed on relentlessly. "Or have children?"

"She never did. She used to drive around the lanes — I remember she had a sure hand with a pony cart — but she never wanted to leave the place, and she never found a match that suited her."

"Is she still, uh" — Althea fumbled for words — "in full possession of her faculties?"

"You mean, is she past remembering what it is you want to know?" Billy said sharply.

"I guess that's what I mean."

"Then you'd best find out for yourself."

Billy seemed annoyed now, and Maura thought it might be a good time to beat a retreat back to Sullivan's. "Althea, I'll see Billy back across the street while you settle up."

"What? Oh, right. I'll follow you over in a few — I'd like to talk to you some more."

"Billy, you ready to go?" Maura asked.

Billy drained his glass. "As soon as I find my way out of this seat, I am." He accepted Maura's offer of a hand to steady him.

Outside the sky was still light — it was near the summer solstice, and it didn't turn full dark until after ten. Maura accompanied Billy back to the door of Sullivan's.

"Are you coming in, Billy?"

"I think not. I seldom have such a meal of an evening, and it's made me ready for my chair at home. That young woman, she's a piece of work, isn't she?"

"She is. Did you tell her the truth?"

"About Eveline Townsend? Sure and I did. I used to share the odd word or two with Eveline, when we met on the road. She was never so full of herself that she wouldn't talk to the likes of me. But she doesn't go out now, and I'm told her mind's more in the past than in the present. I doubt Althea will have any luck with her, even if she gets past the gatekeepers."

"The what?"

"There's a housekeeper and her husband, the O'Briens — they live in to see to Eveline's needs. They've been there for years, but they don't take any nonsense from stray visitors. I was going to warn her, but I think it's best she find that out on her own, if she goes calling at the house."

"Do you think it's possible the painting exists? Could it be there?"

Billy shrugged. "That's not for me to say. I never set foot in the place, not even by way of the back door. Yer gran might have known. I'll see you tomorrow, Maura Donovan."

"Of course, Billy. Good night."

Maura watched as he made his careful way to the far end of the building, where he lived in two rooms on the ground floor. Once he was safely in the door, she turned and pulled open the door to Sullivan's. Things looked under control, with maybe fifteen people scattered around the room. Mick was behind the bar and looked up when she came in, but he was deep in conversation with two men she sort of recognized. She came around the end of the bar and stashed her bag underneath, then started collecting glasses and taking orders, greeting the regulars she recognized along the way. More of them than a month ago, she was happy to see. The longer days were bringing out the locals as well as the tourists. What's more, somehow the rain had stopped while she wasn't looking, and that would help too.

Althea came in a few minutes later and dropped onto a bar stool. She eyed Mick, behind the bar, with obvious appreciation. "Who's that?" she asked, when Maura came over to talk to her.

"Mick Nolan. He works here, part-time."

"Single?"

"Yes."

"You aren't . . . ?" Althea left the question unfinished, watching Maura's expression.

"Nope. He works for me, period. You want anything else to drink?" Maura asked. She wondered what more Althea could want from her, now that Billy had told her what she wanted to know.

"No, thanks. Like you said, I'm supposed to be driving. Any idea where I can find a room for the night? Or next several nights? I was going to try the inn but I don't think Ann Sheahan liked me much."

"What did you expect? You were kind of rude to her. Her husband's family has been running that place for over a century. You can't treat her like the hired help."

"How was I supposed to know?"

"Well, if you want people to help you, it might be a good idea to be nice to them."

"I know, I'm making a mess of this. All I can say is, I'm at the end of my rope, I guess. I'll try to do better. Is Billy's information accurate?"

Maura shrugged. "Got me. I'm the new kid, remember? Probably — he's a pretty honest guy — but you were kind of rude to him too, so he might have mixed up a few details."

Althea sighed. "I'm not handling this very well, am I? I just seem to go around offending everyone without meaning to. Are you pissed at me too?"

"Not really. But I think you need to take it down a notch. This isn't New York."

"I can't blame you for being skeptical, I guess. Here I come out of nowhere with this ridiculous story about a lost artwork, and then I expect instant answers so I can go home and impress the art world. It's pretty unlikely, isn't it?"

"It is. But this is Ireland, and even in a couple of months I've learned that unlikely things happen here a lot. I wouldn't give up yet."

"If you say so. Where are the best places to stay around here?"

Maura herself had first stayed at the Keohanes' place down the road when she arrived, but Althea definitely didn't seem the B&B type. "Depends on what you're willing to spend. There's a nice modern conference center in Rosscarbery — you probably drove past it on your way here."

"How far?"

"Maybe half an hour, by the main road. Or you might try the West Cork Hotel — maybe they'll have a room for you."

"And where's that? Because I really don't feel like driving when it gets dark."

"It's in Skibbereen."

"Where?"

"It's the next town from here. Didn't you get a map when you picked up the car?"

"Yes, but I've barely had time to look at it. And I can't make the GPS work because I don't even know what address to put in. So, please, tell me, how do I find Skibbereen?"

At least she'd asked nicely. "Go out and keep following that road there." Maura pointed out the window toward the right. "Follow it for about five minutes — you'll go past a gas station called Connolly's on the right — and you'll come to a small roundabout. When you come to it, go straight out the other side. The hotel will be on your left, and there's parking behind it. You can't miss it. It's no more than ten minutes from here."

"Got it. Thanks, Maura — if this works out, I'll owe you one."

"And I'll collect, believe me." Maura

laughed.

Mick came over as Althea went out the door. "Who's that?"

"A pushy American on a crazy search for . . . well, I won't say right now because it's kind of a secret. But if she's right, it might liven things up a bit around here."

CHAPTER 4

Maura couldn't stop thinking about Althea's story, even the next morning. What the heck did the woman think she was doing here? She must have some smarts if she held down a job in New York, but she shows up in Leap with a crazy story about a lost painting and doesn't even know where to start looking? Either Althea was dumber than she looked, had some plan she hadn't talked about, or . . . she was on a legitimate treasure hunt. Maura stopped to consider that angle. It might be good for business, she decided. Assuming Althea said it was okay to spread the word, she could put together some kind of evening at Sullivan's where everybody who had any information (or thought they did) could get together and pool their resources, or at least spend an interesting evening talking about the possibilities. The idea cheered Maura up.

Say Althea's crazy theory was true. Would

a discovery like that bring people to Leap? For a day? A week? Maura had been working at the pub since early spring. While business had been steady, had even picked up a little now that summer had arrived, it was still hard to cover the costs of paying for four employees including herself, even if their hours added up to less than full-time each. So far there had been nothing left over for improvements to the place.

Still, it was a better place than it had been when she'd arrived, Maura was proud to say. And she was in a better place personally too. She'd shown up homeless and jobless, not quite penniless but not far from it, with no close family and no idea what she was going to do with her life. Now she had a house and a pub that she owned outright, including the liquor license. She knew the place had potential, and she'd seen enough pubs — from behind the bar, not in front — to have a pretty good idea what it took.

Sullivan's had been around for decades, but the prior owner, Mick Sullivan, had let it go downhill, until only his small circle of faithful friends — and the occasional confused tourist — had kept it going. Maura didn't pretend that she could turn it into a wildly successful place. There simply weren't enough people, either living here or passing through, to make that possible. But she believed there was room for improvement. It was cleaner and better lit than it had been in the dark last days of winter — amazing what a few higher-watt lightbulbs could do for a place. She had installed the espresso machine that had been hidden in the basement, and that had drawn in a few more customers, especially women. She was toying with the idea of serving food, although she'd heard rumors that the regulations for that were scary and to meet them she'd probably have to make some expensive changes, which at the moment she couldn't afford. Not happening this year.

But it was nice to have a sense of purpose. In fact, if she admitted it, it was nice getting to know people and being able to greet them by name and know what their "usual" was. And it was nice being her own boss for a change. At least nobody could fire her. And if the pub went under, she would have no one to blame but herself. Plus she'd still own the license and the property, which were worth something.

She checked her watch: almost eleven, which was her preferred opening time. Old Mick had been kind of casual about keeping to official hours. Maura thought that she should impose some order, and if local people saw that she was open regularly at the same time every day, they might stop by for a quick pint or a cup of coffee or tea. Maybe. She came around the bar to open the front door, only to find Skibbereen garda Sean Murphy standing there, his expression serious, his hand raised to knock.

"Hey, Sean — were you coming in?"

"Good morning, Maura. I'm afraid I've come on official business."

"Okay," Maura answered warily. "Official business" rarely meant good news. "Can I offer you a cup of coffee? Or are you in a hurry?"

"I've been up since first light, so coffee would be grand. I don't think the news will mean much to you, except that you may have a bigger crowd come evening. There's been a death."

Maura loaded the espresso machine for a single cup and waited while it brewed. "Who was it? Anyone I'd know?" she asked when she slid a cup of coffee in front of him.

Sean ducked his head and stared at the foam in his cup. "Doubtful — it's a fellow by the name of Seamus Daly. He worked part of the time at the old Townsend estate, over the road. Kind of an odd-job man and gardener. He is — was — there's no good way to say it — kind of simple. He was a good worker, very careful and thorough, but he was . . . limited."

Yesterday she hadn't known the Townsend estate existed, and now Sean was telling her about a death there? "I get what you mean. How did he die?"

"Struck in the head with his own shovel. He was found on the lawn by the house-keeper's husband this morning — he saw him out the front window, just lyin' there. He must have been out there much of the night."

So it was murder. "I'm sorry." It seemed the right thing to say, even though she'd never known the man. "Do you have any idea who could have done something like that?"

"That we do not. But an investigation's already under way — my sergeant is there now, the chief superintendent has called a meeting for early this afternoon, and the forensic folk are on their way. I've got to get back in a minute."

"So why are you here, Sean?"

"I wanted to ask if you've seen many people from elsewhere here in the last few days."

Ah. Clearly Sean thought — or hoped — that the killer had come from somewhere

58

else. Ireland had a very low murder rate, particularly outside of the cities, and she couldn't blame Sean Murphy for hoping that the killer wasn't someone he knew. "You do know I don't exactly know everybody around here, right? So I can't always tell a local from a visitor. Plus we've been getting a trickle of tourists — there was a family in yesterday in the afternoon, and a few others. But . . ." She wondered if she should tell Sean about Althea. She had trouble seeing Althea, with her fancy New York clothes, bashing someone's head in with a shovel, but Sean should be told about her. Maybe Althea had an accomplice who'd hidden in the car or checked out one of the other pubs while Althea had tried to charm her way to some useful information.

"There was someone here yesterday . . ." Maura began, and she gave Sean the rundown on Althea. "Yesterday a woman named Althea Melville came in, and Billy and I had supper with her over at Sheahan's. Ann served us — she'll remember. Althea's American, from New York."

"Friend of yours?" Sean asked, pulling out a notebook.

"No, Sean, I never saw her before yesterday." As if a blue-collar girl from South Boston would've ever had dealings with a swanky New York gallery girl in the normal course of things. But she didn't say it. Actually, Maura was continually surprised by how many people in Ireland — the whole of which had a population about the same size as New York City's — did know each other, or at least, knew of each other. "She arrived around five o'clock and then spent an hour having dinner with me and Billy at the inn. She said she was looking for a place to stay, so I sent her over to Skibbereen. I don't know if she found a room, but she didn't come back here. I know she was driving a rental car."

Sean was scribbling rapidly. "That's grand. But why do you mention her at all?"

"Because she was asking Billy about local gentry, and he told her all about Mycroft House and the Townsends. She really wanted to see the place. When did this Seamus guy die?"

"Sometime after dark, which is eleven or so these days, or he'd have been noticed sooner," Sean said. "Well, then." He stared at his notes for a moment then snapped the notebook shut. "I'll be going over to Sheahan's to talk to Ann, and I'll tell one of the other gardaí to check with the hotel in Skibbereen. You haven't seen Billy Sheahan yet today, have you?"

"No, it's still a bit early for him. You think he can help?"

"I'll try to talk with him later, if I need him. Thank you, Maura. You've been a great help. Keep your ears open, will you?"

"I will. Good luck, Sean." She stared at his retreating back, troubled. Who would kill a simpleminded gardener, even if it was at a manor house? Had he interrupted a break-in? Did it have anything to do with the painting Althea was looking for? She had insinuated that the thing, if it existed, would be worth a fortune. Maura wished she'd asked Sean if there was any sign of a theft, attempted or otherwise.

Not that it was really any of her business, except, as Sean had pointed out, there might be a few more people in the pub later, eager to trade information. She'd seen it before: murder was good for selling pints at the pub.

Rose let herself in. "Shall I leave the door unlocked?" she asked.

"Sure. Leave it open, in fact. The sun's out, and the air feels good, doesn't it?"

"That it does. How'd your talk with that New York lady go?"

Althea might not be exactly ladylike, but why prejudice Rose? "Oh, that's right — you were gone when I came back, and she

61

stopped in here later. It was interesting. She wanted information from Billy about the local . . . heck, what should I call them? The landowners? The gentry? You know Mycroft House?"

"I know where it is, but I've never seen it. Why?" Rose was checking to make sure they were ready for business — clean glasses, napkins, and so forth. She took up a fresh rag, wet it, and started wiping off the taps.

"According to Billy, the last of one of the old families still lives there. And Althea really wanted to see the place."

"Whatever for? Is it anything special?"

"She thinks there might be a valuable old painting there."

"What's it to her?"

"It's kind of complicated. And now it's even more so, since Sean Murphy came by to tell me there's been a killing there, last night."

That caught Rose's attention. "Who's the victim?"

"The gardener at the estate."

"Ah, not Seamus, was it? He'd never hurt a soul."

"You knew him?"

"He's come in here the odd time or two. Spring and summer are his busy times, so maybe you haven't met him. He's not . . . I mean, he . . ."

"I know — Sean told me. So, who lives there on the estate?"

"Miss Eveline, I hear," Rose said slowly. "She's got to be near ninety now. She's the last of the family there, but I don't think I've ever seen her."

"Sean said there was a housekeeper at the house?"

"There's a couple who live in — the O'Briens, Florence and Thomas, I think it is. They've been there as long as I can remember."

Given Rose's age, Maura thought, that was at least ten years.

"Do they come to Sullivan's? I don't remember meeting either of them."

"They do, but not often. They keep to themselves, and they aren't much for the drink."

"Is anybody in the family sitting on a pot of money?"

"Don't think so. Most of the family's long gone. There's enough for the O'Briens to look after the place and Miss Eveline, but there's not much left for repairs and the like. We'd know if someone had the job to fix up the place, with work so scarce. Da told me Miss Eveline has the right to live there for life, but after that . . . ? I'm sure someone would buy the property, though, once she's gone. It's a fair piece, along the harbor there, and the back road to Union Hall runs along the other side."

"The nephew's not interested in living there?"

"Harry?" Rose's expression turned dreamy. "Nah, things are a bit too quiet for him down here. He stops in when he's about, which isn't too often of late. He has a job in Dublin. I can't say what he does there."

"Not married?"

"No, for all that he's past thirty now."

Maura did some quick mental calculations: clearly too old for Rose to set her sights on, but if she was this interested in him, he must be hot. It was enough to make Maura look forward to meeting him, which she anticipated would happen soon, since no doubt the Skibbereen gardaí would already have contacted him, urging him to show up to sort out this mess.

"Did you tell Sean Murphy about this Althea woman?" Rose asked.

"I did."

"Funny, her asking about the place and that poor fella dying there, in the same day. Think she's a killer?" Was Rose joking? Rose was quick to reassure her, "I'm only teas-in'."

Maura laughed. "No way — it might mess up her manicure."

"And I can't see her tramping about the estate in those shoes. I'd be guessing they cost the earth." Rose tsked. "Her outfit wasn't fit for Ireland, much less murder." In response to Maura's quizzical look, she added, "What? I read the fashion mags."

The first customer of the day came in. "Give me a pint, will yeh? So tell me, Maura Donovan, what have you heard about our murder?"

CHAPTER 5

It was late afternoon when the screen door at Sullivan's swung open and slammed against the wall, signaling Althea's arrival. She stalked in, heading straight for the bar. "Maura Donovan, you ratted me out!"

"As if," Maura shot back. "So, you've talked to the gardaí, I'm guessing?"

"You mean the police? Yeah, the cops tracked me down at that hotel you sent me to. You could have kept your mouth shut."

Where did Althea get her attitude? "Why would I? They asked me if I'd seen any strangers in town yesterday, and you fit the bill. And, yes, I told them you were interested in Mycroft House. I know the gardaí in Skibbereen. I *don't* know you, and I don't owe you special treatment."

"Maybe not," Althea muttered. "But you really think I took a shovel to that guy? Why would I do that?"

"I don't know. Why would you?"

Althea finally realized that the ten or so patrons in the pub were watching their exchange with great interest. "What're you all looking at?" she demanded, eyes sweeping the room. "I'm having a conversation here."

Maura interrupted her. "Excuse me, lady, but this is *my* pub, and these are my customers. So you can either leave or dial it back and we can have a civilized conversation here."

For a moment Althea wavered, and then she dropped onto a bar stool. "I need a drink."

"What do you want?"

"Scotch, neat."

Maura turned and wordlessly filled a glass with an inch of scotch, then set it in front of Althea, who downed it in a gulp. She held out her empty glass. "Another?"

Maura gave her a hard look, but refilled the glass.

Althea wrapped her hands around it but didn't raise it immediately. "Thank you. I apologize — again. I've never had to deal with cops in New York, and I had no idea what to expect with your local guys."

"They're okay. I think they're fair."

"Well, I hope they know something about solving crimes. They want me to stick around until they find someone to hang this murder on."

Maura reflected. "Did they take your passport or just suggest that you remain available?"

"The second door," Althea said, sipping her drink more slowly this time. "I guess it's a good sign that they figured they could trust me not to flee."

"You aren't about to take off on them, are you?"

"Of course not." Althea glanced around quickly; the other patrons had apparently lost interest and returned to their own conversations or to the soccer match on the television. "I still haven't figured out if the painting is somewhere around here," she said in a low voice. "You think the murder has anything to do with that?"

"Why are you asking me? We don't get a whole lot of murders around here — fewer than you could count on one hand, over the past ten years, or so I'm told. But don't underestimate the guards. They're not stupid. I'm pretty sure they think it's suspicious that you show up asking about Mycroft House and the gardener ends up dead a few hours later. Wouldn't you?"

"I guess, but why would I bash the gardener?" Althea demanded. "I still can't believe I'm a murder suspect just because I wanted to ask whoever lives there if they had anything that fit the bill for the painting."

"Wait . . . tell me you didn't go there last night."

Althea looked sheepish. "I did. It was so close, and all I wanted to do was ask . . ."

"How did you find it?" Maura asked. She'd never known it existed, much less where it was.

"I asked someone at that gas station you told me about. It's just down the road."

"So what happened at the manor?"

"Nothing, really. I went up and knocked on the door, and this woman answered, but she wouldn't even let me talk. She just said, 'Whatever you're selling, we don't want any,' then slammed the door in my face."

"Did you see Seamus?"

"Who?"

"The gardener. The man who died."

"I think there was someone somewhere outside there. I didn't pay any attention or talk to him. If that was him, he was definitely alive when I left, poking around the bushes."

"And you went straight to the hotel in Skibbereen from there?"

"Yes. Thank God they had a room for me. I had a drink in their restaurant there.

Several people saw me." Althea sighed deeply. "It's actually a nice place, although it's pretty small. I went up to my room, read for a while, watched the news, and went to bed. This morning I took a walk around town, just to get the feel of it — which took me all of fifteen minutes from one end to the other — and when I got back to the hotel, a policeman was waiting for me. Are they all twelve years old?"

"Clean living and lots of Irish rain — keeps the skin young," Maura joked.

Althea smiled wanly. "I've done this all wrong. You were right before — I've been rude to almost everybody I've met. Why should anyone want to help me?"

Maura took pity on her. "Because they're good people and they're happy to help, if you ask them nicely. I don't think anybody around here is going to steal your precious discovery and publish it before you can get home. Trust them."

"Am I supposed to buy a round of drinks all around? Would that help?"

Why does she keep missing the point? Maura wondered. "Why don't you just relax and talk to people? You don't have to bribe them, you know."

"Right," Althea said dubiously.

Maura leaned on the bar. "Why *are* you

70

in such a hurry?"

"Weren't you listening yesterday? The exhibit is almost ready to go up, and the catalog is at the printer's. I begged them to wait a couple of days. I even said I'd pay for a rush order — that's how important I think this is. And now I'm running out of time, and I have nowhere else to look if the painting isn't here."

Maura considered. Her explanation didn't make much sense in Leap, but maybe it did in New York.

"What time is it?" Althea asked. "I'm starving. You don't serve food, do you? I don't think I can face driving back to the hotel right now. I had to go around that stupid roundabout twice last night before I figured it out."

"Sorry, no food here, beyond a few bags of chips. You could go get something at the express market at the gas station, or go back to the inn, or there's the Motorcycle Café down the street."

"I think I'll try the gas station — it's not far, right?"

"Not far. It's across from the church — you can't miss it. Look, if you want me to, I can try to soften up the regulars, tell them about why you're here . . ."

Althea stood up. "Would you? I sure don't

have much to lose at the moment. And thank you. See you in a few." She strode out the door. Maura was happy to see that her shoes were slightly more sensible than the ones she had arrived in the day before.

"What's going on?" Rose whispered.

Maura cocked an eyebrow at her. "As if you didn't hear every word we said."

Rose blushed. "Well, she has a loud voice. It's not like I was hangin' about to listen in. So now we're all in the hunt for this missing art thing?"

"Seems we are. Call it a treasure hunt."

A few minutes later Billy arrived. He was warmly greeted by several of the men in the place as he made his slow way to his favorite chair. Maura poured his pint and took it over to him. "You're in late today, Billy. I was beginning to worry about you."

"I was chatting with the gardaí, I was. They asked me what I knew about the Townsends, and what I told that nosy woman."

Maura noticed that Althea had been demoted from "lady" to "woman" in Billy's eyes. "You didn't tell them you thought Althea killed the man, did you?"

Billy took a long, slow pull on his pint. "Now, why would I do a thing like that?"

Maura grabbed a chair and set it next to

Billy's. "What can you tell me about the Townsend family that I didn't hear yesterday? Are they broke?"

"In a manner of speaking. They're what you'd call land rich but cash poor. The estate is mortgaged, and it's only Harry Townsend's money that keeps it going. But Eveline is well up in years, and when she's gone . . ." He didn't finish his sentence. Maura realized that Eveline and Billy must be relatively close in age.

"Would there be any buyers for it these days?"

Billy didn't seem particularly worried. "Could be. It's near enough Rosscarbery that it might catch some of the overflow for the conference center there — maybe some business folk who want a pretty view of the harbor. And I hear there's a new place in Glandore as well. But they'd have to put money into the house — it's in sad shape now."

Maura thought for a moment. "You think they've already sold everything they could lay their hands on?"

"I'm not the one you should be asking. I see Tom O'Brien now and then — he says they're trying to keep things much as they've always been for Eveline's sake. I don't how what state she's in, but she'd probably notice if the furniture disappeared out from under her."

Or a large painting, Maura added to herself. "Do you know anyone who would want to do harm to Seamus Daly or the O'Briens?"

"Seamus was never quite right, I told you. He was touched in the head — something happened when he was born. But he never crossed anyone that I know of, and he didn't stray far from the estate — might have come in here the odd time or two. Set in his ways, he was, but he did his job well. Hard to make enemies when you see so few people."

"What about the O'Briens? Could someone have had it in for one of them?"

"Florence has a sharp tongue, but Tom would be lost without her — she rules the place. Besides, the ground around here would be littered with corpses if people were killed for that. And why would they have gone after Seamus?"

Maura thought for a moment. "Okay, so if the reasons weren't personal, it's probably a case of Seamus having tried to stop someone who shouldn't have been there, and that person grabbing the handiest weapon — Seamus's own shovel."

"I'd wager that's how the gardaí would

see it," Billy agreed.

"Would anyone have noticed someone sneaking around the property?"

"I'd be well surprised. The family wanted their privacy, and they made sure the house was set well back from the road, from the beginning. You've never seen it from the road, have you?" When Maura shook her head, he added, "The only other way in is from the harbor."

"By boat? I hadn't thought of that. Are there lots of boaters around in the summer?"

"Not for the fun of it. Most who stop here are serious about their fishing, and powerboats upset the fish. There'd be fishing boats over to Union Hall, but they don't come up here, they go out to the open water. Some fancy yachts at Glandore, now, but why would they stop in here?"

"Billy, if you don't know, I won't even try to guess." Maura grinned at Billy, then asked skeptically, "Can you see Althea doing it?"

"She's very sure of what she's after, though I can't see her swinging that shovel. But it could be that she has a friend to help her — or an enemy who's after the same thing she's looking for."

"I wondered about that. Well, let the

gardaí figure it out. But tell me, who else around here could Althea ask about this painting of hers? If she still wants to find it, after what's happened."

"Him." Billy tipped his head at a newcomer who had just entered.

Maura sized up the newcomer quickly: about six feet tall, past thirty but wearing it well, and . . . hot. Maybe a little too pretty for her taste, but undeniably good-looking. From the look on Rose's face, Maura knew this had to be Harry Townsend. She stood up and walked over to the bar, conscious of the man's frank appraisal of her. At least he wasn't ogling teenage Rose, who was staring mutely at him from behind the counter.

The man smiled, showing very white teeth. "I heard Old Mick passed on. Would you be the new owner, then?"

Maura extended her hand. "I am. Maura Donovan."

He shook it, holding it a fraction of a second too long. "American, by the accent. Yours must be an interesting story. I look forward to hearing it."

"And you must be Harry Townsend."

"Bang on. Called down by the Skibbereen gardaí to sort out this sad mess at Mycroft House. Poor Seamus — he wouldn't hurt a fly. Well, flies maybe, if they got into the roses. But no person. I can't quite wrap my mind around it, that he's dead."

"Have you talked to the gardaí already?" Maura asked.

"I was on my way there when I thought I might stop in for a quick pint. I've been on the road for hours now and I needed the break."

Maura studied him but didn't move.

Harry looked deeply into her eyes. "That pint?"

Maura shook herself. "Of course. What'll you have?" The door swung open again and Althea bustled in, carrying a couple of bags. "You know what, the food there didn't look half bad. I . . ." Then she noticed Harry, slouching gracefully against the bar as he waited for his pint — and he noticed her.

Maura's mouth twitched. "Althea Melville, meet Harry, the heir of the Townsends."

"Well, hello," Althea purred. "What a pleasure."

Maura passed Harry his pint and settled back to watch Althea go to work on him.

CHAPTER 6

For once Maura regretted that the pub was beginning to fill up with both Friday regulars and a smattering of less-familiar faces who all clearly wanted to talk about the murder, because she was enjoying watching the soap opera unfolding in front of her. The presence of Harry Townsend in the midst of the crowd provided an added spark, and Maura guessed that he wouldn't have to pay for many drinks. He looked to be great craic, as the locals would say. As Harry drained his pint, he turned to the group. "I've an appointment with a sergeant in Skibbereen, and I must call in on my poor auntie and make sure she isn't devastated by this terrible event. But I promise I'll be back later and give yeh the whole story, or as much as I know."

Althea laid a hand on Harry's arm. "Oh, please do come back later. I really want to talk to you."

"How could I pass up the chance to talk with such a lovely American? You'll be here at Sullivan's?"

"You could meet me at the hotel in Skibbereen," Althea suggested quickly.

"After I've promised to tell the tale to my good friends here?" Harry replied, ducking her implied invitation neatly. "I'll be back after I've tucked Aunt Eveline in for the night, count on it. Maura Donovan, it's a pleasure to meet you as well. Ta!"

He made his exit, watched by every woman in the room. Althea's expression was a bit calculating, as if she were already plotting some strategy, while Rose sighed. Maura could see why. Harry certainly had charm, and she suspected that he probably could sweet-talk any woman he met. Even without having met Miss Eveline, Maura could picture the elderly aunt doting on this handsome nephew.

But Harry had avoided Althea's obvious come-on. Maybe he had some brains to go with those undeniable good looks . . .

Stop it, Maura! She scolded herself. Her life was complicated enough right now without someone like Harry Townsend in it. Besides, why would someone like him even look at her? He probably had a string of women waiting for him back in Dublin, and he'd be going back there as soon as he'd taken care of things here, which shouldn't take him long.

Mick Nolan and Jimmy Sweeney came in together from the back, arguing about something, but they stopped talking when they noticed Maura. Jimmy turned to Rose. "Goin' to be a busy night, Rosie, love. Why don't you go home and see to supper? We've got this covered."

Maura expected Rose to whine "Do I have to?" but instead she agreed quickly. "You'll stop by to eat, Da?"

"I will. Take care, love."

Althea had watched the exchange, and after Rose left and Mick and Jimmy moved on, she asked Maura, "Just how old is that kid?"

"Sixteen going on twenty-five. Jimmy's her dad. Her mom's dead, so it's just the two of them."

"Is she even legal to work here?"

"There are rules, I gather, but there's some kind of loophole if you're a relative, and she and Jimmy are related somehow to the former owner. Besides, she's finished whatever the local version of high school is. Jimmy's worked here since long before I showed up. So has Mick."

"And now you're the owner? How'd that

happen?"

"It's complicated." Maura waved a hand. "Basically, I inherited the place from an old friend of my grandmother's. She came from around here originally." She didn't want to get into all the details.

"Got it. And that gorgeous guy was Harry Townsend?"

"So it seems. I haven't met him before."

"Married? Attached?"

"How am I supposed to know? Why? You think if you find your painting, you can marry your way to it?"

"It's a thought," Althea quipped. "So, I got some food. Mind if I eat it here?"

"Go right ahead. I'm going to go out and find something myself, plus I need the fresh air. It may be a long night. People will come in to talk about the murder. At least the local people will. I pity any tourists who walk into the middle of it — they'll get an earful."

Mick came up behind Maura, and Maura asked, "Have you met Althea?" He shook his head, so she introduced them. "I saw you in passing," Mick said. *"Fáilte."* When Althea looked confused, Mick added, "That's 'welcome' in Irish. You'll hear it a lot."

"Well, thank you, Mick. Maura, I'm beginning to like this place — lots of handsome men. So, Mick, is this part of the world your home?"

She's flirting again, Maura thought in amusement. Was Althea man-crazy or just working any angle that might get her into Mycroft House? She'd find out soon enough that Mick couldn't help her — at least, she didn't think so — but in the meantime, Maura was hungry, and as she'd said to Althea, it was probably going to be a long night.

Mick and Althea didn't notice her leaving. She walked across the street to the inn, which was moderately crowded, and found herself a stool at the bar. Ann was filling glasses, but when she had a free moment she came over to say hello. "You'll be wanting supper?"

"Yeah. Whatever's easy — I like your soup, and your bread."

"Done." Ann darted into the kitchen.

While she waited, Maura watched the crowd. Not so different from the people at Sullivan's — more men than women in the bar area, some couples, some groups of men. The ages were a mix of old and young-ish, although few people her own age. Where were all the twenty-somethings? Skibbereen? Or were they all off looking for work somewhere else, somewhere there were actually jobs? She'd heard a lot of younger people had gone off to Australia, since there was nothing for them in Ireland.

Ann returned a couple of minutes later with a steaming bowl of vegetable soup and a plate loaded with brown bread. "Where's your friend?"

"Althea? Not, repeat, *not* my friend. She just walked into the pub yesterday. Now the gardaí are looking at her for that murder at Mycroft House."

Ann snorted. "Her, kill someone! Sure and she'd find a man to do the work for her."

Maura smiled. "You feel that way too? Well, I can't blame the guards for talking to her, because I told them that she really wants to get into Mycroft House — she thinks there might be an important painting in there somewhere."

"I've heard that Florence O'Brien shut the door on her."

"How does everyone know everything so fast around here? I only just heard."

"Tom O'Brien stopped in for a pint earlier."

"Why is it he stops in here, rather than at Sullivan's? I don't think I've met him."

Ann shrugged. "Habit, maybe? He's not

much of one for the pint, and his wife keeps him on a short lead."

"Did he say anything useful? Like, does he have an idea who might have killed Seamus?"

"Poor man, no. I don't think Florence lets Tom think — she does it all for him. It was brave of him to come in for that pint. He told Florence he needed something from the hardware store up the road. But they were good to Seamus, the two of them. Looked out for him. He'll be missed. The gardens there are huge — so big they can't even care for them all — and Seamus worked for little more than his room and board and some pocket money. They'll not replace him easily."

"Sounds like it's expensive to keep the place going."

"That it is. The old families, they built on a grand scale, knowing they had the staff to take care of it all. Now . . . there's no money left and no one who wants that kind of work — they'd rather run computers in a city somewhere." Ann leaned closer and said, "Everyone's waiting for Eveline Townsend to die."

"That's sad," Maura said. "What do they think will happen then? Does Harry inherit the place?"

"She has lifetime rights, but he'll be glad to wash his hands of it, I'm sure. And there's hope that whoever buys it will bring some money into the village. I will say, Harry's been good to her, for all that he's not around much."

"You know that Harry's arrived?"

"Has he, now? You've seen him?"

"Uh, yeah. He came into the pub. He's hard to miss."

"He is that. Half the girls in the village have made a run at him, with no luck."

"He isn't, uh, gay, is he?"

"From all that I've heard, no." Ann laughed. "But he has no plans to live here — he likes the city. Sure and there'll be some broken hearts in the village if he ever settles down." Ann shook herself. "I'd better tend to business. Enjoy your supper."

As she ate, Maura pondered. So Harry Townsend was the playboy of West Cork, or at least this small corner of it. But it was hard for her to see how his romantic liaisons could have anything to do with poor Seamus's murder. Seamus was his employee, one he seldom saw, and he worked for pennies. Maura could see no motive for Harry, but then, she had no motive for anyone else either.

She let her thoughts run wild. Maybe

Harry had stumbled upon Seamus with a girl from the village, and the girl had looked upset about it. Or maybe Seamus hadn't known when to stop. What would Harry have done? But if that had been the case, then there'd be a girl, who would talk . . .

Maura, get a grip! Here she went, condemning poor Seamus, whom she'd never met. Ridiculous! Who was it that had said the simplest solution was usually the right one? But what was the simplest solution here? The Townsend household had more or less kept to themselves and muddled along for quite a while. It was too much to believe that Althea's appearance was not connected to their sudden notoriety. Which kind of hinted that the painting might actually exist. But was finding it — or keeping it hidden — worth killing for?

Maura finished her supper quickly, left some euros on the bar, and went back to Sullivan's. The crowd had grown. Maura spotted Althea in a corner, talking with two men who were hanging on her every word. Jimmy was working the room and Mick was behind the bar, chatting with a red-haired woman Maura had never seen before, though she and Mick clearly knew each other, from the way they were bantering.

Mick looked up and saw Maura, then

beckoned her over. "Ah, there you are, Maura. Come meet Gillian Callanan, our resident artist. She's just back for the summer."

Gillian had turned when Mick called out to Maura, and now she extended her hand. She was a few years older than herself — early thirties? — and casually dressed, her red hair cut short and carelessly mussed. Maura could tell she was tall even while she sat on a bar stool. "Mick's been filling me in on what's happened in the last few months. I'm glad you decided to keep the place going, Maura — I'd miss it. Although I'd guess you're quite the change from Old Mick."

Maura slid onto a bar stool next to Gillian. "You knew Old Mick?"

"Everybody knew Old Mick — he was a local institution. The place won't be the same without him."

"I never met him, but his legend lives on. I know I can't fill his shoes, but there was definitely some room for improvement. So far all I've managed to do is clean the place and update the accounting. You live around here?"

"Part of the year, at least. I spend the winters in Dublin, but my family's from one of the townlands, and I rent a place near here, summers — costs too much to keep it warm in the winter."

"Mick said you're an artist?"

"I am that. I make pretty pictures for the tourists, which pays the bills, and paintings that please me the rest of the year, which don't sell near as well. But I get by, with the odd paying job or two. I was trying to talk Mick into hanging a few in here, looking to sell them, but he said you're the boss and to talk to you."

"Oh, yeah?" Maura glanced at Mick. "Can I see some of your work?"

"Of course. Stop by my place in the morning, if you don't mind the mess. Like Mick said, I'm just back this minute from Dublin."

"I'll do that, if you'll tell me how to get to your place. I still get lost in the lanes around here, especially after dark."

"You're living up at Knockskagh, are you? I'm just over the hill from you, at the old creamery in Ballinlough, by the water. Half of it is falling down, but there's plenty of room, and I love the light there."

"Sure, I know where that is. But I'll take the long way around — I'm not a fan of the road down that hill. It's in rough shape." Gillian probably wouldn't know about her run-in with a thug who tried to shove her car down the hill on that stretch of road, and she wasn't about to explain.

"Grand! I'll expect you in the morning — but not too early."

"Deal."

The door opened again, and Harry Townsend walked in. The men in the room only glanced at him and looked away, but Maura could have sworn that Althea's ears pricked up like a cat's. And at the same time Gillian's face lit up. Harry came straight to the bar. "Gillian, my love — I was wondering if you'd show up." They exchanged what Maura would label "friend" kisses, on the cheek, though Gillian's eyes lingered on him for a bit after.

And it was pretty clear that Althea noticed. She said something to her two companions, then stood up and came over, laying a hand on Harry's arm. "Harry, you're back! Did the police grill you mercilessly?"

"Nah, it wasn't too bad. I couldn't tell them much, after all, seeing as I was in Dublin at the time of the murder."

"What's going on?" Gillian interrupted.

"You haven't heard? There's been a death up at the house — Seamus, the gardener. He was killed by a blow to the head. Tom O'Brien found him on the lawn this morning."

"How sad," Gillian said and sounded like she meant it. "Do the gardaí know what happened?"

"Not yet."

Althea, not to be distracted, said, "Harry, I'm sorry to bother you at such a difficult time, but I really need to talk to you. Can I buy you a drink?"

"Sure, darlin'. Gilly, I'll ring your mobile when I know what's what and we'll get together, all right?"

"Fine, Harry."

Gillian smiled, but Maura watched her gaze follow Harry and Althea to the farthest corner of the room. *Uh-oh,* Maura thought.

Gillian turned back to the bar and finished the glass in front of her. "I'd best be going — I still have masses of unpacking to do. Maura, I'll see you in the morning. Mick, good to see you again."

"Glad to have you back, Gillian."

When Gillian had left, Maura turned to Mick, then tilted her head toward Harry, sitting close to Althea. "Trouble?"

Mick shrugged. "Maybe. Harry and Gillian have a long history. But it's none of my business if Althea seems to have set her sights on Harry."

"Is that going to be a problem?"

"Depends on who you ask. He's not one

for, uh, long-term relationships."

"I don't think that's what Althea's looking for," Maura said wryly.

"No more do I," Mick replied. "So I wouldn't waste my time worrying on it."

Maura agreed, then recalled something she'd meant to ask earlier. "What were you and Jimmy arguing about when I came in?"

Mick shrugged. "The same. He's still upset about what Old Mick did, shutting him out of the will."

"Like that's my fault?" Maura muttered.

Mick noticed. "No, but it falls to you to keep him in line. You're the owner here now."

"I've never managed anyone in my life. You think he'd be better off somewhere else?"

"That's not for me to say. And there's Rose to consider."

"I know, I know. I want to help her, but I don't know how." Maura looked up to see more people arriving. This was a discussion that would have to wait.

CHAPTER 7

The evening passed quickly, as Maura, Mick, and Jimmy kept busy filling glasses and collecting empties. While she worked, Maura overheard snippets of information about the death, but no one seemed to have any idea who would have wanted poor Seamus Daly dead. The Townsend family received mixed reviews: most people liked Harry well enough, but he hadn't lived here "for donkey's years," and the last resident Townsend, his great-aunt Eveline, had been nearly a recluse for years, so no one seemed to know her. The manor house itself, concealed from the road behind a thick forest, had been all but forgotten by local residents.

Maura also learned a bit more about the O'Briens, since they had to come out and buy supplies occasionally, although there were some grumblings that they took their trade to Union Hall instead. The consensus was that they kept to themselves, and they were seldom if ever seen in any of Leap's pubs. Maura wasn't exactly surprised: they had sole charge of caring for Eveline and keeping a large, crumbling estate going, not to mention the large gardens — a job made more complicated now that Seamus was gone. When would they have time to socialize?

Maura had seen Althea and Harry leave together, shortly after ten. They hadn't come back. She drew her own conclusions. Now it was a bright summer morning, and Maura was pottering around in her own kitchen. *Her* kitchen, in *her* house. She still wasn't used to that. Nor was she used to the silence and the solitude — she'd spent her whole life in a cramped apartment in an old triple-decker in South Boston, surrounded by people and cars and buses, and now here she was practically alone in the midst of rolling green fields. The old building was small and no-frills, but it was structurally sound and had what people around here called "mod cons," as in "modern conveniences," like electricity and indoor plumbing, thank goodness. The small stove was fueled by a propane tank out back, not that she used it much. There was electric heat, and a few times in the early spring Maura had been tempted to build a fire in the massive open fireplace that took up one end of the building, but in the end she'd just put on another sweater and waited for summer. Maybe she'd reconsider her heating options when winter came. It was looking more and more like she'd still be around then.

She had a few neighbors on the Knockskagh hill. She had learned that "knock" meant hill anyway, and the "skagh" part mean white thorn, a kind of bush or tree that she couldn't identify yet. Most of the neighbors had hooves, but Mick Nolan's grandmother, Bridget, lived just down the lane. Bridget had known Maura's grandmother, and she loved sharing her memories, so Maura tried to see her as often as possible, usually in the mornings when Bridget was most alert and before Maura had to be at the pub.

Maura was not surprised when Bridget rapped on her door frame. "Have you had yer breakfast yet? I've made two loaves of bread and I thought you might like one."

"Just getting around to it now, Bridget." Maura still felt funny calling the older woman by her first name, but Bridget had insisted that "Mrs. Nolan" was too formal. "It's nice to see you out and about."

"Ah, I love the summer," Bridget said, settling into a chair at the table. "I'm awake with the birds, and my bones don't ache as much." She unwrapped the crusty round loaf of bread from the tea towel she had brought it in and laid it on a pretty china plate on the table. "I hear there's been some excitement in the village."

"Did Mick tell you about it?" More likely one of the friends who kept an eye on Bridget when Mick couldn't, Maura thought.

"No, one of the neighbors stopped by for tea yesterday."

Maura found two clean if mismatched plates and pulled butter out of her tiny refrigerator and set them all on the table. "Did you ever know the Townsends?" she asked.

"The likes of me and the likes of them? I might have had work there, when the house was full, but my husband didn't want to see me working. Different times, they were. Now all you young girls have jobs and go everywhere on yer own." Bridget laughed briefly. "I might have met Eveline Townsend a time or two. She wasn't a Lady Muck, stickin' her nose in the air like the rest of the family. Ah, but they're all gone now, except for her."

"What about her great-nephew, Harry?"

"Now, there's a lad. A wild one, he was, when he was younger. And now he's off to Dublin for work."

"He's back in town now, because of the murder."

"Poor Seamus Daly. He was a good boy. Mebbe a bit touched, but no trouble to anyone. I knew his mother, years ago. When she died, the O'Briens looked after him. It's a shame."

"It is." Maura sliced some of the still-warm, crumbly soda bread and placed slices on each plate. "Will you join me?"

"Is there tea made?"

"There is."

They enjoyed their simple breakfast, then Maura checked her watch. "I hate to rush you, but I said I'd meet Gillian Callanan at the old creamery before I open at Sullivan's. Do you know her?"

"She'd be the artist over the hill? I can't say I've seen much of her since she was a child, and a lovely thing she was. Sure and her family's from up near Reavouler, not far. She's stayin' in the old creamery?"

"That's what she tells me. I thought it was abandoned."

"Time was, all the farmers here delivered their milk to that place, by horse cart. Now it's all big trucks over to the new place in

Drinagh."

"I've driven past that one. It's a big business."

"That it is. It's good they've done well. People do still want their milk and butter, don't they?" Bridget stood up carefully. "I'll be on my way, then. Mick said he'd stop by later in the day. *Slán agat.*"

"*Slán abhaile.*" Maura smiled. Bridget kept trying to teach her a few phrases in Irish, even though languages had always been hard for Maura in school. It felt a little funny to be wishing her "safe home" when home was only a couple of hundred feet away. Still, she admired Bridget for holding on to her home — and her independence, despite Mick's gentle pressure on her to move in with his sister.

Maura glanced again at her watch and speeded up her pace, wrapping up the bread and collecting the breakfast dishes, dumping them beside the sink. She could worry about washing them later. She had to get going to Gillian's place. She'd never met a real artist before, and she was curious about the woman.

She collected her bag, keys, and a sweatshirt to wrap around her shoulders — it was still cool in the morning, before the sun reached the old stone house — and set off.

The lane that ran along the south side of Bridget's property led to the Ballinlough road and brought her quickly to the former creamery, next to the small lake that had given the road its name. She knew that "lough" meant lake, much like the more familiar Scottish "loch," but she wasn't sure about the "Ballin" part — person or thing? She'd have to ask Bridget. She could already see a few fishermen in rowboats out on the water. She pulled off the road in front of the creamery, which had once been painted an unlikely shade of bright blue, now faded. As Gillian had said, one end, where the milk had probably been delivered years ago, was falling apart, leaving the interior visible and cluttered with large pieces of unfamiliar rusty machinery, the big doors hanging precariously, windowpanes broken. But around to the left, there was a people-sized door, in front of which sat a couple of chairs and a parked car. Maura headed for that door.

The brightly painted door — a sunny yellow — was open, and Maura could hear music inside. She knocked on the doorjamb and called out, "Hello?" A voice inside called out, "Coming!" and thirty seconds later Gillian appeared, wiping her hands on a dirty and colorful rag and bringing with her a strong smell of turpentine. She gave her hands one last scrub and extended one to Maura.

"Come in, come in." Gillian stood back to let Maura enter. "Can I offer yeh a cup of tea?"

"Sure." Everywhere she went, Maura found people offering her tea, and it always seemed rude to say no. "I'm not interrupting anything, am I?"

"Come on through. No, I was just finishing something up, and I'm ready for a cup myself." She led Maura toward the back of the building.

The smell of turpentine grew stronger. They stepped into a single large room than ran parallel to the road and the shoreline.

"Wow! I can see why you like it," Maura said. The space had been cleared of whatever milk-processing equipment had been there, leaving a single open space with a patchy concrete floor. At the back a bank of large windows opened onto the lough. The light that flooded the space was clean and bright, with a bit of a sparkle from the reflections off the water.

Gillian was watching her with a smile. "Grand, isn't it? As you'll see, no one could live here in winter — it's impossible to heat. But I like to spend summers here. Mostly I camp out. I've an old mattress in the corner there, behind a screen, and an electric kettle for tea. I don't do much cooking, and if I want a real meal I go to Skibbereen."

"Do you own this place?"

"The owner's a friend who has no use for it, but he keeps the power and water on and I pay for it when I'm here. It works just fine for me. Let me see to that tea."

While Gillian filled the kettle then rinsed out some cups, Maura wandered around the room. At one windowless end, Gillian had hung a variety of unframed canvases as well as some watercolors. The latter were clearly more commercial, with views of hillsides and sheep, or what she recognized as the harbor at Leap, but painted with a quick, sure hand — Maura could easily see tourists wanting one. The oils were more intense in color and more abstract, but still compelling. Together they made the echoing space come alive.

"Here you go," Gillian said, handing her a hot mug. "Milk? Sugar?"

"This is fine, thanks. These paintings are great, all of them."

"As I told you before, the pretty watercolors are mostly for the tourist trade. People like to take home a nice souvenir of the Old Country, and I'm happy to oblige. I sell them through a couple of shops in Skib, and a gallery in Schull, which gets lots of summer people. I'm trying to sweet-talk my way into something at Glandore, or even Rosscarbery, for the corporate types who visit. The oils are more personal. I use some acrylics too."

"I'd be happy to hang a couple in Sullivan's, if you want," Maura said before wondering if Jimmy and Mick would see that as "fancying up" the place, something they had argued against.

"That'd be grand," Gillian said. "Sit." She motioned at Maura. "Talk to me. Sometimes when I get to working, I lose track of time. I can go days without even exchanging a word with a living soul. So, tell me about yourself. How on earth did an American girl like you arrive at the ends of the earth here?"

Maura smiled. "It's a complicated story. My father was born up the hill there, but he and my grandmother went to Boston when he was a child. He died when I was very young — I barely remember him."

"Sorry," Gillian said. "We've lots of stories of people who went away. Nowadays some of them or their kids come back to visit, looking for their history, but there's not

much to be found. Do you see yourself staying?"

"I never planned on it, but then, I never
had much of a plan back in Boston either.
I'm still getting to know the place, but I like
it. I think. It takes getting used to. What
about you? Did you say you spend part of
the year in Dublin?"

"I do, when it's too cold to stay here. I've
done a show or two there — you can guess
there are more places for that kind of thing
in the city — but the competition is wicked.
I know my limitations as an artist, and I
guess you'd say I'm not terribly ambitious.
I like it here. I come here to clear my head."
Gillian stared out at the view. "Truth be
told, this is home. I can come and go as I
please. Paint all night, if I want, or not at
all. I don't have to answer to anyone. Things
are easy."

"I'm beginning to see what you mean. I
grew up in a part of Boston where there
were always people around, and they weren't
exactly quiet. And then there were cars and
trains, and planes overhead. I don't think I
knew what real quiet was like until I got
here. But it's not scary, just peaceful."
Maura took a swallow of tea. "Listen, can I
ask you something?"

"Sure," Gillian said quickly.

"Do you know the Townsends?"

Gillian's mouth twitched. "Are you asking, do I know Harry?"

"Yeah, I guess so."

Gillian laughed. "Tell me you haven't fallen for him too?"

"Nope, not my type. Too pretty."

"Good for you. The bottom line is, Harry's a fine thing, as you noticed, and he knows it, so he can have almost anyone he wants. But he really likes women, too much to settle on just one. I've known him all my life, and we usually get together every couple of months."

That was more or less what Mick had said. Maura guessed that they did more than play darts on those occasions. "Does he spend much time here?"

"Harry lives in Dublin most of the time. Drives down when the spirit moves him. He gets to play lord of the manor and impress the local girls."

"He won't go after Rose, will he?"

"Of course not. He's not a bad person, just easily distracted by a pretty face. He does have some scruples."

"What about a job?"

"That too, to his credit. He's an accountant."

Maura almost spit out her mouthful of

tea. "Really? No wonder he likes it better here. Playing lord of the manor beats number cruncher any day. I understand he manages whatever's left of the estate and takes care of his — what is she, great-aunt?"

"Right. He'll probably be around for a few days now, sorting things out."

"What's Miss Eveline like?"

"The last time I saw her, last summer, she seemed frail, and her mind travels to the past a bit, but given her age, I'd say she's doing well."

Interesting that Gillian had actually spent time with Eveline. "Not senile or feeble?"

Gillian smiled. "Not at all. And I'm pretty sure she knows about Harry's girls and doesn't approve — she'd rather see him settled. Why do you ask, if you've no dog in the hunt?"

Maura wondered briefly whether she should ask her next question, but she decided it might save her some trouble. "You saw Harry with Althea last night, didn't you?"

"She the one with fancy shoes, who left with him?"

So Gillian *had* noticed. Did she care? "That's her."

"Friend of yours?"

"No, but she is a fellow American." Maura

had a lightbulb moment. "Hey, you may be able to help her — if you don't hold it against her for hanging all over Harry."

"How'm I supposed to help?"

"She's here looking for what she says is a long-lost painting — a Van Dyck, I think she said — that will wow the New York art world and save her career, and she thinks it may be at Mycroft House. That's her story, at least."

"Wow. That *would* rock the art world," Gillian said with something like admiration. "So Althea thinks it's a real possibility?"

"She does. Have you ever been inside the manor?"

"Yes, but not all of it. But we've had tea there on occasion."

"So you wouldn't know if there was a rare and valuable painting lurking somewhere in the house?"

"Not personally. Harry might be able to tell you, but he's an eejit about art, much less historical art — to him it would just be something that's been hanging on the wall as long as anyone can remember. And under the terms of Eveline's father's will, she has the right to live in the place for the rest of her life, and she has complete control of the furnishings until she goes. I guess her father felt sorry for his poor unmarried daughter.

So even if Harry knew of such a treasure, he wouldn't be able to do anything with it until Eveline's gone. What's Althea's game?"

"I think she's making it up as she goes. But I think she made a run at Harry last night to get into the house, not because she's after him. When she tried to get in on her own, the night before, Mrs. O'Brien barred the door to her."

"It doesn't do to cross Florence O'Brien. She's very protective of Eveline, bless her. And I'm sure you know there are those who would prey on older folk, particularly during these times, so that's a good thing."

"Can you fill me in on the setup? What I've heard so far is that Harry lives in Dublin most of the time. Eveline lives at the manor and doesn't even go out anymore. The O'Briens look after her and take care of the place. Seamus did the gardening."

"Poor Seamus," Gillian said, and Maura thought she sounded like she meant it, rather than making polite noises. She shook her head, then looked at Maura. "He was a good lad. The O'Briens took in Seamus some years ago, and he lived on the estate, but he seldom ventured as far as the village. They were very kind to him, and he was well treated. I don't know what they'll do with the gardens now — let them go wild?"

Gillian hadn't offered any reason why the O'Briens would have done any harm to Seamus. Let the gardaí sort out his death. Maura returned to something she could do something about. "So let me ask you this, and you can go ahead and say no: are you willing to help Althea look for this painting?"

Gillian regarded Maura steadily for a moment. "You think I'd put her off because she's made a play for Harry? I have no claim on him. Although she did set on him rather quickly, didn't she, now?" Then she said slowly, "I'm willing to help look for it if it means that there'll be a bit more money to make sure that Eveline is comfortable for the rest of her days. I'd bet she wouldn't want to sell the painting, if it exists, but maybe Harry could borrow money against it. I know he's worried about the money running out, and the old place does need a lot of work. As far as I know, the O'Briens are working for no more than a roof over their heads and their meals. So I guess that's a yes, as long as Althea doesn't spirit the piece off in the middle of the night and sell it for her own reward."

"Thank you — that's generous of you. Can I tell Althea? And I'll beat it into her head that she should be grateful to you. She doesn't seem to get how things work around here. New York and West Cork don't mix well." Maura checked her watch. "Shoot, I've got to get to town. If I see Althea I'll tell her, but I don't have time to go looking for her." Althea was probably in Harry's bed, Maura guessed, but she wasn't about to say that to Gillian.

"I'll stop in later. Can I bring you some of my paintings?"

"Please! I'll bet they'll brighten up the place, even if Old Mick is rolling over in his grave."

CHAPTER 8

Maura and Rose were hip deep in customers later that morning when Althea dragged herself in, wearing the previous night's clothes, and found an empty stool at the bar. Maura acknowledged her but her hands were full; she noted that Rose took her order and gave her a cup of coffee a minute later.

At about one there was a lull in the crowd, and Maura wondered once again if providing light lunches or hot food might keep people around. If they had to go elsewhere to find their lunch, they might not come back. Still, she had to keep reminding herself that she shouldn't make any big decisions without a better idea of how things worked around here — including the regulations about serving food. She asked Rose to cover the taps for a bit, then moved down the bar to where Althea sat, gloomily stirring her coffee. "How you doing?"

"I screwed up."

"Harry?" Maura asked.

"How'd you guess?"

"You want to talk about it?" Maura asked the traditional bartender question.

"I don't know. I'm not sure I can fix this, and it's my own stupid fault."

"Try me." Maura tried to ignore the fact that Rose was near enough to overhear. But if Rose was old enough to serve at the bar, she was old enough to hear about Althea's bad behavior.

"Harry . . . invited me home with him last night."

"I think everyone in the bar figured that out."

"Oh, great. I keep forgetting how small everything here is. Anyway, yes, he took me to his palatial estate — which, believe me, needs a whole lot of work. I'd had a drink or two here, and then we had a drink or six when we got there, and you can guess the rest. I can't say much about Harry's performance because I don't remember much of anything." She looked around the room. "Did you all hear that, guys?" Every man in the room averted his eyes quickly.

Althea smiled bitterly and continued. "Doesn't do to burn any bridges, does it? So after our night of passion, the sun came up, and I went down the hall wearing Harry's shirt and not much more, looking for a bathroom, and ran smack into Aunt Eveline. She started shrieking, and that brought Mrs. What's-Her-Name and her hubby running, and then *she* started yelling at me, and then Harry finally woke up and stumbled out in his tighty whities and the housekeeper started yelling at *him.* So he grabbed me and dragged me back into his room and suggested rather strongly that it might be a good time for me to make myself scarce, until the shouting stopped. I pointed out that he'd driven me there and was I supposed to walk? So we both kind of threw our clothes on and left as fast as we could. He dropped me here, which is where I left my car. I don't know where he went, but I'm pretty sure it wasn't back to the house."

Maura was enjoying Althea's story more than she wanted to admit. Althea had been asking for trouble, and it looked like she'd found it. "Just to review, you and Harry hooked up last night, right? Did you have a chance to talk about the painting? Or look around the house?"

Althea shook her head. "Never quite got to that. We, uh, didn't do a lot of talking, just drinking and . . . other stuff." She glanced at Rose, who was suddenly very busy polishing glasses.

"But you've managed to tick off both Aunt Eveline and the housekeeper who runs the place? The one who had already thrown you out once?"

"Yup, two for two."

"Did Harry have anything to say?"

"Beyond 'Thankyouverymuch, that was grand, I'll ring you'? Nope."

"Well, at least *he* wasn't yelling at you, was he?"

"Nope. But I think he was embarrassed, in front of his aunt. Men don't like that." She shook her head again, but gingerly. "I really messed this up."

"You still want to find this painting?" Maura asked, even as she wondered how willing Gillian would really be to help.

"Like I have a chance in hell of getting anywhere near the place now."

Maura leaned her forearms on the bar. "I have an idea. But you're going to have to play nice."

Althea looked at her. "You mean, not insult or annoy anyone else?"

"That's a good start. I know someone who I think can help you. You may not be able to get into the house, but she can, with Harry."

"I will owe her my firstborn child, although she may have to wait a while to collect. And my undying gratitude, which probably isn't worth much right now. Who is she?"

"Gillian Callanan. She's a local artist."

"Why would she help me?"

Good question. "She wouldn't be helping *you,* she'd be helping Harry and Eveline. She knows they need the money."

Althea thought for a moment, her eyes unfocused, and then she said, "That sounds like the best deal I can hope for, under the circumstances. Okay, what do we do now?"

"Wait until Gillian comes in. I talked to her this morning, and she said she'd be along shortly."

Althea looked frustrated, even though she agreed. "What about this murder thing? Does that screw things up?"

"Is it related to the painting?" It was only then that Maura realized that there might be other scenarios — ones that involved Althea. "You think someone else could be looking for it?"

Althea considered briefly. "Believe me, I didn't go trumpeting this around to all my colleagues. Of course there's Nate Reynolds, the guy at the auction house who called me in at the beginning. When we met with the woman who had brought it to Nate, all she could tell us was that the woman who'd originally owned the sketch had come from Ireland somewhere. We never talked about whether there was another painting, but Nate could have made the same leaps of logic that I did."

"So you did meet with the woman who brought it in?"

"Dorothy? Yes. After Nate showed me the painting, we met with her once, the three of us together, after I'd done a little digging."

"What did you tell her?"

"That we both believed her little painting could be an important work of art and worth a good deal of money."

"Nothing about a big painting to go with it?"

Althea shook her head. "The poor woman was confused and overwhelmed enough as it was. I mean, what does she know about art or the art market? It's a wonder she didn't sell the thing at a flea market. And I didn't want to tip my hand to Nate — I hadn't really thought it all through. It was only after I got home again and did some more research that I realized there might be more to the story. And that's when I decided to come to Ireland."

"What's to stop this Nate person from doing exactly what you're doing?"

"You mean, heading over here on a wild-goose chase?"

"Exactly. How well do you know him?"

"We've met at various events here and there, and we're part of the same community, sort of. I don't know that he's a friend exactly. He's someone to hang out at the bar with, after an opening, say. Look, he called me because he knew I was up to speed on Van Dyck and he wanted an outside opinion, fast. I was close. When we all met, I didn't get the impression that he was holding much back. He just wanted to know what he had."

"Is he honest?"

"How should I know?" Althea shot back. "To a point, sure, but dangle a few million dollars in front of someone, and how honest are they going to be?"

"Wait — where does money come in?"

"I guess I should explain. Nate is an employee of the auction house. If he brings in an item for sale, like this painting, he gets kind of a finder's fee. The little painting might do very nicely in the right sale, so he'd see some reward for that. But if he found the big painting that goes with it, you can multiply that by a whole lot."

"What's in it for you? And don't tell me it will save your job. Would he pay you part of his share?"

"It doesn't usually work like that. All I asked for was that he let me exhibit the oil sketch, with a suggested attribution to Van Dyck, before it went up for sale. Period. I know you don't believe it, but I swear, for me it wasn't about the money. Though before you ask, even a fraction of what we're talking about would seem huge to Dorothy Ryan. And no one's out to bilk her either — it would be a fair auction and she would get whatever the market decided the painting was worth."

"Okay, I think I understand better now." Maura considered for a moment. "Did you tell the gardaí any of this?"

"I told them why I was here and what I was looking for. Do you think they'll figure out how valuable the big portrait could be?"

Maura struggled with how to answer that. "They're not stupid, but they don't have a lot of experience in some areas, and probably not when it comes to artworks. Just looking around and asking questions isn't exactly a crime, and that's all you've been doing, right? Their interest is solving Seamus Daly's murder. If what you told them — including the value of the painting — helps them with that, they're interested. Otherwise, probably not so much. Now, if this Nate guy had killed you . . . Seriously, do you think he might be in Ireland?"

"I really don't know. I mean, he never struck me as much of a go-getter, but then, he may never have had such a valuable item in his hands. All I can say for sure is that he hasn't gotten in touch with me." Althea swirled her empty coffee cup, staring at the grounds. Then her head snapped up. "Wait — are you saying you think this person who killed the gardener, assuming it's not Nate, might come after *me*?"

"Not if he — or she — finds the painting first. Let's say it is Nate, or someone like him, and he shows up here — what would his pitch to Harry be?"

"Something like 'It's worth millions . . . spotless provenance . . . I know an auction house that would jump at the chance to sell it . . . yadda yadda.' "

"Provenance?" Maura asked.

"Where it came from, where it's been. Odds are, this painting has been in the family since it was painted — if it's there." She ran her hands through her hair in frustration. "This is ridiculous! We aren't even sure the painting exists. I *have* to get into that house — or someone with a good eye does."

"And that would be me," Gillian said, sliding onto the stool next to Althea. She stuck out her hand. "Gillian Callanan. You're Althea?"

"I am." Althea shook Gillian's hand enthusiastically. "Gillian, great to meet you. Maura here says maybe you can help me? Let me say before you start: I don't deserve it, and I will be forever grateful. If there's any money involved, I'll see that you get your share."

Gillian cocked her head. "You really are American, aren't you? I'm not looking to be paid for whatever I can do. I've told Maura, I've known Harry all my life, and I like Eveline. If finding this thing and seeing that it sells, now or down the line, can help them, that's enough for me."

Althea looked uncomfortable, and Gillian pressed, "Is there something you're not saying?" She glanced briefly at Maura, and Maura wondered if she had winked.

"Well," Althea began, clearly embarrassed. Then her words came out in a rush. "Last night I went home with Harry Townsend, and early this morning his aunt Eveline caught me coming out of his room with not much on and now she's mad at me and will probably never let me near the place again, ever. And that Mrs. O'Brien threw me out for a *second* time. I'm sorry. You don't have to help me. I know it was stupid of me."

Maura held her breath, waiting to see how Gillian would react. Gillian managed to surprise her: she burst out laughing. "Wouldn't I love to have been a fly on the wall? Yes, I'm sure Eveline was not at all pleased — she belongs to a very different generation. And it is her home. Sounds like you managed to bollocks this up."

"Huh?" Althea said, confused.

"You messed up, wouldn't you say, Maura?"

"I would, Gillian," Maura agreed happily.

"What about Harry?" Althea said meekly.

Gillian laughed. "I've known Harry forever, so I can't say I'm surprised. You aren't hoping for anything more from him, are you?"

"No. No way. Not that he's a bad guy or anything," Althea hurried to add. "But I'm not interested in anything longer term. And I'm pretty sure he isn't either."

"You'd be right about that."

"Gillian, are you still willing to help me?"

Gillian studied Althea's face. "Before I make up my mind, tell me why you're so sure this painting is here."

Althea took a moment to gather her thoughts. "The woman who had the little painting when she died — she came from Cork, although the records I found didn't say where. I knew that Van Dyck had worked in Cork, or at least he had Cork connections. There's a nice portrait by Van Dyck of Richard Boyle, the first earl of Burlington and the second earl of Cork, in the National Gallery in London. Boyle was born in Youghal, and that painting dates to around 1640. There aren't a lot of surviving manors, or at least old families, in Cork from that period, and Mycroft House is the last one that I haven't seen. The timing and the connections fit, don't you think?"

"You may well be right," Gillian said. "Have you a picture of it?"

"Of course." Althea reached into her large handbag and pulled out an envelope, from which she extricated a glossy photograph. "This is Dorothy's painting." She passed it over to Gillian.

Gillian studied it. "Nice. I can see why you're excited. But I haven't seen a larger painting with that likeness in my visits to Mycroft House, though there are plenty of rooms, even on the ground floor, that I haven't visited. Do you think it resembles Harry?" She handed the picture to Maura, who looked at it briefly — to her it just looked like a kind of dull painting of a guy with long hair — then returned it to Althea.

Althea looked at it again. "You know, that

never occurred to me. But I think you're right."

Gillian went on, "So, where do things stand with you and the gardaí? What did they ask you?"

While Althea reviewed the events of the past day for Gillian, Maura went back to working, going around the room, greeting people who had come in recently, and collecting glasses. Somehow Billy had slipped in while she wasn't watching and was settled in his chair by the fire, a pint glass on the table next to him. Rose must have taken care of him.

Maura perched on the arm of his chair. "Hello, Billy. How are you on this fine day?"

"Happy to be here. I see that our artist has come home for the summer."

"That makes her sound like a bird. I should have figured you know her."

"Only since she was as high as my knee. Knew her father before her, and her grandparents as well, may they rest in peace."

"She a relative of yours?" Maura asked, only half joking.

"Well, her mother's sister married a nephew of mine . . ."

"She asked if she could put up some of her paintings here, maybe sell a few. Will anybody object?"

"Nah, she does good work. I don't think Old Mick would mind."

"You think he's keeping an eye on things from up above?"

"I'm sure of it." Billy took a swallow of his stout. "Those two look thick as thieves." He tilted his head toward Althea and Gillian, who seemed to be getting along well.

"All things considered. If you haven't heard already, Althea has also now managed to tick off not only Mrs. O'Brien but even Eveline Townsend herself, so I don't think she has a chance of getting into Mycroft House again. But Gillian can."

"Gillian is a generous woman indeed."

"Have you had any other ideas about Seamus Daly's death?"

Billy sighed. "Nothing's come to me. He wasn't the full shilling, but he was a harmless lad. Most likely he startled someone in the act . . . but the act of what, I can't say."

If this was one of those boring English novels Maura had been forced to read in high school, Seamus the gardener would have come upon a poacher with a couple of rabbits, and the poacher had dealt him a fatal blow. Of course in this case, the stakes might be a lot bigger than rabbits. Maura wondered how the Irish police handled forensics. If this was *CSI,* somebody would announce that Seamus had been hit with an antique shovel used for digging turf, bearing traces of rust and a waterweed that could only be found along twenty-two feet of harborfront. And the person wielding the shovel was five foot ten, left-handed, and had grown up in Albania. If there still was an Albania. Maura's sense of geography was a little fuzzy.

"You've customers waiting, Maura," Billy reminded her gently. "I'll be here for the afternoon, and I'll see what people have to say."

"Thanks, Billy. I hope it helps."

She went back behind the bar to help Rose fill orders. Business was picking up again, and it looked to be a busy afternoon.

When she came around the bar, Rose nudged her. "There's a fella over there — no, don't look — who's been keeping an eye on the three of you women."

"Why shouldn't he?" Maura asked. "From what I've seen, Gillian attracts a lot of attention." And Althea in her New York clothes and shoes simply looked out of place in a shabby pub.

"Dunno," Rose replied. "Oh, here he comes now."

Maura checked him out. He had close-cropped hair and a cheap leather jacket, and he didn't quite look like a typical sightseer. Whether or not he noticed Maura's examination, the man came up and leaned against the bar. "Can I get another?" *American*, Maura noted, as he pushed his empty glass toward her.

"Sure. You're American?" Maura asked conversationally. *This couldn't be Nate, could it?* she wondered, then immediately stopped herself. *Good grief, Maura, you're running a pub! See a stranger, assume he might be a murderer? You can't be suspicious of every unfamiliar face that walks in!*

He gave her a perfunctory smile. "Yeah. First trip to Ireland. You're American too, aren't you? What're you doing here?"

Maura watched the pint she was filling. "Actually, it's my first trip too." She grinned. "Came over and never left. I'm behind the bar because I own the place now. Are you enjoying your visit?"

"Kinda quiet. I've only been here a day or two."

"I'm Maura," Maura offered. "And you?" His eyes kept drifting toward Althea and Gillian. Of course, Gillian was a striking woman by any standard, and Althea was dressed to attract attention.

He turned back to Maura. "Oh, uh, Ray. You sound like you're from Boston."

"Southie, born and raised."

"Ah," Ray said. "So, what should I see?"

Maura topped off his pint and pushed it back toward him. "On the house, for a fellow American. Have you thought about visiting the Blarney Stone?" Their talk shifted to touristy things, and the man proved to be clueless about what to see, leaving Maura wondering why he had chosen this end of the country for his first visit, rather than someplace like Dublin. Maura made some suggestions, based on her own scant three months' worth of knowledge, and he seemed interested — but his gaze kept returning to the corner table where Gillian and Althea sat with their heads together. Well, if he wanted female company, Maura wasn't about to set him up. If he was lonely, he could go over and introduce himself. Maura was pretty sure that both Gillian and Althea could brush him off if they wanted.

As the afternoon wore on and local people drifted in, talking about the death of Seamus Daly, Maura didn't see the American leave.

CHAPTER 9

Gillian and Althea went off to strategize their approach to Harry and Mycroft House. There was finally a lull in mid-afternoon, and Maura realized she hadn't ever eaten lunch. "Did you eat, Rose?"

"I brought a bit from home. There's some left, if you like."

"If you're sure you don't want it."

"Most recipe books have recipes for at least four people, and there's only the two of us at home, when we're at home at all. Please, help yourself."

"Thanks." Maura rummaged in the small refrigerator and came up with a half-full container of something that smelled wonderful when she opened it.

"It's better hot, but it's fine cold."

"As long as I didn't have to make it, I'm happy," Maura said.

"You don't like to cook?" Rose seemed to find that idea surprising.

"Let me put it this way. I *can* cook, well enough to keep myself going, but I don't *enjoy* cooking. You do?"

Rose beamed. "I do. When . . . me ma was sick, a few years ago, I kind of took it over. She'd tell me what to do, and after a while I started trying things out. You know me da expects his supper, though I never know when."

Maura sat down at the end of the bar with the container and a spoon and tasted it. It seemed to be a cross between a soup and a stew, but whatever it was, it tasted really good. She looked closely at it: there wasn't anything she couldn't identify, but she'd never managed to put those ingredients together in a way that tasted like this. "Rose, you can cook!" she said. "This is great."

"Ah, it's nothin' special." Rose blushed and concentrated on polishing the already shining top of the bar.

Maura wondered again if there was some way to fit a kitchen, even a tiny one, in the back of the building. It was clear that Rose had a knack for cooking, and it would be a shame to waste it, but she had a feeling that even trying to add a new electric outlet in the old building could be a nightmare. Still, she'd keep the idea in the back of her mind.

Mick unexpectedly appeared from the

back. "What are you doing here?" she asked. "You aren't on the schedule until five."

"Just checking supplies. You've been busy?"

"We have. It's an awful thing to say, but death is good for business."

"Too bad about Seamus. He never did anyone harm, and to go like that . . . it's not right."

"No, it isn't." They both paused respectfully for a moment. Then Maura asked, "You have a minute?"

"You need something?"

"I have some more stupid questions, and I'd rather ask you than a stranger."

"There's nowhere I need to be, if you don't mind a minute while I make meself a cup of tea," he said. "Want one?" Maura declined, and he went around behind the bar and fixed himself a mug, then came back and sat down. "What did you want to know?"

"I guess I'm kind of confused by this whole class thing — you know, the big manor house, and who gets to go in the front door and who has to go around back. We don't exactly have that in the States. I know that here it's kind of a holdover from another time" — as was a lot that she had seen in Ireland, Maura added to herself —

128

"but it seems kind of relevant right now, doesn't it?"

"You mean Mycroft House and the Townsends?"

"Yes. I mean, they still have servants, right? Wasn't that what Seamus was?"

"More or less." Mick stopped to think for a moment. "I'll give you the short course on Irish cultural history, shall I? Starting with Harry Townsend."

"You don't much like him, do you? You were kind of, I don't know, stiff with him, when he was in here."

Mick answered carefully. "I don't know him well. I don't like his type. Do you want the history or not?"

"Sorry. Go ahead."

Mick sipped his tea. "Harry's the bitter end of an old Anglo-Irish family that's been settled here since the late seventeenth century, although most of the house is a bit newer than that. The Anglo-Irish used to be the important people — socially, politically, legally — and they owned much of the land in Ireland. They were Irish but they weren't, you know what I mean? Most of them were English, if you went back far enough, or even Norman, and most were Protestant. They didn't have much to do with our kind, except to hire us to work on their estates."

Maura was surprised at the faint bitterness in Mick's tone. The Irish held on to their grudges for a long time, it seemed — centuries, even.

Mick went on, "Like most wealthy people, they built a lot of grand houses — a lot of the city of Dublin too. They did do some good — the Anglo-Irish were very involved with Trinity College there, and they produced plenty of writers. Jonathan Swift, for instance — surely you've heard of him?"

Maura replied, tartly, "I'm not a total idiot, you know. We had to read *Gulliver's Travels* in school. So these Anglo-Irish families, they were sort of the big fish in a small pond, huh?"

"That's about the shape of it. Like I said, the Townsends were one of the old families, and they held some power in the old days, but Harry's branch was pretty junior. You know, third son of a third son sort of thing — and they just gradually faded. They didn't put enough back into their estates to make them productive, and to make ends meet they sold off bits and pieces of land, which didn't help. They apparently thought the good life was going to go on forever. I guess a lot of people thought that until the bottom fell out after World War One. Actually Harry's family was lucky that they've been able to hang on to the house this long. But the land around the manor's all that's left of the estate. Eveline is the last of her generation, and from what I hear, Harry's having trouble enough keeping the roof over her head. To his credit, I've never heard talk of him trying to move her out of the only home she's ever known, but aside from a few rooms, most of the place is closed up because they can't afford to heat it, and of course it's also falling down. The roof leaks, the plaster's crumbling, and so on."

Maura shook her head. "This whole class thing is so sad and stupid. Why didn't the Irish rebel against the way the Brits treated them? In America we fought back and forced them out. Why not Ireland?"

"They did, but they weren't very successful. You have to remember, until nearly the end of the nineteenth century, most of the Irish had no rights. They couldn't own land. They couldn't learn their own language. Your country is, what, a couple thousand miles away from England? It's different when your oppressors' seat of power is right next door. Here the British could all but spit at us. Do you not know that in the Famine, the landlords insisted that the Irish keep paying their rents and shipping the crops? When their tenants were starving?"

Mick was as angry as she'd ever seen him. "I'm sorry, but how was I supposed to know?" Maura protested. Maybe it was time to get away from history and back to the present. "Harry has a job in Dublin, right? Gillian told me that he's an accountant."

Mick took a moment to calm himself, then said, "She did, did she?"

Maura debated asking Mick about Gillian's relationship with Harry, but decided that would be tacky. Besides, he might not even know anything; men could be kind of blind about things like that. She went back to the topic at hand.

"Mick, my question is, does any of this matter, here and now? Okay, you've got this big old house, even if it is falling apart, and you've got the last two heirs hanging on by their fingernails, with a couple of servants or whatever you want to call them. And now one of them has been killed. But do you think it has anything to do with class?"

Mick shook his head. "Seems unlikely to me. No one cares anymore. A century ago, the gentry provided jobs for a lot of farmers' children, particularly the girls. The boys would work on the land or in the stables, and the girls'd put in a few years in service here, and then they might emigrate, with a better chance of getting a job in an American city. That went on for a very long time. Didn't I hear that your gran worked in the kitchen there as a girl?"

"If so, she never mentioned it." Like so many other things, Maura thought with regret. "In the U.S. she never did that kind of work, but she sure held her share of dead-end, low-pay jobs in Boston. So Harry is more or less the end of the line, any way you look at it?" When Mick nodded, she added, "Anyway, thanks, Mick, for filling me in. All this doesn't show up in our high school history classes."

Mick smiled. "Fair enough. I think your Revolution gets about three pages in our textbooks." He looked up to see a group of men coming in. "Welcome, fellas. What can I get you?"

Maura set to work pouring more pints and serving, and the next time she looked up, it was three o'clock. Althea and Gillian hadn't come back. Maybe Althea was promising Gillian a show of her own in a New York gallery, or maybe they'd cornered Harry somewhere and forced him to slip them into the manor house. No matter which, Maura felt a little left out. After all, she was the one who had put them together.

Sean Murphy, in uniform, came in the door and crossed to the bar.

"Hey, Sean," Maura greeted him. "Or am I supposed to call you Garda Murphy when you're on duty?"

"Sean is fine," he said. "Hey, Mick."

"Sean," Mick said. "Can I get you anything?"

"Not right now. I stopped by to talk to Maura, if you can spare her."

"Hey, I'm *his* boss, not the other way around," Maura protested. "What did you want?"

"Would you walk with me, outside?" Sean asked.

"Sure." Maura wondered what all the mystery was about, but as Althea had already commented, there were a lot of eager ears in the pub, and apparently Sean wanted a private word. "Where do you want to go?"

"How about along the harbor?" Sean suggested.

Well, that would certainly be more private than Sullivan's. "Okay." She followed him in silence until they'd crossed the road and descended to the rough lane that ran along the water. "So, here we are. What is it you wanted to talk to me about?"

Instead of replying directly, Sean pointed. "Look across the water there."

Maura looked. Trees, fields, cows, and a

few swans on the water. "What am I supposed to be looking at?"

"Straight on, over the water — that's
Mycroft House."

When Maura looked harder, she realized
that, on the other side of the harbor, she
could see small glimpses of a structure. "I
can't see much, but I guess I can tell there's
a building there. Why? Is this about the
murder? Have you arrested anyone?"

"We're no further along than when we
first found Seamus Daly's body. Nobody
saw anything or heard anything, and you
can see why — it's well hidden away. But
nobody had reason to want him dead. He
had no money, and he'd made no enemies.
I don't think any of this was about him."

"So, what do you think it was about,
then?" Once again Maura was faced with
the dilemma of whether to conceal information from the gardaí. "Uh, you talked to
Althea, right?"

"We did. She claims not to have seen
Seamus, but she admitted to trying to gain
entry to the house, though said she was
turned away by the O'Briens, which they
confirm."

"Well, she found a way in last night. With
Harry Townsend. Do you know Harry?"

"I spoke with him yesterday as well. He's

not been around much since I joined the guards, but I know of his reputation. But what does it matter if she was there the night *after* Seamus Daly's death?"

"I can't say, but I thought you should know that she's still looking for that painting, and she seems pretty determined. Did you talk to Eveline Townsend?"

"I did not myself, nor did any other garda, as far as I know."

That sent off a faint alarm for Maura. "That's weird. Shouldn't someone have talked to her, to see if she saw or heard anything?"

"We asked the O'Briens if she'd be up to an interview, and they warned us off, said it would upset her too much. Florence O'Brien went on to say that Eveline has been more and more vague in her mind of late — her old memories are clear, but not the newer ones."

"Does she even know that Seamus Daly is dead?" Maura asked, still incredulous.

"I'd imagine the O'Briens would have broken the news to her, carefully. Maura, you have to remember, the lady's not young."

"Well, yeah, but I'm just wondering . . . Look, maybe I'm out of line saying this, but it seems like there's still a class thing going on here. I mean, 'She's the fine lady from the Big House, so she shouldn't worry herself about one of the hired help getting killed right under her nose'? And then your people don't want to bother her, not even to solve a crime?"

Sean stiffened. "We spoke with those who know her best, and they said she wasn't up to it. Did you want us to barge in and harass a poor old woman? And there's none of us competent to assess her mental state. What is it yer asking?"

"Shoot, I don't know. I'll be willing to say that Eveline Townsend didn't take a shovel to the gardener in the middle of the night, but she still might know something useful." Maura once again thanked the stars that her own grandmother had remained mentally alert to the end.

"Maura, let the gardaí do their jobs, will you? Was there anything else?"

In for a penny, or whatever the silly slogan was. "Do you really think that Althea is a suspect?"

Sean sighed. "Truth be told, no. And she hasn't been all over us asking to go home. If she'd whacked someone, I'd expect her to clear out as fast as she could, if she had the chance."

"Like I said, she really wants that painting, and I don't think she's leaving until she's sure it's not at Mycroft House. And it seems to me that if the painting is there in the house, Seamus's murder could be somehow related to that. Has anybody come up with a better idea?"

"I shouldn't be telling you what I've already done. Will you be speaking with Althea again?"

She noticed that he hadn't exactly answered her question. "Yes. You want me to tell her something?"

"She's cooperated with us so far. We have no right to tell her what to do, seeing as she's a private citizen, and an American one at that. But if she comes upon something about this painting, could you ask that she tell us?"

"Of course. I think she'll be happy to cooperate, especially if she knows she's not a suspect. She wants to find this painting, but as far as I can tell, she wants to do it legally and as publicly as possible. She wants the credit for finding it."

"I understand."

"Was that all?" Maura asked. "Because we're expecting another busy night and I should get back."

"Well, yes, there was, in a manner of speaking. Not garda business. You see . . ."

He hesitated, and Maura noticed a red flush creep up his face. "I was after wondering . . . might you be wanting to have dinner with me one night?"

Well, that sure wasn't what she'd been expecting! Sean Murphy was asking her for a date? A real date? Maura wasn't sure she'd ever actually gone on a real date — people her age back in Boston had mostly just kind of hung out together, which was kind of hit-or-miss. Maybe things were different in Ireland. And now here was Sean, in his slightly too big uniform, his blue eyes anxious, asking her out. Did she want to date an Irish cop? *Maura, it's one dinner, not a lifetime commitment.* Would people in Leap talk? Of course they would. There'd be no hiding it. Was she okay with that? Maybe. Yes. "If you'd rather not, it's no big thing," he hurried to add, and Maura realized she'd been silent for too long.

"Sorry, it's just that you surprised me. Sure, I'd be happy to have dinner with you," she said firmly, before she could change her mind. "When?"

Sean Murphy looked like a huge weight had been lifted from his shoulders. He also looked about fifteen years old. "Grand. I know you're busy weekends. Monday, maybe?"

"Sounds great."

A date with Sean Murphy. Who would have thought?

CHAPTER 10

Maura and Sean said their good-byes before she went back into Sullivan's. As they'd walked back toward the pub, it hit Maura: she had exactly nothing to wear on a date. She'd have to ask somebody about that.

Althea and Gillian were back and had snagged a corner table, opposite Billy's chosen spot. They beckoned Maura over. Maura checked to see that someone was taking care of the taps and raised a hand to Jimmy Sweeney, but everything looked under control, so she joined them. "What's up?"

"Gillian's been giving me the whole history of the manor house," Althea said. "The dates fit, if the painting has been there since it was painted. But I still don't get why you haven't been inside it, Gillian."

"That's not the way things are done around here. Well, let me explain a bit. I've been inside, as Harry's guest, and once or twice to have tea with Eveline, but it's not like she gave me a guided tour of all the rooms. I think Eveline and I got along well — at least, I didn't offend her." Gillian shot a pointed look at Althea, who looked away. "Besides, it's Harry that's my friend, and he isn't around much, so that's limited my access. Maura, as I've told Althea, if the painting is there, it's probably in one of the rooms they're not using anymore. Florence O'Brien might know where it is but may just see it as a big old painting on a wall somewhere, not as a priceless possession. I doubt she'd recognize a specific artist."

"Oh, God," Althea moaned. "I can just see the painting moldering away. Too cold in winter, too hot in summer, and isn't every place in Ireland damp? With my luck, all the paint has already fallen off the canvas. We've got to find it before it's too late!"

"I'd say be patient, Althea, but I'm guessing that's beyond hope." Gillian winked at Maura. "Have you found anything new, Maura?"

"Sean Murphy stopped by while you were out." Maura debated with herself about telling them that Sean had asked her out, and decided that she wasn't ready to go there. "The gardaí have no suspects and no leads. They've talked to both of the O'Briens and to Harry, but not Eveline. They are officially stumped. I can't say that I blame them."

"Well, my gut still says it's got to be about the painting," Althea said firmly.

"Althea, we don't even know if there *is* a painting!" Maura protested, "and if there is, that it's in that house!"

"No one would kill a harmless gardener without a good reason," Althea insisted. "A very valuable painting is a good reason. Ergo, Seamus was killed because of the painting, which therefore must exist."

Gillian laughed. "That is the most circular piece of reasoning I've heard in a while!"

"You have anything better?" Althea demanded. "Anything? Huh?"

"Cool it, you two," Maura said. "What's your next step, Althea?"

Althea slumped in her chair. "I don't know. I was thinking about calling my buddy Nate at the auction house and seeing if I've missed anything. Maybe Dorothy Ryan shared something with him that he didn't pass on to me — he could have been in contact with her who knows how many times, while I've been running around here."

"Wait, isn't he one of the only other people who knows about the oil sketch?" Gillian asked.

Maura refrained from pointing out that

half of West Cork must have heard by now — but Nate had known earliest.

"How much do you trust him?" Gillian asked.

"As much as I trust anybody in the art world in the greater New York area, which isn't saying a heck of a lot."

"How well do you know him?" Gillian asked.

"We don't hang out together socially. We see each other at professional events sometimes, and we have mutual friends. Look, he knew enough about me to get in touch with me when he saw the oil sketch, and I was definitely the right person to consult. I don't think he had anything underhanded in mind — at least, not at the time. He could have changed his mind."

"Is this auction job full-time, or does he do something else for a living?" Gillian asked.

"That's it. It's a small house in New Jersey. They're trying to get established, but this is a lousy time for it. Or maybe not — the big auction houses are stuck in New York with a lot of overhead costs, just when people are counting their pennies and not spending big on artworks the way they used to, or they're looking for a really good deal. Either way, the income of the big houses is down. So being in Jersey, with lower over-head and a younger, less expensive staff, may be a plus. And he may be hungry for business."

"So why'd he pass the question on to you?"

"I don't know. Maybe he didn't trust his own judgment and wanted somebody to confirm what he thought he had, and because he knew about this show I was working on, he thought of me first. My eye would already be tuned to a Van Dyck frequency, so to speak."

"Did you tell him you thought the sketch really was a Van Dyck?" Gillian asked. "Who brought up the name first?"

"He let me take a look at the painting first, without giving any hints. But it was obvious to me immediately, and then he said he thought it might be a Van Dyck work but he wasn't sure."

"No poker face, huh?" Maura said.

"Hey, I was excited, all right? It was so cool to handle the painting, up close, and to find even a hint of a major work that isn't even in the catalogue raisonné would be huge. It just came out of my mouth."

"Uh, English please?" Maura said.

"What? Oh, you mean catalogue raisonné? That just means all one artist's works —

everything he's done in his life, as far as is known."

"Okay, got it," Maura said. "So the guy knows you think the sketch is for real, and nobody in your museum or auction world knows about it, and Nate knows that the owner came from Ireland originally. If — and that's still not for sure — if he came up with the same idea that you did, that there's a bigger, more important painting somewhere, this would be the first place he would look for the painting too. Have I got the outline about right?" When Althea nodded, Maura asked, "And if he thought like that, what would he do next?"

"The same thing I'm doing, of course," Althea said glumly. "If he wants his auction house to have the right to sell the sketch, it would be a whole lot more valuable if he can prove it really is a Van Dyck. It would definitely be worth it to him to at least take a stab at finding the final painting."

"And he knows as well as you how to research the provenance of an artwork," Gillian said. "Are you sure he isn't in Ireland right now?"

Althea glared at her. "You two really know how to cheer a girl up! You're right — he could be on the same trail, right here."

"And he could be involved in Seamus Daly's death!" Maura said, exasperated. "Did you tell the gardaí about him?"

"Well, no. I told them the facts — why I was here, why I wanted to get into Mycroft House. They didn't ask about anyone else. Can they find out if he's here, if I tell them?"

Maura sat back and sighed. "The local garda station is about twice the size of this room and has at most ten guys on staff. I sincerely doubt they have the resources to see if your pal has entered the country or to track his mobile phone to find out exactly where he is or whatever. In theory I guess they could, but not easily, and it would probably require a lot of paperwork. So that's not happening, not without a good reason. Besides, why would they look? It's not like they have any reason to think this Nate guy is involved in a crime."

"But you're the one who keeps telling me how small this place is!" Althea protested. "Wouldn't Nate be easy to find, if he's here somewhere?"

Maura looked at Gillian. "Help me out here, will you? You must know more than I do about how this works."

Gillian reflected a moment, then said slowly, "Like Maura said, if somebody was looking, they might be able to find him. But it's tourist season. There are lots of unfamiliar people about. If — still an if — your Nate is in this area, there aren't many places he could stay, but it's not as if the gardaí have any reason to go looking for him. Why don't you just call the guy?"

"What, now? This minute?"

"Why not? Catch him off guard — ask him where he is."

Althea stared at Gillian. "What time is it in New Jersey?"

"Five hours earlier than here," Maura replied promptly.

"Oh, but it's Saturday. Isn't it?" When Maura said yes, Althea went on, "The only number I have for him is his work number, and he may not be there on a Saturday."

"Don't they hold auctions of a Saturday?" Gillian asked.

"Well, yes, I think so."

"So somebody should be answering the phone there. At least you can find out if he's in town."

Althea hesitated for a long moment, then said, "You're right." She rummaged around in her large handbag and pulled out a small notebook as well as her phone. She held up the phone. "Will this work here?"

Maura recognized the type of phone. "Wait, hold on. Does that have international calling?"

"Uh, yeah, because I work with museums all over the world," Althea said. "Why?"

"Because whatever number comes up on his end might tip him off about where you are."

"But it's my regular number — he'd recognize that."

"Yes, but there are international prefixes and the like, aren't there?" Gillian asked.

"Oh, shoot, you're right. I'll text him." Althea tapped on her screen for a bit, then keyed in some text. "There, done. I said I needed to check something about Dorothy's painting ASAP, but I didn't say why. I know Nate lives on his smartphone, so it shouldn't be long. I can ask if we can get together or something and see what he says — he doesn't know I'm here." She stood up. "I'm going to hit the ladies'," she said and walked off toward the other end of the room.

"So, what do you think of Althea, now that you've spent some time with her?" Maura asked Gillian when they were alone. "Is she being straight with us?"

"You know, I think she is. She's pushy, but I think part of that is the New York style. Does she know what she's talking about when it comes to the art? I believe she does. I'm no expert in her area of specialization, but I know a fair amount from art school, and I know a bit about galleries and museums. She talks the talk well enough to convince me she's legit."

"So she's not an international art thief?" Maura smiled, then answered her own question. "If she was, she'd be more quiet about it, wouldn't she?"

Gillian smiled. "You mean she wouldn't tell the whole pub, and for all I know the whole hotel in Skibbereen, all about her business? I'd agree with that. Subtle is not her strong suit."

"You've got that right."

Althea came back in and dropped back into her seat. "Now what?"

Maura scanned the room — she was supposed to be running the pub, not looking for lost paintings. Rose waved as she left for the day; Mick and Jimmy seemed to have things in hand. Maura turned her attention back to the conversation with Althea and Gillian.

"Tell me more about how this all works," Gillian said. "Say your friend Nate finds the painting here at Mycroft House. Can he make an offer to Harry or whoever the official owner is to sell it through his auction house? Does he have that authority? And who makes the money?"

"There are a couple of different ways this

works, depending on the house. He could be on salary or working on commission. He works for Goodham's, in New Jersey — do you know it?" Althea asked. Gillian shook her head. "They're relatively small and eager. I don't know the details about their sales policies, but if Nate is really here in Ireland, which we don't know for sure, and he's hot for this painting, then I'd bet he's working on a commission basis. Which would be a nice piece of change for him, even for the sketch. For the pair of paintings, it could be huge."

"Why would Nate get first shot at it?" Gillian asked. "I mean, there are much bigger auction houses out there — even Harry knows that."

"Sure, but they'd also take a bigger cut. Look, this would be a real boost for a small place like Goodham's, and for all I know they'd waive their fees just to get the publicity. So Harry might make more on it by going with the smaller place. I'm just guessing here, but it's a possibility."

"In that case, why would Harry or Eveline lend the painting to you, Althea, if they could get cash in hand much more quickly by going with Nate's auction?"

"Because if it goes into the exhibit the publicity would attract more buyers and drive up the auction price. Everybody wins. But I have to get in first, before Nate makes his pitch."

"Althea, I know this may not come naturally to you, but why couldn't you and Nate simply work together?" Gillian asked with a smile.

"Because if I find it first," Althea shot back quickly, "I have some leverage. I'd be happy to let Nate and Goodham's sell it — *after* I get what I want, which is the recognition for finding it. I want to save my job at the museum, because if I can't pull off this discovery thing, I'm out on my ear when the grant money runs out. And even if I get dumped regardless, at least the local arts community will know my name, which will help if I have to find another job. Seriously, I love what I do. Of course money would be nice, but it's not the most important thing."

Gillian gave her a searching look before saying, "Althea, I don't know if you're being straight with us, but I'll confess, I'm curious — I'd like to know if this painting really exists."

A muffled tone sounded from Althea's pocket. She pulled out her phone. "It's Nate," she said. "That was fast."

"And?" Gillian asked.

Althea was still looking at the tiny screen.

"He says he's at the auction and can't chat now. He hasn't talked to Dorothy lately but he plans to see her next week. What do I tell him?"

"Do you believe him?" Gillian asked. "On either count?"

"You mean if he's in New Jersey and if he's planning to see Dorothy?"

"Yes."

"What difference does it make? Right now I can't prove he's *not* there."

"Then tell him you'd like to be there when they talk," Maura suggested. "That way he might think you're still in the States."

"Good, right." Althea keyed in a response, then hit send. She got a reply almost immediately. "Done. He agreed that I could tag along. How very friendly of him — ha!"

"So now we go back to worrying about what's going on here," Gillian said. "What are you going to do?"

"Find that damn painting," Althea replied.

Chapter 11

Maura checked the crowd again: definitely growing. "I've got to get back to work, ladies. Let me know when you've figured out what you want to do."

Gillian turned to Althea and held her gaze. "I'll talk to Harry and lay out what we think. He can probably get me — and Maura, if she likes — into the house." As Althea started to object, Gillian went on. "Eveline likes me, Althea, but I doubt she thinks kindly of you right now, after your last encounter, and we need her goodwill. Eveline's moral standards are those of another age, so if you're a guest in her home, she'd be polite to your face. You know and I know that you and Harry are willing adults, but throwing your . . . recreational activities in Eveline's face, even by accident, was not a smart move."

"I'm sorry!" Althea protested. "Harry didn't warn me — we were kind of caught up in the moment. It's not like I planned for her to see me like that. What planet are we on, anyway? This is the twenty-first century!"

"This is still Ireland, and Eveline is north of eighty," Gillian said sternly. "It's her house, so you play by her rules."

Maura stood up. "Okay. Gillian, you talk to Harry and see what you can set up, and let me know. I've got to get to handle the bar."

"What am I supposed to do?" Althea pouted.

"Go sightseeing, go fishing, go shopping. Just stay away from Mycroft House, all right?"

"Yeah, right." Althea didn't looked satisfied, but she stood up and stalked out of the pub.

"You're welcome, Althea," Maura called out to her retreating back. "Sorry, Gillian, but I've still got a pub to run. Let me know what Harry says, will you?"

"I will. Go on, then," Gillian replied.

Back behind the bar, Maura told herself that Althea and her mystery painting really weren't her problem, except where they involved the police. Specifically, Sean Murphy. Who had found the body, or at least been first on the scene, and who, given the small number of Skibbereen gardaí, was going to be in the thick of the murder investigation. Who had just asked her out on a date. Which meant what? She didn't know.

She'd never had a serious long-term relationship with a guy. Back in Boston, she'd convinced herself that she didn't have time, but the truth of it was that nobody had interested her. Most of the guys she'd met there seemed immature, and most of them had wanted nothing more than to get into her pants, and she didn't want that, not from some townie jerk who probably couldn't spell her name right. Sean seemed nice, but she didn't want to lead him on. At the same time, she didn't want to disappoint him. She had too much to sort out, what with the pub and the house, and she'd be willing to bet that after having dinner with Sean in a public place, half the people who came into Sullivan's the next day would ask if they'd had a nice time, and how was the food? If you messed up with someone around here, it was hard to avoid that person, which meant you had to tread really carefully.

"Hey, Maura — two pints waiting for those guys in the front." Mick's voice broke into her thoughts.

"Right, got it." For the next hour, Maura

worked steadily. The pub was packed wall to wall. Maura saw Gillian fight her way to the bar where she was pulling pints, one after another. Gillian shouted something at her, and Maura yelled back, "Can't hear you!"

Gillian cupped her hand around her mouth. "Tea with Eveline, three, tomorrow, at Mycroft House. I'll meet you here."

Maura yelled, "Great! Thanks."

"What's that about?" Mick asked, when there was a brief lull.

"Gillian's arranged with Harry to show us around Mycroft House so we can look for Althea's painting. I'll be off for an hour or two tomorrow afternoon."

"Hobnobbing with the upper classes, are we, now?" Jimmy said. He'd come up behind her when she wasn't looking. "Tea and crumpets? Think they'll bring out the good silver for the likes of you? Oh, that's right — they pawned it a while back to fix the roof."

Maura was surprised at the edge in his tone. "Jimmy, what's your problem? I'll have a chance to see the house tomorrow, and that's it. I don't expect to make Eveline Townsend my BFF. What are you, a reverse snob?"

Jimmy sniffed. "That Harry — he's been

known to skip out on paying his bill now and again. Thinks he still owns the village, like back in the old days." Jimmy picked up a couple of pints and left to deliver them.

Maura turned to Mick. "What was that about?"

"Don't mind Jimmy — he's jealous of Harry. Harry seems to have it all and gets away with a lot. So you're going calling, are you?"

"I am. Shoot, I'd better wear my good pants — oops, you call them trousers here, right? Has Eveline ever even seen blue jeans?"

"On Seamus, of course."

"Oh, right. He'd work in them, in the garden. Well, if that blasted painting is really in Mycroft House, we might be one step closer to figuring out why he's dead."

"I'm sure Sean Murphy will be pleased."

Maura gave Mick a sharp look, but he'd turned away to talk to a customer, and she didn't feel like pushing it.

The next day was moderately busy but provided no excuse for Maura to back out of her appointment for tea. Not that she wanted to. She was curious. Not many ordinary tourists had the chance to visit one of the big houses, even a crumbling one, in a social way. She didn't assume Eveline Townsend would warm to her; in fact, she wasn't even sure that Eveline would talk directly to her, not if Gran had worked for her family, years back. Would Eveline even remember? But as she'd said to Jimmy, she didn't expect Eveline to become a friend; Maura wanted to be no more than another pair of eyes, and that would be the end of it.

Harry pulled up outside Sullivan's with a flourish, in an aged but well-maintained Mercedes convertible — a relic of earlier, wealthier days? — and Gillian waved from the passenger seat. Maura told Rose, "I'm off. If I'm not back by sundown, drag the harbor for my body."

Rose looked bewildered. "What?"

"I'm having tea with the Townsends. I shouldn't be more than a couple of hours, okay?"

"Got it. Have fun, and mind your manners. And tell me all about it when you get back!"

"Will do." Outside, Maura climbed into the small backseat of Harry's sporty two-door car. "Hi, Gillian, Harry. Thanks for letting me tag along. I'll keep my mouth shut."

"You'll do no such thing," Gillian said

promptly. "Eveline is a very nice woman, and she'll be quite polite to you. Right, Harry?"

Harry concentrated for a moment on making a sweeping U-turn and heading back toward Skibbereen. "I'd guess Aunt Evie will be so glad to see a friendly new face that she won't care who you are."

At least as long as that friendly new face isn't in her skivvies in Harry's bedroom, Maura thought, but aloud said only, "Do we have a strategy?"

"I wouldn't bring up the painting per se," Gillian answered. "I haven't seen much of the building, and you haven't seen any of it, Maura. We'll just ask for Eveline's permission to let Harry show us the rest of the place. I think it's better than sneaking around and possibly startling her coming around a corner, which has been known to happen." Gillian glanced toward Harry, a slight smile on her face.

Harry ignored her jibe. "So, if the painting is there, when is it meant to have been painted again?" he asked. "I'm wondering which illustrious ancestor of mine it could be."

"Around 1640, maybe. Who would that make it?"

"Given the era, I'd guess probably Colonel

Richard Townsend, the founder of the family, or possibly one of his sons. Aunt Evie would be able to tell you — she's the family historian, although I'm not sure how much of that she remembers now. If I recall, he was part of the court of Charles the First, in England, and he was lucky enough to grab quite a big chunk of land in Ireland. He built this house, or at least part of it. He married well and had several sons, and they outgrew this place, so he moved the family seat to Kilkenny. One of his younger sons inherited Mycroft House, and we've been here ever since."

He pulled off to the left and followed a long driveway that paralleled the harbor; Maura, bouncing around in the backseat, guessed it was long overdue for paving, or at least another load of gravel. The driveway was flanked by old trees that hung over the single lane — they looked as though they could use some pruning, but Maura guessed that not too many vehicles passed this way.

"Look there, ahead, Maura," Gillian said.

Maura leaned forward for her first glimpse of Mycroft House. She was surprised: in her mind she'd expected something far grander. At the end of the drive, the house sat on a rise and faced the gardens and the water. The white stucco-clad building with a slate roof consisted of a central part flanked by two symmetrical smaller wings, and the whole appeared to continue toward the back. The ground-floor windows extended nearly to the ground and had to be six feet high; the front door was sheltered by a covered portico. The lawns between the house and the water were punctuated with strips of formal garden, including a wealth of rosebushes, many blooming. Seamus's work, no doubt, and their lushness was a tribute to him. Who would take over now? Maura wondered.

Theirs was the only car in sight. Maybe there were garages or stables out back, out of sight; surely the O'Briens must have some way of getting around. They could walk into Leap but not to Union Hall.

Harry pulled up in front of the door and parked. Gillian climbed out without waiting for help, then turned and offered Maura a hand to extricate her from the backseat. Harry paused in the doorway, looking for all the world as though he was posing for a society portrait. All he needed was a pipe and a dog, or maybe a waiting horse, to be the picture of the perfect Irish country gentleman.

Harry waved theatrically at the facade. "Welcome to Mycroft House, Maura. What do you think?"

Maura nearly laughed. She felt like she'd wandered into some novel, or maybe an old movie. "Oh, my, sir, it looks real grand, it surely does." She faked a curtsy.

Gillian elbowed her in the ribs. "Maura, be nice. It really isn't his fault that he owns a manor house."

"And if I could get rid of it, I would, believe me," Harry said, although he was smiling. "Are you lovely ladies ready to go in to tea?"

"Sure," Maura replied cheerfully, "and I promise not to steal the spoons."

As Harry opened the massive front door and ushered them into the broad central hall, Maura tried not to gawp. Her first impression was how big everything was — the entire apartment she had grown up in could fit in the entrance hall. High ceilings, a checkerboard marble floor, and a bunch of paintings in heavy gold frames were all she could take in quickly. The only time in her life she could recall being inside a building this big was probably some field trip to a museum when she was a kid. "You said your family has lived here for centuries. Is that true?"

Harry responded modestly, "Well, the land's been in the family for quite a while, and, as you can guess, a lot of the ancestors took a whack at building, not always successfully. If you go down to the basement, there are actually some medieval walls from some earlier building, probably a monastery, but most of the shell is early eighteenth century, with a few later additions. My grandfather peeled off some of the worst of the Victorian efforts — although probably even those would be considered gems now. Tastes do keep changing."

"Did you grow up here?" Maura asked, with real curiosity.

"Mostly, when I wasn't off at school. I'm an only child — the last of my line — but there were always a lot of cousins visiting, so it was a lively place. We used to have a lovely time sliding on the hall floor here, in our socks."

Maura looked across the vast expanse of polished marble and tried to imagine a tribe of young boys and girls scooting around. The idea made her smile.

"Ready for tea?" Harry asked.

"Yes, Harry," Gillian said. "Let's get this started, if you please."

Maura hung back, feeling shy. What was she doing here? Billy had told her that Gran was a servant here, a long time back. Now she was coming through the front door —

164

as a guest? Would she be welcome?

Harry led them through a series of increasingly smaller corridors, finally arriving at the back of the house and outside. There were more gardens here, though less formal and smaller, bordered by the thick stand of trees that hid the house from the road that Maura knew led to the village of Union Hall. Harry guided them through a gate into a small walled garden, filled with lushly blooming flowers that Maura couldn't begin to identify. More of Seamus's work, no doubt. The household was really going to miss him.

Ahead Maura could see a grouping of white-painted cast-iron chairs around a table laden with teapot, cups, and plates. One of the chairs was occupied by a small, white-haired lady, who appeared to be dozing and hadn't noticed their approach.

Harry called out, "Aunt Evie?"

The woman gave a start, then focused on them. She stood up carefully, and Maura noted that while the cut of her flowered dress suggested another era, as did the long string of handsome pearls, her hair was neatly combed and her pearl earrings matched the string around her neck.

"There's no need to raise your voice, my dear boy. I heard you coming. Gillian, it's lovely to see you again. And you must be the new American." She extended a well-manicured hand to Maura, who shook it carefully. "Welcome to Mycroft House. I'm so glad you could join us for tea."

Eveline's smile was warm, and Maura returned it. "Thank you for inviting me. You have a beautiful house."

Apparently she had said the right thing, for Eveline beamed at her. "Isn't it, though? And you should see it when there's a party, all the windows lit up — just wonderful. Harry, will you pour? I've been a bit stiff lately — it must be all the gardening . . . I asked Florence to set up out here — the weather's been so lovely."

"The garden's looking grand, Eveline," Gillian said. "Would you mind if I came by and did a few pictures here?"

"Please do, my dear. It's no trouble."

With all this talk of the garden, Maura wondered if anyone was going to mention Seamus, but it seemed wrong for her to bring it up on this polite social occasion. She felt tongue-tied. What was she supposed to say?

"I asked Florence to make us some fresh scones. Ah, here she is — she'll tell you that scones are best eaten warm."

Maura looked toward the house to see a

plain woman who appeared to be around fifty, plodding carefully in her sensible shoes, balancing a tiered silver tray bearing the promised scones as well as some other sweets. Florence set the tray down on the table and looked briefly at the group, without warmth. "Is there anything else you need, Eveline?" she asked.

"No, thank you, Florence. I think we're all set. I'll let you know when you can clear the table." Eveline turned back to Maura. "Please try a scone while they're hot, Maura. Florence is an excellent cook. Tell me, how does a young American girl come to own a pub in a small Irish village?"

Maura took a plate and helped herself to a scone and butter. The butter knife looked old — was it real silver? Not that she'd seen much in her lifetime. "It's kind of a long story, but the short version is that my grandmother left here when my father was young, but she kept in touch with Mick Sullivan, and he left it to me." Maura hesitated before adding, "You might have known my grandmother — Nora Sullivan?"

"There was a young woman named Nora who was employed here, oh, some forty years ago, when we kept a full staff," Eveline said thoughtfully.

"That could have been her. She left when

she got married." Clearly there was nothing wrong with Eveline's memory, at least for the past, if she remembered a housemaid who'd been here only a couple of years, decades earlier.

"How very interesting. And here you are, back in Ireland after so long. Are you settling in well? I'm so impressed by you young girls today — you do so many things that we never would have considered when I was your age."

"I'm enjoying it, so far. It's a beautiful country, although I haven't seen a lot of it." And after that, the conversation rolled forward smoothly. The tea was excellent, as were the scones and small sandwiches. Gillian seemed at ease with the older woman, and Harry was attentive to his elderly relative, which was nice to see. Maybe even a horndog like Harry had a good side.

An hour slipped past. Maura realized she was enjoying herself: this was certainly another way of life, or what was left of what it had once been. Kind of a time warp. Eveline dominated the conversation, if gracefully, and Maura wondered if Harry had been right about his great-aunt's hunger for new faces, people who hadn't heard her stories. Much like Billy Sheahan, even if the setting was different. One of the minuses of a small Irish town: everybody had heard everybody else's tales.

Soon, though, Eveline's energy began to flag — it was clear she had expended quite a bit entertaining her guests. Maura was pleased to see Harry notice; another point in his favor. Standing up, he said, "Well, Aunt Evie dear, we shouldn't keep you." He offered her his hand, but it took Eveline a moment to collect herself.

"Well, if you must go, my dear, perhaps I'll just take a little nap. Oh, have you shown Maura the rest of the house yet?" She turned to Maura. "I heard you were particularly interested in seeing it, though I'm afraid it's a pale shadow of what it once was. Still, you might enjoy it."

"I'd love to see it," Maura replied promptly. "And thank you for having me. You've been very kind." She was touched that Eveline had made such an effort to entertain them.

Harry, with Eveline's hand tucked under his arm, led a slow procession back to the house and saw Eveline to the door of her own sitting room, near the front of the house on the ground floor. Maura doubted the old lady could have climbed stairs at that point.

Maura and Gillian remained in the hall

while Harry settled Eveline.

"So we're in," Gillian said.

"With an invitation, no less. How big is the house?"

"I've never counted the rooms. Actually, though, this is on the small side for a manor, although this was only a minor branch of the Townsend family."

"If you say so," Maura muttered.

Harry emerged from the sitting room, closing the door quietly behind him. "She's all tucked in. Let me have a quick word with Florence and tell her she can clear up in the garden, and then we can begin."

"Harry, can I do that?" Maura volunteered, and then she struggled to come up with an excuse, apart from curiosity about what went on "backstairs." "I wanted to introduce myself properly, since we're neighbors now." It was lame but good enough.

"If you want. The kitchen's in the back, on the left. Oh, and warn Florence that we'll be pottering around the place so she won't think we're burglars. I daresay she hasn't been in some of the rooms for years herself."

"I'll do that. Meet you back here." Maura set off toward the back of the house and found the kitchen mainly by following the delicious odor of baking. When she arrived there, Florence was busy chopping something at a well-scrubbed wooden table. She looked up when Maura walked in. There was no sign of her husband.

"Yer the new girl at the pub, eh?"

"Yes, I am. We haven't met. Maura Donovan." She held out her hand, but Florence held up her own, covered with chopped onions.

"I don't hold much with drinking," Florence said with a sniff. "Nor do we have the time fer hangin' about the pubs, me and my husband. And now with Seamus gone . . ."

"What a terrible thing to happen. He'd been with you a long time?" Maura asked.

"Near as long as Tom and myself have been here at the manor — it's too much to manage for only the two of us, so Seamus was a godsend, like. He loved his work, and he never asked for much." She resumed chopping, looking away from Maura.

"It's a beautiful house. I don't suppose you use all of it, if it's just Eveline here now."

"She's content with the few rooms — she doesn't get around as well as she used to, but she does enjoy the sun in the garden. Although how she'll manage now I do not know." Florence shot a hard glance at Maura. "And why should I be telling you this?"

171

"Harry sent me back to tell you that we've finished in the garden and he's settled Eveline now. And now he's going to show us the rest of the house."

"So that's why he sent you, instead of telling me himself. Tell him to mind the dust," Florence said, a touch defensively, Maura thought. "We keep the rooms Eveline uses nice, but the rest're shut up, mostly. Excepting ours and Seamus's at the back."

"I haven't met your husband yet."

"He's somewhere about the place — he handles most of the work outside the house, and I do for inside. And don't expect to see him at Sullivan's, neither. We haven't the money for drinking."

Definitely defensive, although Maura wasn't quite sure why. She wondered if she should play the Gran card and decided it couldn't hurt. "You know, my grandmother was in service here, before she married. That was a long time ago, so I don't suppose you would have known her."

Did she sense a slight softening in Florence's expression? "We've been here only the last ten years, since Harry asked us to look out for Eveline. Yer gran would've been here well before my time."

Time to play one last card. "She's gone now. I wish I could have asked her what life was like here in the house when she knew it."

Florence unobtrusively crossed herself. "I'm sorry to hear that. So that's what brought you back here?"

"It is." Maura decided her bid for sympathy had done its work. "Well, I won't keep you, Florence. I'd better go join Harry and Gillian."

Florence definitely sniffed this time. "Harry could do worse than settle down with Gillian. Instead of messing around with some other people I could name."

Like Althea? Maura decided against getting into that. "I hope I'll see you again. Nice to meet you." She found her way back to the main hall, where Harry and Gillian were waiting, without any trouble.

CHAPTER 12

"So, did you two come up with a plan?" Maura asked.

Gillian began, "If Harry's ancestor was important, and he could afford to pay for a big-name artist, then it's probably a life-size painting. So it's big. It wouldn't fit in a bedroom. It's probably down here on the ground floor somewhere."

Harry agreed. "That narrows it down a bit, but not enough. There are quite a few large portraits lurking in dark corners here, though, so plenty of possibilities. But it may not be easy to make out a lot of them — they're pretty dark now, from years of smoky fires, age, et cetera."

"I know that, Harry. I don't suppose it would help to say it should be a 'good' picture?" Gillian made air quotes.

"Oh, so now you want to debate aesthetics, do you?" Harry said with a smile. "What's the man look like?"

Gillian fished in her bag and pulled out a print of the sketch Althea had given her. "Here he is, in the oil sketch."

"Ah, this *is* nice," Harry said.

"It is, isn't it?" Gillian said. "I'd say you take after him. This is a quick sketch, but it does capture the spirit of the subject. A formal portrait would be stiffer and more pompous. The whole goal was to impress the beholder with how important the sitter was. It was kind of a political statement. Does it look familiar?"

Harry held out his hands. "How am I supposed to know? I've never paid any attention to the paintings until now, to be honest." He squared his shoulders. "Right, so we're looking for a big, dark portrait of a pompous rich guy, who may or may not be Richard Townsend, which may or may not look like this sketch. Well, let's begin with the main hall — there's a whole crowd of portraits there."

Maura and Gillian dutifully followed Harry back to where they had come in. The hall measured at least fifteen feet across, with an equally high ceiling, and as Maura had noticed, it was lined with time-darkened oil paintings in massive, ornate gold frames. Some were landscapes, and about half were portraits. As they walked down the length of the hall, Gillian muttered to herself, "Too late . . . Too late . . . So covered with dirty varnish that I can't see a thing . . . Wrong clothes . . ." Once they'd completed the circuit, Gillian said to them, "No, it's none of these. Where next, Harry?"

"Follow me." They wandered from one room to another, coming in one door and going out another, so that after a half hour or so Maura was completely lost — the place seemed bigger than it looked from the outside. She knew she had seen a conservatory at the back filled with lush plants — more of Seamus's work? — and a music room and a drawing room, and there was a ballroom somewhere. And that was just the first — no, over here it was the *ground* floor.

"Why did you never think of selling some of these, if you're strapped? Even the bad pictures must be worth something," Gillian asked.

"I can't do that to Eveline." Harry raised a hand. "I don't just mean by the terms of her father's will, for all that she still owns everything, but knowing how sad it would make her if I started taking away the things that she's always known and loved. There'll be time enough for that. We'll get by."

Maura's estimation of Harry went up another notch. He seemed to be taking good care of his great-aunt, not just seeing to her physical needs but also respecting her wishes. Maybe that earned him the right to have a little fun now and then. Maybe he wasn't as much of a jerk as she had thought.

Maura's general, admittedly uneducated impression of the place, beyond the sheer size of it, was of a hodgepodge of styles, varying from room to room, and sometimes within a room. Maybe that was what happened when so many generations lived in the same place, and each one wanted to leave his or her mark. And never got rid of anything. Maura had little experience with that kind of continuity. But overall she sensed a slight but pervasive seediness — frayed edges, chipped corners, and the dust of long neglect. Maybe nowadays that would be labeled "shabby chic," but here it had come naturally, over centuries.

"Are we done yet?" Maura asked, sounding to her own ears like a cranky child. Harry had made dismissive noises about the kitchen, the wine cellar in the basement, and the servants' quarters up on the third floor under the eaves.

"Attic?" Gillian had asked.

"Too low for a major painting," Harry said. "Besides, it leaks. If the painting was there, it's probably destroyed. Heck, maybe they folded the damn thing up and stuffed it in a trunk."

"Heaven forbid," Gillian said fervently. "But you're probably right that the changes in temperature in the attic combined with the damp would probably have all but destroyed any painting kept up there."

"There's only the library left, at the back. My father loved the room, probably because that's where he kept the liquor. This way."

Harry opened the door and politely stood back to let Gillian and Maura pass. It was quite a dark room, its walls lined floor to ceiling with shelves filled with books in antique leather bindings, and heavy velvet drapes drawn nearly closed. Harry crossed the room and threw open the nearest set of drapes, sending up a cloud of dust in the process. Maura looked around the room with interest. She could visualize gentlemen retreating here after a six-course dinner and enjoying their vintage port and cigars — definitely not a room for the ladies.

Gillian was staring at something over the mantel, carved from mottled dark marble that to Maura looked like salami. There was a large painting on the wall, maybe six feet tall by three feet wide, its gilded frame extending nearly to the fancy molded plaster ceiling, and Gillian approached it almost

178

reverently, just as Harry opened more drapes on the opposite side of the room, throwing light directly on the painting.

"Yes," Gillian whispered, and then more loudly, "Yes!" She turned to her companions. "Look at it! This has to be it!"

Harry came up to stand beside Gillian. "Good God, I think you're right."

It was a three-quarters-length portrait, and the man in it was wearing a sumptuous suit of clothes, all satin and lace, but the face was the same as in the sketch, as was the air of arrogance, cockiness, and good humor. They all stared silently for several seconds.

"Do you know, that painting's always hung there, as long as I can remember, but I never paid attention to it," Harry said.

Maura turned to Gillian. "Is it —"

"A Van Dyck? I won't say no." Gillian's eyes were bright with excitement. "Althea would know more than I do, but the style is right, and the clothing, and it matches the sketch."

Harry looked pained. "I'm not sure I can bring Althea back, unless I smuggle her in, in a suitcase."

"You can work around Eveline's schedule, or at least keep out of her way, can't you?" Gillian said.

"It's not Eveline I'm worried about, it's Florence O'Brien. The O'Briens are very protective of Eveline, and I don't think they ever sleep. Maybe in shifts. We know that Florence had a run-in with Althea and didn't take kindly to her."

"Harry, you have every right to bring someone into the house — isn't it at least part yours? And by the way, if the O'Briens are so alert, how come they didn't hear anything when Seamus was killed?" Maura demanded.

"You know, I hadn't stopped to think of that," Harry said slowly. "I really can't say. Tom's been known to slip off to a pub the odd time or two, and Florence pretends she doesn't know. They're never both out at the same time. They take their job here quite seriously."

"So Florence would give him an alibi anyway? Swear they'd been together all night?"

Now both Harry and Gillian were looking at her oddly. "What?" Maura said. "There's been a murder. We're standing in front of an important painting, possibly worth millions, that more than one person may want to get his or her hands on, and it may have something to do with the murder. If you tell us that the O'Briens keep close watch on anyone who comes and goes here, then why didn't they notice something? I'm guessing you don't have alarms and motion sensors and that kind of stuff?"

Harry said absently, "Too expensive. You make a good point, but the O'Briens' room is at the back of the building, and Seamus was found on the front lawn. Maybe they simply couldn't hear whatever happened."

"Maybe." Maura wasn't convinced. "So what do we do now?"

"First I'm going to get some pictures," Gillian said, pulling a mobile phone out of her bag. She spent several minutes prowling around the picture, taking multiple shots, both up close and from a distance. Maura meanwhile wandered around the room, looking at books. She noticed that the dust layer was the same everywhere — on the shelves, the tables, and the floor. Florence hadn't dusted in here for years, she guessed. The good news was, if someone else had been looking for the painting, they hadn't been in this room, because the dust hadn't been disturbed until they arrived. Nobody had visited this room for a long, long time.

"Okay, I'm done," Gillian said. She turned to Maura. "Ready to go?"

"Sure." On the way to the car, out of Harry's hearing, Maura said in a low voice,

"What are you going to tell Althea?"

"I'm . . . not sure. I suppose I could text her one of the photos of the picture, but I'd really like to see Althea's face when we tell her we've found the painting. Let me text her and have her meet us at Sullivan's, all right? I won't give her any details."

Maura grinned at her. "You want to make her suffer, right?"

"Just a bit," Gillian said. "After all, she's the one who thinks the rest of us have to drop everything just to do what *she* wants. She can wait a bit longer." She raised her voice. "Harry? Let us break the happy news to Althea, will you? We want to surprise her."

"And I'd be in the way, eh?" He didn't look very upset.

He was right, whether or not he was joking. Getting together with both Althea, after their recent, rather embarrassing encounter, and Gillian, with their long history, could prove uncomfortable for almost everyone involved.

"You would," Gillian said decisively. When they were settled in the car, Gillian turned to Harry again. "Would you consider selling the painting, now that you know what it could fetch?"

Harry stared straight ahead as he started the car and didn't answer right away. "I'd be curious to know what anyone thinks it might be worth," he said carefully.

Gillian swatted his arm. "Harry, that's not answering the question. Althea's going to want to know whether she can borrow it for her museum's precious exhibit, and once the word gets round, there'll be a lot of interest — the cat'll be out of the bag. If the painting passes all the authenticity tests, you'll want to be alerting potential buyers."

Harry turned to her. "You mean after all this running around, you're not sure it's genuine? It's been in the family since it was painted!"

"That may be, Harry, but it could have been done by a pupil or a follower of Van Dyck's, not the man himself, which would make it worth less. And appraisals take time. Now, if Althea were to convince her museum to ship it to New York for this exhibit — at their expense — then there'd be plenty of chances for the experts to take a good look at it."

"They'd pay, eh? Assuming the poor old thing survived being taken off the wall and shaken up a bit." The car was running, but Harry made no move to drive. After a moment he said, "Gillian, let me think about this, will you? I'm not asking that you keep it a secret from Althea, even if you could, but I need to consider how to tell Eveline any of this, and what she might want to do."

"Fair enough. After all, it is your painting, and it's yours to deal with. But you already know that Althea will be leaning on you to act fast."

"That I do. What's the saying, 'a New York minute'? I think she needs to see what an Irish minute looks like."

He finally engaged the clutch, and the car shot down the drive, back toward Leap. Gillian was busy texting on her mobile phone. "Will it be quiet at Sullivan's, do you think?"

"Sunday evening? Probably. Why?" Maura asked.

"I don't want to tell her we've found the painting in front of a room full of gossips."

"I know what you mean. I'll find you a quiet corner." She could tell Gillian to go see Althea in Skibbereen, where she had a hotel room that would offer some privacy, but Gillian was right: she wanted to see Althea's reaction too. She felt personally involved in this hunt. "Should we tell the gardaí what we've found?"

"I hadn't thought about that," Gillian said, putting her phone away. "Maybe we should. But will it change anything? We've found no tangible connection between the painting and Seamus's death."

"Yet," Maura replied. "But if the gardaí don't look for one, they won't find it."

"There is that," Gillian agreed. "I'll leave it to you, then, since you seem to be on good terms with them. Harry, take us back, will you, now?"

"My pleasure," he said, but Maura thought he looked like he was thinking of something else. What would this discovery change for him?

CHAPTER 13

Gillian and Maura had been back at Sullivan's no more than five minutes when Althea rushed in. Maura hadn't had time to respond to the curious looks from Rose, Mick, and Jimmy, but she knew she'd have to report on her tea with Eveline when the dust settled, as soon as Althea left. Sometimes Sullivan's felt like a fishbowl, with everyone watching your every move. The interest wasn't exactly unfriendly, but it did take getting used to.

Stopping just inside the door, Althea scanned the room. Maura caught her eye and gestured toward Gillian, seated at the table in the corner. "I'll be . . . over there," she muttered to no one in particular and headed to join the two women at the table.

Althea was talking before she sat down. "So? What did you find?"

Gillian regarded her levelly. "What makes you think we found anything?"

"Because if the answer was 'no' you would have just said so. Okay, tell me."

Instead of saying anything, Gillian pulled out her mobile, opened the photo app, and handed it to Althea. Althea stared intently at the first picture, then scrolled through the next few, and by the time she was done she could barely sit still. "Yes, yes, yes! I knew it! I told you, didn't I? Didn't I? Damn, why didn't you get better pictures? This is like looking at a postage stamp. But it looks right. Doesn't it, Gillian?"

Maura suppressed a smile: everyone in the place was sneaking glances at Althea, and a few were watching openly.

"How does it compare with the oil sketch?"

"I think it's a good match. What do you think, Maura?"

"If it was a police lineup, I would have recognized the guy from the sketch."

Althea looked at her with a bemused expression, then burst out laughing. "You know, that's a good way of putting it. I'll have to remember that. So, tell me all about it."

"The painting measures something less than two by three meters — oh, for you that would be . . . three by eight feet, at a guess — and the frame looks original. As near as I

187

could tell, it's in good condition, although the varnish is soupy, as you might expect after three centuries. Harry says it's been hanging there forever, in what he called the library, which isn't used now. The good news is, the room is kept dark; the bad news is, it's unheated. But I'd guess the conditions are pretty stable, and I don't think the painting's condition is too bad."

"Good, good . . . Did Harry know anything about the subject?"

"A bit. He thinks it might be Richard Townsend, some earl back up the line. He's not much into family history, although he thought Eveline might know more."

"Great work, you guys," Althea said. "Okay, there's just one more thing . . ."

Gillian and Maura looked at each other. *Why do I think this isn't over yet?* Maura wondered. She answered herself, *Because that would have been too easy, and this is Althea.*

Althea leaned forward with an air of conspiracy. "What we have to do now is find the contract."

"What?" Gillian and Maura said at the same time. "Althea," Gillian said, "we found the painting for you. What you do from here is your business. There is no 'we.' "

"No, look, please . . ." Althea fumbled,

then took a deep breath. "I'm sorry; you're right. You've been great. So if I want anything else, I need to ask you. Nicely. It's just that this is so important to me, and I'm so excited. Please, Gillian, can't you help me just a little more? Maura, give a hand to a fellow American in need? Sisterhood and all that?"

When Maura just stared at her, Althea turned to Gillian. "You — you know how important this work could be to the art world. You know what it could be worth and how Harry and his aunt would benefit. And a work like that shouldn't be left to molder in the dark in a backwater like this. It should be taken care of and shown to the public. It's a treasure."

Gillian sat back in her chair and smiled. "Althea, you are not to be believed. You waltz in to this 'backwater,' as you so graciously call it; you pump everyone you can for information; then you try to sleep your way into the house to get what you want. And when that doesn't work, you enlist us to do your work for you. I'm not sure why we should agree with whatever scheme you've cooked up. Do you agree, Maura?"

"You've got that right," Maura answered. "To be blunt, why should we, Althea?"

Althea's eyes narrowed. "You want money?"

"This isn't about money," Maura protested. "I know I haven't been here all that long, but I've seen it over and over — people here have gone out of their way to help me. If you don't change your attitude, no one will step up." She glanced at Gillian, who nodded her encouragement. "Gillian and me, we've already taken time from our jobs or our lives to do you a big favor, so don't act all surprised when we expect something in return, especially when you decide you want more."

To her surprise, Althea didn't protest. After a long moment, she said, "You're right — again. I'm sorry — again. And I'm guessing getting credit in a footnote in an exhibition catalog isn't going to mean a whole lot to either of you. What do you want, if you help me?"

Gillian spoke first. "A bit of respect would be nice. Beyond that . . . you could get some of my paintings into a New York gallery. That could make a world of difference to me."

"Whoa! You seriously think I can get you a show in New York?"

"Did I say anything about a show? But you can put me in touch with the right people, maybe get a few of my paintings into the right places. If you've got the job you claim to have, you ought to be able to do that much at least."

Althea didn't answer immediately. Then she said slowly, "I'd have to see your work. If it sucks, though, there's no deal."

Gillian smiled. "I wouldn't expect anything less. I'll be happy to show you what I've done."

Althea turned to Maura. "What do *you* want?"

Maura thought hard. "Publicity." Althea arched an eyebrow in question. "You said you wanted to make a big splash when you go public with your find, right? Make sure you get some stories in the Irish papers too. And mention Leap — and Sullivan's. Tell whoever writes about the painting that Leap is a beautiful, unspoiled area with friendly natives and lots of history and full of surprises like your long-lost Van Dyck portrait. And great pubs. Why not tell 'em Michael Collins stopped in for a drink when he happened to be passing by? That'll bring 'em in." Maura had to fight a case of the giggles.

"When did Michael Collins drink here?" Althea sputtered.

"Hey, we don't know that he did, but he

came from near here, and the building's been here for a long time, so it's possible — barely. Can you prove he didn't? Be creative, Althea."

"You know, that's a smart idea, Maura," Gillian said with admiration. She turned back to Althea. "And it won't cost you a penny — you just have to contact the right people, and I'm sure your museum can make it happen. So there's the deal. If you want our help."

"You two aren't as dumb as you look." When she looked at their expressions, Althea was quick to add, "Joke! If I can do what you ask, it's a deal — and I promise I'll try my best. Now can I tell you what I need?"

Maura held up a hand. "Before we move on, there's one thing we keep leaving out: Seamus Daly's murder. Even if it has nothing to do with the painting, it still makes things more complicated. Look," Maura began, then hesitated — was she right to share what she had seen, or rather, not seen? She decided it was easier simply to tell everybody everything, excepting the bar patrons. "When we were in the library and Gillian was drooling over the painting, I was looking around the room. The place was really dusty — Harry said nobody's used it for years, and all the draperies have been closed for who knows how long. But there was dust on *everything,* including the floor. Which means that if somebody else was looking for the painting — and we're still not sure about that — that person never got into the room where the painting is and never saw it. Maybe Seamus ran into someone sneaking around the grounds and tried to stop them and got whacked, and the killer left in a hurry. So they still don't know that the painting is there for sure. Unless, of course, someone here blabs to the rest of the world." Maura raised her voice. "Think you can keep a secret, boys?"

"Will it get us a free drink?" someone called out.

"When the official headline shows up in the *Irish Times,* the first round's on the house." Maura's announcement was met with cheers. Mick looked at her from across the room and shook his head, but with a smile.

Maura turned back to Althea. "Okay, what is it you want us to do?"

"I have to back up a bit to explain," Althea began. "I believe with all my heart — and my gut — that this is a real Van Dyck. But at the museum, I'm not considered one of the experts, I'm just a midlevel employee. If somebody identifies what may be an important find, they go to the scholars, the academics, usually more than one, and even they don't always agree. If I come back with photos of this painting and say to my bosses, hey, I've found this great picture that I really believe is a long-lost work by Van Dyck, and I think it has to go into the exhibit that we've been planning for two years and which is going to open, like, tomorrow, they're going to laugh in my face."

"Wait a minute," Maura interrupted. "Isn't that why you've been looking for this in such a big hurry? To get it into the exhibit?"

"Well, yes. I know, bad timing, but the sketch surfaced very recently, and when I saw it I figured it was worth taking a chance. If it doesn't work out with the painting, I'll probably lose my job for going AWOL right now when I know it's crunch time. But I'd be losing it anyway after this show is up, so I figured, why not go for it?"

"So what's going to make a difference now?" Maura demanded.

Althea leaned in and said in a lower voice, "The people at the museum aren't going to take my word for it that this is the real thing, and we don't have time to go through an official review process. But I could jump right over that if I could show them the original contract, a letter to the artist, something from the period that establishes the commission and purchase of the portrait. If that proof exists."

"What makes you think the Townsend family would've kept a piece of paper from sixteen-whatever?" Maura asked. "They've got the painting, and they don't seem to care who painted it. They sure didn't treat it like it was anything special."

"I know, it's a real long shot. It's one of the things I wasn't even going to bother worrying about until I was sure I'd located the painting. Now I'm hoping somebody maybe stuck the estate records someplace and forgot about them, so they're still there. Do you think it's possible, Gillian?"

"Maybe," Gillian said dubiously. "We'd have to ask Harry, and I have trouble seeing him ferreting around in a batch of dusty old documents from sixteen-whatever about managing the estate. You may have noticed he has a rather short attention span. What's more, he has no interest at all in his own family's history, and I'm sure you've already noticed he's never looked at the paintings in the manor."

"He wouldn't help even for something this

important? Not to mention valuable?" Althea exclaimed. "Fine, I'd be happy to look for them myself."

"Althea, you know that's not going to happen," Gillian said. "If we agree to help you — again — you will have to tell us exactly what we're looking for. What kind of paper, what language it's written in. Details like that. And even if we find something that looks like a contract for a painting with the right date, what if it says no more than 'Big picture, eight hundred of . . . whatever was currency of the day'? Will that be of any use to you?"

"Maybe. It would be better than nothing. And can you do this fast?"

Gillian sat back and looked at Maura in disbelief. "Is it only me, or is she really this thick?"

Maura made a face. "Althea, didn't anybody ever teach you any manners? You don't exactly make people want to help you, no matter what you dangle in front of them."

"Maura, being pushy has gotten me where I am today. Somebody once said, 'I'd rather beg for forgiveness than ask for permission,' and that about sums it up for me. You know how many unemployed art historians there are? I *have* a job. I want to *keep* that job. And I'll do whatever it takes."

196

"Including murder?" Gillian said quietly.

"*No,* not that," Althea said, contrite. "I'm sorry if my shtick doesn't play well here, but that doesn't mean I'm a killer. I'll swear on as many Bibles as you want that I had nothing to do with the death of Seamus the gardener and I have zero knowledge of what happened aside from what you and the police have told me. Is that good enough for you? Are you in?"

Maura waited for Gillian's answer. This was much closer to her territory — art and Harry both. Of course, she herself knew nothing about historic documents — she'd never even seen one, unless she counted photos of the Constitution and the Declaration of Independence in her high school textbooks. The most she could add to the hunt would be an extra set of eyes.

"All right," Gillian said at last. "I'll help. But as I said once before, I'm doing it for Eveline and for Harry. Were things different, I'm not sure I'd cross the street to help you, Althea, the way you're acting. Maura, will you help?"

"You know I don't know anything about all this stuff, but if you really think I can help, I'll be there. Are we going to tell Eveline Townsend what's going on?"

"Grand. If there are more of us going

197

through the papers — assuming we find them — things might go faster. And let's allow Harry to tell Eveline what he thinks she needs to know."

Maura said quickly, "Then I'll help. Tomorrow and Tuesday are pretty slow days here, so I can get away for a few hours."

Gillian stood up. "Right, then, I'll give Harry a ring." She grabbed her mobile and walked out the front door, leaving Maura and Althea alone at the table.

"You know, Althea, you really are a pain in the ass," Maura said.

Althea grinned. "You're not the first person to tell me that. But I usually get what I want."

While Gillian made her phone call, Maura got up and collected a few glasses around the room, taking them back to the bar.

"So, what's that all about?" Mick asked Maura, his eyes on Althea.

"As if you haven't heard every word, just like everybody else in the place," Maura said. "I'll fill you in later. I may need to take some time off over the next couple of days. Can you and Jimmy cover?"

"Maura, you're the boss. You can bunk off whenever you want. You tell us what the schedule is."

She didn't feel like anybody's boss, but he

was right, at least in theory. "We'll figure something out. Oh, and I'll be out tomorrow night."

"That'd be your date with Sean?"

"You know about that?"

"It's a small town."

Figures, Maura thought. Was there no way of having a private life around here, short of living in a cave? Eveline Townsend and the O'Briens seemed to have managed it; no one knew much about any of them. But was becoming a recluse the only way?

Gillian approached the bar. "We're on for tomorrow. I'll pick you up here at eleven, Maura, if that suits — Harry won't be awake earlier than that. And you're to wait to hear from us, Althea, so don't just show up."

"Got it. I'll be waiting on pins and needles."

CHAPTER 14

After a while Gillian and Althea left to find dinner. The pub had filled gradually, keeping Maura and the others comfortably busy. *This is the way it should be,* Maura thought. Happy people, chatting, sharing a drink and a pleasant hour.

"Will you be wanting me to stay, Maura?" Rose asked.

"Only if you want to. I think we've got it covered." Maura hesitated, reluctant to go on. "Look, Rose, I, uh, need some help with something different."

"I'd be happy to help you. If I can, that is. What is it?"

"I'm kind of going out for a meal with Sean tomorrow night, and . . . jeez, this sounds so stupid, but I don't have anything to wear."

"Ah," Rose said wisely. "Do you know where Sean's taking you, then?"

"No idea. I don't think I've been to a

restaurant since I got here. You and everyone else in Leap know more than I do about this date. Where do *you* think he's taking me?"

Rose dimpled. "Well, if he wants to impress you, I'd guess either the hotel or the Church."

"He'd take me to church?" That was not what Maura expected to hear. Was it some weird local tradition, to pray before a date? Rose giggled at the look on Maura's face. "It's a restaurant that used to be a church. Oh, no — they don't do dinner of a Monday. Probably the Voyage, then. More likely than the hotel."

Maura knew nothing about any of them. "Okay, so what do I wear to any of those? I don't want to make a big thing about it. I just don't want to look out of place and embarrass Sean."

Rose seemed to be thinking hard. "There's not time for real shopping. Wait — I've an idea. Can you meet me here early, say, at ten tomorrow morning? I know where we can go."

"I'm supposed to meet Gillian at eleven. Will that be time enough?"

"No worries."

"Then I'll see you here at ten."

Rose looked excited as she waved good-bye — maybe *too* excited. *Oh, man,* Maura thought, *what am I letting myself in for? And why did I have to ask a sixteen-year-old how to dress?*

The next morning Maura woke early and lay in bed listening to the birds. And the cows. And the sheep. A rooster crowed somewhere nearby. She almost laughed out loud: she never would have seen herself as a country girl, but here she was, living right where her father and grandmother and great-grandparents and who knew how many other ancestors had lived, where there were still more cows than people. It was barely past seven, so she was in no hurry. Monday was usually a slow day at the pub, and she often spent the time cleaning and going over the accounts. But today was going to be different: first, she had to do the girly thing and buy something pretty to wear for her date with the nice young policeman. Ick. No, not ick to the idea of going out with Sean, but ick to the whole idea of dating. In Boston it had been easier — she could just hang out with a gang of people. But a lot of them had paired off over the past few years and disappeared from the group, leaving her the odd woman out more and more often. Was she odd for not wanting to be half of a couple? But she wasn't looking for a string of casual hookups either. She wasn't sure what Sean wanted. She didn't want to give him the wrong impression, and she had no idea what he expected from her. She knew that a lot of twenty-somethings had left the area and even the country to find work. Maybe the pool of available females of the right age was kind of small, and Sean was desperate. Did he think he was going to court her? Or to go to the other extreme, did he think all Americans were casual about sex?

Somehow she didn't think so. She couldn't claim to know Sean well, but he seemed nice and sweet and dependable. Wow — not the first things she thought she would have looked for in a date. Maybe a sense of humor, or some electricity between them. But she couldn't think of a good reason *not* to go out with him at least once. After all, it might be useful to have an in with the cops — no, she liked him too well to use him that way. She didn't want to hurt his feelings or insult him tonight and drive him away altogether. She sighed. This was why she hadn't dated much. It was just too complicated.

She still had time to fill before meeting Rose at the pub, so she decided to walk down the lane and see if Bridget Nolan was awake. Bridget claimed she slept less and less, now that she was older, although Maura had caught her napping during the day more than once. But Bridget was a bit like a cat looking for warmth — she sought out the sun when it was out or the fireside when it was wet. Maura pulled on a sweatshirt and wandered out her front door, leaving it unlocked and open to the summer air, although it still unsettled her to do that. Off to one side, cows grazed contentedly in a field. Maura went the other way and walked down the hill to Bridget's cheery yellow house. As she had guessed, Bridget was not only awake but out in the front garden, picking dead flowers off her lush array of potted plants.

"Good morning!" Maura called out, not wanting to startle Bridget.

"And to you!" Bridget replied, straightening up slowly. "It's another fine day we're having."

"Looks like it, yeah."

"You're out early. Busy day ahead of you?" Bridget cocked her head and regarded her with a bright eye, like a small sparrow.

What had she heard? Maura wondered. Bridget had an amazing network of friends who kept her up-to-date on what was going on in the townland, the district, maybe even the county, for all Maura knew, even though Bridget seldom left her house. "I do. Rose is taking me shopping for my date tonight, and then I'm meeting Gillian and we're going back to the manor with Harry to look for — well, I guess you'd call it a bill of sale for the painting. You know we found it?"

"I heard. Is it worth all the shouting?"

"You know, I think it is. I don't know a lot about art, but I was impressed." As she had suspected, Bridget's friends had updated her since yesterday. Clearly there was no way to keep a secret in Leap.

"There's tea made, inside, and a bit of bread. Help yourself. Then come back out and sit with me and keep me company."

Maura went into Bridget's clean and tidy home and poured herself a cup of strong tea, as instructed. She buttered a piece of brown bread and went back outside to take a seat next to Bridget. Bridget had her face turned to the sun like a flower, with a small smile on her face. When Maura sat down, she opened her eyes and turned to her. "Sean's a good boy."

"I'm sure he is."

"But? Yeh don't seem all that pleased about stepping out with him."

"It's not that. I guess I just don't know if

I want to go out with anybody."

"And why would that be? I know you young girls are so independent these days, what with jobs and education and all, but wouldn't you like to share your life with someone?"

"I don't think about it a lot. Look, Bridget, you know about my family. My grandfather died, leaving Gran alone with a son to raise. She did her best for him, and then he died too, and my mother just . . . left. So I guess I don't have much of a model for happy relationships, you know?"

"There's no sure thing, but my Michael and I were happy."

"I know some people are, I just don't know how. And I'm still not sure what I'm doing here."

"Would you rather be back in America?"

"No, it's not that. But I'm still trying to get used to owning a business, and a house. There was never anything that permanent in my life before. I don't want to blow it at the pub, because now other people are counting on me to keep Sullivan's going. Like Jimmy and Rose and Mick."

"I learned long ago not to meddle in other people's lives. Mick's a grown man, and he'll find his own way. It's not on your head. Jimmy, now, I'm not so sure how he's doing, but the likes of Jimmy always land on their feet somehow."

"I know what you mean," Maura said, smiling. Then her smile faded. "I worry more about Rose. There are so few jobs, it seems, and so many people fighting for them. She has no skills or training beyond working at the pub. What can she do? Jimmy's no help at all."

"She's young yet. And I seem to recall you did much the same work at her age."

"Yeah, and I wish I could give her better advice than I ever got. Though I don't know how helpful I'd be — do you know, I had to ask her what I should wear tonight?"

"For Sean? Sure and he won't mind, whatever you wear."

"I guess. But I don't want to disappoint him."

"Do you like him?"

"He seems like a good guy, and he's helped me with a couple of messes. But it never occurred to me to date him."

"He comes from a good family, and he's steady. Give him a chance, is all."

"And if it doesn't work out and I stay around, I'm stuck with seeing him for the next fifty years or so. It's tricky."

"And now you're worrying yourself about the next half century? It's only the one meal you're having."

All right, Maura admitted, she was nervous. Stupid, at her age. And a lot of her questions about dating in modern Ireland, she couldn't ask Bridget — too old — or Rose — too young. Time to change the subject.

"I really like Gillian. It's almost like she's two artists — one for the tourists and one for herself. The styles are very different. It must be hard to make a living that way. I told her I'd hang a couple of her paintings at Sullivan's, where people would see them. If a tourist comes into the pub and sees something she likes on the wall, she might think about buying it, right?"

"I'm sure the pictures will brighten up the place," Bridget agreed.

"Gillian . . . seems to have a history with Harry Townsend." Maura was curious to see how Bridget would respond.

"There's little future in it, I'd say. Harry doesn't want to settle down. He's been good to his great-aunt, I'll give him that, but once she's gone, I suspect he'll sell up."

"Gillian can see him in Dublin, can't she?"

Bridget just shook her head. "He won't change. Now, Sean — that's a lad you can depend on."

Maura was hit by the thought that maybe,

somehow, Bridget had sent word through her grapevine that Sean should ask Maura out. Would she do that? Was there any harm in it? If it was true, at least Bridget meant well.

Maura stood up. "I should be going. I've got to meet Rose at ten, and then Gillian at eleven."

"You go on your way, dear. I'll just sit here a bit longer. Mick said he'd be by later."

Maura took her cup inside, then said good-bye to Bridget on her way out. She wasn't sure Bridget heard her, since she seemed to have dozed off.

She drove into Leap and parked up the street from Sullivan's. She was waiting in her car when she saw Rose walking toward her. "Right on time," she called out. "Where are we going? Skibbereen, I assume?"

"Yes. You've said you've little money for clothes, so I thought I'd take you to the charity shops."

Maura had never considered that. "There is such a thing in Skibbereen?"

"Oh, yes. More than one. They're mostly for Oxfam and the like and support good causes, like raising money for wheelchairs or for taking in stray animals. There are a couple on the street leading to the square. Have you not noticed them?"

"Guess not." Back in the States, thrift stores had begun to achieve a little class, especially if they labeled themselves as "vintage." She hadn't spent much time in them around Boston — she didn't like the idea of wearing someone else's rejects and preferred to buy what she could afford and wear it as long as it lasted. What would an Irish thrift store be like?

After they had traveled a couple of miles on the highway, Maura asked, "What do you think I should be looking for?"

"A nice sweater or shirt, say. No sequins or strappy things, if that's what's worrying you."

"Where on earth would people wear stuff like that around here?"

"There'd be clubs over to Clonakilty or Bandon, I've heard."

They drove past the roundabout, and a half mile further on, Rose pointed. "There. Pull in and park where you can." Maura complied.

Forty minutes and two small shops later, Maura emerged with a lightweight wool sweater that would do for any season. She'd been pleasantly surprised by the experience, and she liked what Rose had chosen for her. The sweater had a modestly scooped neck-line, and Rose assured her that the teal blue color looked great with her coloring. "Too bad you haven't time for a trim," Rose said.

"A haircut? I never even thought about it, but it's kind of late now. I've got to meet Gillian in about seven minutes."

As they drove back toward Leap, Maura asked, "Are you . . . seeing anyone?"

"You've only now begun to wonder?" Rose laughed. "No. Most of my old classmates are somewhere else now, and you might have noticed there aren't many fellas around to choose from. Not that any of those have asked."

"Does that bother you?"

"Not so much. I've me da to look out for. And I'm *far* younger than you." Rose grinned wickedly at her.

"Oh, right."

Gillian was waiting when they returned. When Maura climbed out of her car, Gillian said, "You know, your place could do with a slap of paint."

"Among a lot of other things, I know. I'm working on it. Are we still on?"

"We are. Shall we take my car?" After they'd settled into it, Gillian said, "I talked with Harry already — this whole thing seems to have finally caught fire with him. He actually got up before ten, the dosser. He says that very likely the estate records *are* there, in a storage room in the attic."

"Well, that's good news, isn't it? Did you tell Althea?"

"I thought I'd wait a bit for that, until we've seen what's what. She can be rather . . ."

"Obnoxious?" Maura volunteered.

"I was thinking 'demanding,' but that works as well. In any case, this may take some time. Harry says the records are all jumbled up in crates and such — there's no order to them, and he has no idea how far back they go. He never cared."

"No wonder these old families ran out of money. Not that Old Mick did any more with Sullivan's books, I have to say. But since I started, I've been trying to keep an eye on what comes in and what goes out."

Gillian shook her head. "Smart woman. On the other hand, we should count ourselves lucky that the family stuck them away and forgot about them, if Harry's right."

"Good luck for Althea, maybe. We're the ones doing all the work."

"Aren't you curious? This is a snapshot of over three hundred years of Irish history, in one place. Who knows, maybe your ancestors worked for the Townsends, or leased land from them."

"Well, I know Gran did, if only for a short

while, and I don't expect her to show up in any record book. As for earlier family members, I haven't a clue. Sorry — I've never been interested in Irish history."

"Well, maybe this will change your mind. We're here." Gillian pulled up in front of the portico, where Harry waited.

Chapter 15

"Hello, Gillian. Maura. I hope you don't mind getting dirty."

"That bad, eh?" Gillian said.

"Nobody's been up there in years, so you can well imagine."

"Does Eveline know we'll be up there? I don't want her hearing thumps and bumps over her head and worrying."

"She hasn't gone above the ground floor for quite some time."

"What about the O'Briens?" Maura asked.

"I don't owe them an explanation for my activities in the house," Harry said, annoyed. "They work for me."

"Harry, that's rude," Gillian protested. "They've taken good care of Eveline, so they deserve a little courtesy."

He held up his hands in surrender. "Sorry, you're right. I'm only half awake. I'll see if they're in the kitchen."

"I'll come with you," Maura said, although

she wasn't quite sure why. To make sure that Harry didn't make things worse?

When they arrived at the kitchen, Maura saw Florence O'Brien and a man she didn't recognize sitting at the kitchen table, with mugs of tea in front of them. They stood up quickly when Harry walked in.

"Tom, have you met Maura Donovan?" Harry asked. "She's the new owner of Sullivan's, in the village."

"Florence mentioned her. *Fáilte,* Miss Donovan."

"Maura, please. It's good to meet you."

"Did you want something, Harry?" Florence said, effectively cutting off the pleasantries. "Will you and yer guests be stayin' for dinner?"

"No, don't worry about us, Florence," Harry said. "I wanted to alert you that we'll be poking around in the attic, so don't worry if you hear a lot of noises. No ghosts or burglars."

"Thank you fer lettin' me know. But it's no doubt a right mess up there, with dust everywhere."

Harry smiled, turning on the charm. "Don't worry yourself, Florence. I promise we won't track ancient dust on your nice clean floors."

"Right, then," Florence said, smiling

grudgingly. Tom silently raised a hand as they left.

He led Maura back to the dim entrance hall, where they rejoined Gillian, then all three headed up a set of stairs toward the back. On the second floor he stopped in front of a door, pulling a ring laden with keys from his pocket. "I warn you, it's pretty dark and dusty up there. There's electric light, if you count one bulb about every twenty feet, but it won't be much to see by. Let me see if I can find some torches or rig up something. Wait here a moment." He disappeared the way they had come, presumably in search of flashlights.

Gillian looked at Maura. "Shall we say a prayer to St. Anthony, patron saint of lost things?"

Maura shrugged. "If you say so. What're the odds of finding what we're looking for?"

"Not so bad, now that we know the records should exist. As you may have noticed, the Townsends never threw anything away. I'll wager the attic is full of stuff — as are the cellars. Now and again, Harry stumbles on some really nice wine left in a dark corner. You never know."

"Ready, ladies?" Harry stood before them, armed with not only flashlights but also lamps with long electrical cords. He held one up. "Borrowed these from Tom."

"Lead on, sir," Gillian said.

Harry unlocked the door. On the other side, a flight of narrow wooden stairs led up into darkness. Harry turned a knob on a ceramic base attached to the wall, and a feeble light drifted down from above.

"Ah, it works. I wasn't sure it still would." He handed each of the women a flashlight, then led the way up. As they mounted the stairs, the air grew increasingly hot and stuffy, and Maura guessed that the old slate of the roof had held in the heat. There were partitions that broke up the rambling expanse of attic, but the ceiling rafters were exposed, with nothing like insulation. So this was what the bones of a seventeenth-century building looked like? She reached out to lay her hand on a rafter. It was darkened and twisted with age, but it felt hard, almost sinewy. Plainly this building had been built to last — and it had.

"Coming?" Harry and Gillian were waiting some twenty feet away, and Maura hurried to catch up with them. Harry stopped before another cubicle, this one with a door. It was padlocked, and even the lock looked antique. Harry searched through his keys, then found one that would open the lock. He pushed the door inward and stepped back so Maura and Gillian could look.

It took Maura a moment before her eyes adjusted to the dim light: there was no lighting within the cubicle, only the reflected light from the string of bare lightbulbs that ran along the roof spine. The small room looked to be about fifteen feet on each side, and the perimeter was stacked with wooden crates, a few chests, and piles of large books — nothing as modern as a cardboard box. Unfortunately there looked to be few, if any, labels on anything. They were going to have to go through the boxes one at a time.

"Where should we even start?" Gillian said, looking around the room in dismay.

"Depends on what we're looking for," Harry said.

Gillian took a deep breath. "Best case, if I understand what Althea told me, is a bill of sale presented by Anthony Van Dyck to Richard Townsend or his representative, dated between 1632, when he was appointed court painter to King Charles the First of England, and 1641, when he died. Richard would have been around twenty, which looks right for the painting." When the others gaped at her, Gillian said, "I wrote it down, all right? If the document's not in English, look for anything that resembles 'Van Dyck' — I have no idea what

218

language they used then. Second best, a household account book of some sort from the same era listing a payment to the painter Van Dyck — *that* would be in English, even if the handwriting is tricky. But I'd settle for an inventory, from any era, that identifies specific paintings and calls one a Van Dyck, not just 'large painting of the earl.' Or a will, if it's itemized or includes an inventory. I don't know enough about either Irish or English history to know if there were such things as property taxes or assessments, particularly on things other than land. But we've got to start somewhere."

Gillian surveyed the room. "Can we pull a couple of these crates together to make a table or something flat we can put books on? God, I wish we had more time to prepare for this — I'm really shooting in the dark — but Althea wants this ASAP. It's a shame we can't do a proper inventory of all this. There must be some really interesting documents in here somewhere."

Harry laughed. "Ah, no mind — if we can prove the painting is authentic and sell it, I'll hire an archivist, I promise you. How's that?"

The three of them separated and began to prowl around the room, prying off box lids and trying to determine which crates held the earliest materials. It was, as Harry had warned, both dark and dusty — and hot. Maura found quickly that the leather bindings of very old books tended to shed when touched, so her hands were soon covered with reddish powder that looked disconcertingly like dried blood. She wished she had any idea what she was looking for; her concept of an old book, as compared to a *really* old book, was unfortunately pretty sketchy. And heaven help them if the oldest ones had been rebound by some thoughtful later Townsend and now looked like merely middle-aged books. She sighed and moved on to the next box in her row.

Gillian called out from across the room, "Here's an old batch. Come look." Maura and Harry joined her. Gillian had pulled out a volume that was over two feet tall, and when she opened it Maura could see its pages were covered in spidery brown writing. She guessed it was an account book of some sort, with columns of figures at the right of each page. She searched for a date and was disappointed to find the page was headed "1754": old but still more than a century later than the papers they were looking for.

"Let's put that aside and look at it more carefully later," Gillian suggested. "It's the right kind of thing — day-to-day operations of the estate — but too late for the original painting. But it still might list the thing, so let's put it in the 'maybe' pile in the middle and work through the whole lot first, before we start reading individual books."

Two hours later Gillian stretched and announced, "Hey, I'm good for another few hours, but I'm parched. I need to drink something to wash this dust down. Harry, anything on ice?"

"I think there's some cans of lager, down in the kitchen."

"Be a love and fetch us a couple, will you?" Gillian said.

Harry made a mock bow and clattered down the stairs, tossing a final comment over his shoulder. "If I'm not back in an hour, send out a search party."

"Will do."

Maura noticed how much dust they had stirred up, as the motes danced in the wavering light of the old bulbs. She too was tired, thirsty, and filthy. She suddenly realized that she would need a shower before heading back to work — not to mention her date that evening. "How much longer do you think this will take?"

Gillian surveyed the mess. "I think we've collected all the books from the right time period. But we need to go through them page by page. Do you have to go soon?"

"I guess so. I hate to leave you with all of this, but I need to get cleaned up." There were still many piles of old volumes and loose papers that had to be looked at.

"Don't worry about it. I think Harry's gotten into it, and I can use his help, since he knows the estate."

Harry came up the stairs, carrying three oversized cans. "Here you go, ladies."

"Keep them away from the documents," Gillian cautioned. "It wouldn't do to spill beer on them after they've been safe for the last three centuries."

Harry looked around. "Can we get through all this today?"

"Doubtful," Gillian told him. "Why don't we assemble all the likely candidates, then set them aside and read them tomorrow? Maura needs to be on her way, anyway, and I'm going cross-eyed trying to read in this light."

"We can keep looking if we use the dining room," Harry suggested. "The table there seats a dozen, without adding the extra leaves."

"Thanks, Harry. That sounds ideal. Maura, why don't I run you into Leap while Harry hauls this lot downstairs?"

"Sure. Can I help carry something?"

"We'll take care of it. I'd hate to muddle up what little order we've established. I'll be back in a short while, Harry."

Maura followed Gillian down the stairs and out the front once again. Daylight confirmed that she was caked with filth and a few spiderwebs; so was Gillian. "Drop me at my car, will you? I'm going home to clean up."

Gillian looked at her and laughed. "An excellent idea. And I'll stop by Sullivan's later and tell you if we've found anything."

They climbed into Gillian's car. "What do you think, now that you've seen the stuff?" Maura asked.

"I'm more hopeful than I was when we started. I hadn't realized how interesting this stuff is, especially if you know the area the books tell about. I'd love to come back to it, after we've satisfied Althea."

"If you say so," Maura said. She had learned quickly that she wasn't very interested in old things, or at least, not just because they were old.

It took them only three minutes to reach the pub, and Maura went straight to her car, then home to scrub off the dirt of three centuries. After her shower she considered her options: wear her "good" clothes all day at the pub or wear her usual jeans and shirt and bring her date clothes to change into later? The latter, she decided. No need to advertise to the entire population of West Cork that she was going on a date — as if they didn't already know.

She arrived at Sullivan's at three and glared at Mick and Jimmy as if daring them to make a comment about her whereabouts — gadding about the manor house while they were working. Then she sighed inwardly: sure, she was the boss and she had every right to take time off if she wanted to. But at the same time, she had to set a good example for her staff. She was still finding out that management was a challenge. Rose winked at her but said nothing.

Althea stayed away, which was a relief. Maybe Gillian had called her to report on their progress at the manor. Certainly Maura had nothing to add. Yes, they'd found old books and files. No, she didn't know what was in them, how long it would take to figure that out, or whether there was anything that might relate to the painting. Maura knew that Althea must have chewed her nails to the knuckles, waiting. Or maybe not: Althea had one serious manicure, and she'd probably paid good money for it. Maura looked at her own short, ragged nails, with some dirt still embedded even after her shower and a good scrub, and grimaced.

At six thirty Maura grabbed her bag and went into the ladies' room to change. It didn't take long: she had only to swap one shirt for another, and her jeans for her black trousers. No makeup — she hated the fuss. She finger-combed her hair and, thinking of Rose's comment, tried to remember the last time she'd had it cut — and then she remembered: her gran had trimmed it, a couple of weeks before she'd gone into the hospital that last time. Maura stared at herself in the cloudy bathroom mirror, tears suddenly in her eyes. *What am I doing, Gran?*

Impatiently she scrubbed the tears from her face, splashing water on it. Gran had sent her here, but Gran hadn't been to Leap or Knockskagh or Skibbereen for a very long time, and there was much she wouldn't recognize. She would have trusted Maura to make her own decisions and find her own way. Wouldn't she?

Maura straightened her new teal sweater and went back to the bar to wait for Sean Murphy.

CHAPTER 16

Maura almost didn't recognize Sean when he walked in, and it was only Mick's nudge that made her look again. She realized she had never seen Sean without his garda uniform. In ordinary clothes he looked . . . ordinary. But nice. And at the moment he looked nervous.

Sean took in the whole of the room — habit? Maura wondered — then his face lit up when he saw her behind the bar. After greeting Mick and Rose, he said to her, "Are yeh ready to go, Maura?"

"Sure. Just let me grab my bag."

Outside he led her to a battered small car, but at least it was newer than her own, which was actually a hand-me-down from Bridget Nolan's late husband. Sean courteously opened the passenger door and waited until she was settled in the seat before closing it. When he climbed in the other side he said, "Seat belt," then he blushed. "Sorry —

but it is the law here."

"No problem," Maura said. "I always wear mine anyway. After . . . you know." She didn't have to mention the accident on the hill to Sean, who'd been the one to come to her rescue, after all.

"But that didn't put you off driving?" he asked, starting the car.

"Do I have a choice? If I don't drive, I'd have to walk everywhere, and even that's not safe, since the lanes are so narrow. If I meet anyone on the road, I'd have to climb into the hedgerow."

"There is that. Are you still borrowing the same car?"

"Yes." She looked at him, trying to guess at his interest. "Is that a problem?"

"No, not at all, as long as Bridget Nolan has kept up the paperwork."

"I think Mick takes care of all that. So, where are we going?"

"There's a nice restaurant on Bridge Street in Skib — I know a couple of the managers there. Small, not too fancy, but the food's great."

Maura's experience with eating in nice restaurants was limited, and she wasn't sure what she would consider "great" food, so she'd have to trust Sean's judgment.

"How long is it you've been here now?"

Sean asked, skillfully navigating the round-about.

"Uh . . . three months? I arrived in March."

"And are you settling in well?"

"I guess. I don't have much to compare it to, since I lived all my life in the same place."

"With your gran, was it?"

"Yes. In South Boston. Have you ever been to America?"

"I have not. I joined the gardaí as soon as I left school."

"Do you just apply for that?"

"You have to have certain grades in your Leaving Certificate — that's what you get when you've finished your secondary schooling and passed the tests — including in two languages, one of them being Irish, with an oral test for that."

"I'm impressed," Maura said. "Can you actually speak Irish?"

"Not well, but there's little call for it. My other language was German, since there are a good number of blow-ins from there in Cork, but I'm no better at that than the Irish." He followed the road that looped around the town center, pulling into the parking lot behind the market. "Do you mind walking from here?"

"Of course not," Maura said. Out of the car, they followed a path along the small stream toward the main street. "So after you apply and you're accepted, then what?"

"You're sent to the Garda College for training, and then you spend half a year at different stations. Then you're attached to a station, and then there's a probation period, for another two years."

"Do you get to choose your station?"

"Not always, but you can make a request."

"Is this where you wanted to be?"

"It is. I come from here." He stopped in front of a small restaurant the width of a single storefront, facing the main street. "We've arrived."

Inside it smelled wonderful, even to Maura's uneducated nose. Sean waved to a woman in a simple black dress, clutching a stack of menus, and she came over quickly. They exchanged a familiar if hurried hug. "Sean, good to see you! It's been too long."

"The work keeps me busy. We're always shorthanded these days. Marie, this is Maura — she's just moved to Leap, to take over Sullivan's."

"*Fáilte romhat a Mhaire!* Me da loves that place, although he says it's not what it once was, this past couple of years. But then, he says that about a good number of things.

How's the business now?"

"Picking up a bit, now that it's summer. Tell your father I've been cleaning up Old Mick's messes since I got here."

Marie laughed. "I'll do that, and I'm sure he'll have to go in to see for himself. American, are you?"

"Yes. From Boston."

"Well, welcome. It's good to meet a friend of Sean's. Where'll you sit, Sean? You've plenty of choices." Only half the tables were occupied.

"Could we sit round the corner, near the window? Maura, you can watch the kitchen from there, without all the noise."

"That sounds good," Maura said cautiously. Did she *want* to watch the kitchen? Sean seemed to think it would be a treat.

Marie led them to a table on the far side of the restaurant, covered with a crisp tablecloth; there was a single flower in a slender vase in the center. "Here you go. Order whatever you like — I'll give you time to decide."

When Marie had left, Maura said, "How do you know her?"

"As a garda it's my business to know people, but Marie and I went to school together. She went off for a few years to cookery school, then came back and opened this place a couple of years ago."

"It *is* nice," Maura said, looking around, and meant it. The decor was simple, and all the staff appeared to be about her own age and seemed to be working comfortably together in a relatively small space. "What's good here?"

"I've never had a bad meal, but the set meal is a good value."

"Fine," Maura said, without looking at the details.

When Marie came back, Sean quickly ordered two of the fixed price dinners. Maura was doing some quick math: if he'd left whatever they called high school around here and spent two years at the Garda College and then another half year rotating through different parts of the country, just how old was he? When Sean turned his attention back to her, she said, "So, have you finished probation?"

"A few months past. The case that you were a part of, when you'd only just arrived, was my first. And my first under the detective superintendent."

So he was maybe . . . twenty-three? A bit younger than she was. "The detective's quite a guy. What's he like to work with?"

"Smart. Fair. He works as hard as anyone in the station, doesn't just pawn off tasks to the rest of us. He's a good boss. It's hard when we're so poorly staffed — we're even closing down some of the small stations out in the townlands."

"Budget cuts?" Maura asked sympathetically.

"Yeah — orders from the top. Although in fact there's less need for those stations now. So many of the younger lads have left, looking for work, that small crimes are down. Don't jump on me, now — we've a few women gardaí as well." A server appeared and deposited their appetizer course. "Did you want a glass of wine?" she asked. "Comes with the dinner."

"That'd be grand. The white, Maura?"

"Sure," Maura said. She seldom drank wine and didn't pretend to know what was what, above what people asked for at the various bars where she had worked. She'd had few requests for wine at Sullivan's, although she'd noticed that the market in town here sold a large variety. Maybe because Ireland was closer to the source of some European wines?

The server brought their glasses quickly. Sean picked his up and raised it to her. "Thank you for joining me."

"Thank you for asking me," Maura replied. "Why did you?" She didn't think she was exactly a prize.

Poor Sean looked startled by her question. "Why are you asking?" he countered.

Now she'd embarrassed him — and herself. "Never mind — rude question. I don't date much. Clearly. This is a date, right?"

He smiled. "That's what I'd meant it to be. And to answer you, from what I've seen, yer an interesting woman. Was I wrong to ask?"

"No, not exactly. I just didn't expect it. And I don't know what you expect."

"I expect a pleasant evening with someone I'd like to get to know better, nothing more."

Something in Maura relaxed. No pressure. He *was* a nice guy, right? "Okay, then." As a diversion — so she didn't have to look at him for a moment — she dug into her appetizer. "Wow, this is good!"

"I told you, they're great cooks here. When you're at home, do you not cook for yourself?"

"As little as I can. I'm not even sure how to turn on the oven at my house, or if it works. It scares me."

And the talk turned to lighter topics. Maura found herself liking the wine as well as the food. Sean proved easy to talk to, and Maura stopped worrying about his intentions or unknown social signals in a country she didn't know well at all. She realized that he must in fact be good at his job — he was drawing her out without making it obvious, paying attention to what she said, asking good questions. She was enjoying herself.

"So, tell me — I've been told there are few murder investigations in Ireland. Is that true?" she asked.

"There are few murders, right. At least compared to your country."

"What's few?" Maura asked, curious.

"Over the last ten years, no more than three in this district, and only one of those since I came on here. You'd remember that one."

She did, only too well. "You know, it's kind of hard to get used to. I mean, people don't even lock their doors around here — not that I have anything worth stealing. But it's hard to break old habits, after living in Boston."

"So you couldn't trust yer neighbors, where you lived?"

Maura shook her head. "Heck, half the time I didn't even know my neighbors. It's not like here, where everybody knows everybody else." This was not what Maura wanted to talk about, so she decided to change the subject. "How does an investigation work around here? Seamus Daly's death isn't like the last one, so in Seamus's case, what happens? That is, if you can talk about it. Who does what?"

Sean sat up straighter in his chair, as if preparing to recite. "The gardaí receive a call reporting that a body has been found, and a uniformed officer like me is sent out to investigate. If that officer determines that the death was not natural — the deceased is found lying on the lawn with obvious injuries, say — then he will call the station and tell the sergeant. The sergeant will inform the superintendent, who will gather his officers and assign tasks. A record book for the crime will be started. The coroner will be called in, and the body will be sent for an autopsy — at the hospital in Cork. Those working on the murder will assemble at least once a day and report on their assignments, until someone is arrested. And an arrest warrant must come down from Dublin headquarters, once we've presented the case to them."

"All the warrants have to come from Dublin, for the whole country?"

"They do. It's not a large country, Maura."

"Yeah, I keep forgetting that. I mean, this whole country has, like, half the population of New York City."

"True, and we've lost many a good Irishman to that place, and to Boston as well."

"So, what's the progress on Seamus Daly's murder?"

"I shouldn't talk about that."

"Sorry." And then Maura realized that Sean didn't know a lot about what Althea had told them and the wild-goose chase that she and Gillian had taken on. She looked around the restaurant — it had filled in nicely, but nobody was paying any attention to them. "Sean, I think I need to tell you a few things."

"About the murder?"

Maura would swear that he looked disappointed, and she realized that discussing murder was not exactly the best thing to do on a first date with a guy who liked you. "Possibly. Look, it can wait. I don't want to spoil the evening."

"You mean you didn't say yes to this date just so you could worm information out of me?" He was smiling, but his eyes were cautious.

"No!" Maura protested quickly. "Really. It has to do with Althea Melville. I kinda wish she'd never walked into Sullivan's and decided I was her new best friend — or at least, that I could be useful to her. And then

I made the mistake of dragging Gillian into it, and then Althea messed things up with Harry . . ."

"Hold on. I've lost the thread here," Sean said. "I understand where Althea comes into it — she's here to look for a painting at the manor."

"Right, and you brought her in for questioning right away, because she arrived just about the time Seamus died. Not that you can seriously believe she killed a gardener she had never met."

"I can't say." Official Garda Murphy was back on duty.

"Okay, okay, I get it."

"How did Gillian Callanan become involved?"

"You know her?"

"I do. She was at school with my older sister."

"Oh, right, she told me that she'd grown up here. Well, here's the story: Althea was hunting for that painting and she tried to get in through the front door of the manor, as you know, and was turned away by Florence O'Brien. But she's determined, so when Harry Townsend showed up, she made a play for him, and it worked to get her into the house. Then Miss Eveline came upon her by accident and found her wearing not much and pitched a fit, and Florence threw her out *again,* so now she's definitely not welcome in the house. So Althea enlisted me and Gillian to do her snooping for her. Gillian wasn't sure about helping her at first, but then she figured if things worked out it would be good for Harry and his great-aunt, so she agreed. And yesterday we did get in, with Harry, and we did find the painting."

Sean's expression had changed several times during Maura's explanation, and now he looked as though he was trying not to laugh. "Take a breath, will you, now, Maura?"

"What's so funny?"

"I'm trying to imagine how to write this up in a report! So the painting's been found, has it? That's news to me. Is it what Althea was looking for?"

"Seems to be, though Althea hasn't seen the painting because Harry won't let her back in the house, but Gillian showed her some photos. Now we're looking for any kind of records for it."

"We?"

"Harry, Gillian, and me, although I'm not much help." Maura paused to gather her thoughts. "Oh, and there's one more thing that might help you."

"And that would be?"

"The room where we found the painting? Everything was covered with dust. Thick dust. Clearly, no one's gone in there for a very long time. So if Seamus Daly's death had anything to do with the painting, whoever killed him was never in that room, and he couldn't have seen the painting from outside because all the curtains were closed tight."

Sean brightened at that. "That's worth knowing. You've a good eye for detail, Maura."

Maura was startled by the compliment. "Sean, I really don't think Althea had anything to do with this death. Any other suspects?"

"That I will not tell you, Maura." Sean's phone buzzed in his pocket. "Sorry, I have to take this — with so few officers, we're always on call." He stood up and walked toward the window, keeping his back toward their table, as he spoke briefly on his phone. He returned quickly. "There's been a report of shots fired at Mycroft House, and I've got to go check it out. I'll drop you back at Sullivan's on the way."

"All right." *What was going on at Mycroft House?* There were questions she wanted to ask, but this was not the time. Sean was all business now. No doubt someone at Sullivan's would fill her in quickly enough. Maura retrieved her bag from under the table. Sean located Marie and spoke briefly to her about the check, though she waved him away. Maura stood awkwardly by the door until he joined her.

"Sorry about this," he said.

"I understand." At least she didn't have to worry about an awkward ending for this date — did he expect a goodnight kiss? Moot now. Would there be other dates? She was surprised to realize she might like that.

After they retrieved his car, Sean drove silently back to Leap and deposited her in front of Sullivan's. She climbed out quickly, but before shutting the passenger door she leaned in and said, "If you can, come tell me what happened. I'll be here until close."

He smiled briefly. "If I can, I will. Got to go." Maura shut the door, and Sean pulled onto the road, toward the drive for Mycroft House.

CHAPTER 17

Rose was gone when Maura walked into Sullivan's, so she didn't have to tell her all about her "date." Had she blown it with Sean? A guy asks her for dinner and she ends up pumping him about police procedures? No one had ever called her romantic, but this might've been going too far.

"You're back early," Mick said. "Everything okay?"

"Fine and dandy," Maura said. "Nice guy, nice restaurant, nice time. I'm back early because Sean got a call from the station and had to leave — something about shots heard at the manor."

Mick's mouth twitched. "Glad to hear you enjoyed your dinner. We've had no reports here of trouble."

"Wow, you mean the grapevine doesn't pick up everything as soon as it happens?"

"I'm sure we'll know soon enough," he said and went back to pulling pints.

Mick was proved right no more than a half hour later, when someone Maura didn't recognize came in and asked for a pint. Leaning on the bar while he waited for it, he said, "A bit of trouble up at the manor."

"And how would you know about that?" Maura said, keeping an eye on the pint she was pouring.

The man settled himself on a bar stool. "Sure and I was driving along the Union Hall road, with me windows open to the wind, and I hear a 'boom.' Or maybe it was more a 'bang.'" He stopped, searching his mind for the memory.

"And?" Maura prompted, setting the glass aside to settle.

He leaned his forearms on the bar. "And I think to myself, that sounds for all the world like a shotgun. Now, who would be firing off a shotgun at the manor this late hour? I wondered."

"A good question," Maura said, although she had no idea how unusual this might be.

"Who indeed?" another man chimed in, coming up behind him.

"There was nowhere else it could have come from except the manor?" Maura asked. "What about the other side of the road?"

"It's all rock there, now, isn't it? Not a

house for a mile or more."

"So what did you do?" the second man asked.

"I was near to Union Hall when I decided it might be right to let someone know, given the trouble they've had up at the manor lately, so I pulled up and called the gardaí."

"Did you, now? And did they laugh at you?" the second man said, clearly incredulous.

"No, they said they'd send a man over, to see if there was any trouble. Since there's already been one death there of late."

And that would be Sean, Maura thought as she topped off the pint and slid it across the bar to the man telling the story.

"Ta," he said and slid a few euro back, then he and his companion found themselves seats across the room.

Mick looked at Maura. "Sean?" he said. Maura nodded.

It was close to closing time when Sean came in. The crowd had thinned, and Maura was wondering whether it was worth staying open, when he walked through the door and scanned the room. He smiled when he saw her, and crossed to the bar.

"How are yeh, Maura?" he asked.

"I'm grand, Sean," she said — at least she'd figured out the right local greeting.

"Are you here to tell us about the gunshots at the manor? Because we've already heard several versions from the guys who were in here earlier."

Sean sighed. "I'm off duty now, so I'll take a glass of the black stuff, if you don't mind. I'm not supposed to talk about these things, as I told you. But so far we have no evidence of a crime, apart from an unlicensed firearm."

Maura started his glass. "So there *was* a shot at Mycroft House."

"There was," Sean said. "Tom O'Brien fired a shotgun at what he thought was a prowler. He said he's been feeling nervous after what happened to Seamus, and it was getting dark . . . he admitted he could have been wrong."

"Did anyone break in?"

"Not that he could tell. If so, this person was on his way out, not coming in, when Tom fired."

"Did he think it could be a woman?" Maura's mind went straight to Althea. She couldn't be that stupid. Could she?

"It was dusk, and his eyes aren't what they once were."

"Did he hit anything?"

"He says he fired as a warning only." Sean accepted the glass Maura handed him and peered into its foamy depths.

Was he avoiding her eyes? "But?"

"I took a look outside, where he said he'd seen something. There was blood."

"Oh, my God!" That wasn't good. "A little or a lot?"

"Not much. If he hit someone, they walked away. Of course, it could well have been a stray dog."

"What now?" And what if it *was* Althea? Not that she really believed that, but still . . .

"I file a report."

"Is it illegal to fire a shotgun around here? I mean, I don't know anything about who's allowed to do what, or gun registration, or all that." She hadn't known much about it in Boston either, although she had known people who carried firearms there, legally or otherwise. Here, not even the cops carried guns.

"Our laws are fairly strict. Most civilian firearms in the country are shotguns and hunting rifles. The shotgun Tom fired belonged to Harry's father, and nobody'd given it a thought until after Seamus's death, when Tom pulled it out and made sure it was in good order."

"So the short answer is, it's not licensed to anyone."

"That's right."

"What happens now?" Maura ignored Mick, who was watching her exchange with Sean with a half smile.

"I've told him to register it or get rid of it. The chief superintendent has to issue any certificates, and Tom'd have to show a good reason for having it."

"What about whoever he might have shot?"

Sean took a long drink from his pint, then pushed back his stool to look at her. "And why would you be so concerned?"

"What if it's Seamus's killer, come back to look for the picture again?"

"Then he's not very smart. Maybe he thought no one would be looking out for him at the manor now, but they're all on edge there. Possible the fella's been hit badly and has crawled off to die somewhere, though that's unlikely, given the relatively small amount of blood. More like, he's only been hit by a few pellets and might get by with some sticking plasters, which he could buy any number of places."

"What if the injury was somewhere in between, and needs stitches?"

"If he goes to an A and E or a clinic, they'd be required to report it. Maura, you're far too interested in all this. Are you planning to apply for the gardaí?"

She swallowed a laugh. "No. At least, I hadn't considered it. I'd bet it's less risky to be a garda around here than a cop back home, though. And it couldn't pay less than this place does." She sneaked a look at Mick, who ignored her comment. "Is it okay if I tell Gillian and Althea about this?"

Sean shrugged. "Seems as though half the world knows already. As I said, we have no direct evidence that a crime was even committed. Tell away." He drained his glass. "Walk me out?"

"Sure." Maura came around the bar, and Sean let her pass before he followed her out the door. "Did you want to tell me something?" she asked.

"Only that I enjoyed our dinner tonight, even with all the talk of murder. Can we do it again sometime?"

She smiled at him. "Sure. I had a good time too. And thanks for coming by."

"I'll see you, then." After a brief return smile, Sean turned on his heel and went back to his car, leaving Maura feeling a little confused. Had she really expected him to try to kiss her? And what would she have done if he had?

"Good, you're still open!" Gillian emerged out of the gathering dark. "Am I too late for a drink and a chat?"

"Hey, I'm the owner — I can do what I want. Come on, we'll have a lock-in. I've only just learned how that works."

Inside Sullivan's, Maura went around the bar. "What're you having?"

"Paddy's, no ice."

"Hard day?" Maura said, pouring a glass.

"I spent most of the evening with Althea."

Hearing that, Maura added another half inch to the glass before pushing it across to Gillian. "That must have been fun. Learn anything?"

"Not for lack of gab. That woman could talk the hind legs off a donkey. But I figured it was better I stayed and kept an eye on her than leave her alone to get into trouble."

"How did you and Harry do with the records?"

"We ran out of steam a couple of hours after you left, and I went home, but I think we can finish up tomorrow — it's slow going, trying to decipher the old handwriting — thank God it's in English, even if it's old-fashioned. Oh, tell me — how was your evening with Sean?"

"My date? Fine, except we spent half of it talking about Seamus Daly's death, and then he got a call to the manor."

Gillian sat up straighter. "Indeed? What was that about?"

"Tom O'Brien fired a shotgun at some-body or something he thought was a prowler. Whatever it was, Tom hit it — Sean found blood, but not a lot."

"And you're thinking that this must be related to the painting and Althea again?"

"From everything I've heard, West Cork is a pretty peaceful place. So when we get a rash of crimes in a couple of days, I'm going to think they're connected, though I can't tell you how. Anyway, keep an eye out for somebody wearing a bandage or limping or whatever." She thought for a moment. "Gillian, I had to tell Sean about what we've been doing. I mean, he knows why Althea is here, but not that we're helping out — or not how much. I told him we found the painting, which he didn't know. He's going to have to report what I told him to the crime meeting in the morning, or whatever it is they call it."

Gillian didn't say anything immediately. "I suppose there's no harm done. After all, we've broken no laws. And we don't know anything new that points to the murder. Save that the painting is real and it's in the manor."

"I told him about the dust in the library too. I mean, the fact that it hadn't been disturbed."

"Ah," Gillian replied and then fell silent. "So you're guessing that Seamus's killer really *was* looking for that painting and he hadn't found it yet? Did you tell Sean that?"

"I did. I thought he should know, although he wouldn't comment. Like you said, we aren't doing anything wrong. Unless Althea is hiding something, which wouldn't surprise me."

"Nor me." Gillian drained her glass and stood up. "I'd best get home. I need to get some painting done in the morning, if I want to eat this month."

"Don't forget to bring some of your stuff by here and we can see what looks good," Maura offered.

"I'll do that, maybe after Harry and I finish looking through the papers tomorrow."

"Good." Relieved that Gillian didn't seem to want her help again with the musty old documents, Maura started to say good-bye, and then a thought hit her. "Gillian, did you say you were with Althea all evening? Until you came here?"

"I was — we had dinner at the pub at the hotel, and I've only just come from there. Why?"

"Then Althea couldn't have been the one Tom O'Brien was shooting at, at the manor. Assuming it was human."

Gillian laughed. "I'm not sure that Althea is quite human, but she definitely wasn't at Mycroft House tonight. So maybe there is someone else involved . . . Let me think on it. See you tomorrow, Maura."

CHAPTER 18

Tuesday morning Maura awoke to the sound of rain on her slate roof. She lay in bed for a while, considering what that would mean. If it was wet and dark, would that drive tourists into Sullivan's? The older ones, maybe, but not the families with children. For a few seconds she considered adding video machines of some sort and then shuddered and dismissed it. The noise and flashing lights would be sure to drive her regular patrons away quickly — and drive her crazy. She should remember to light the fire when she arrived, to take the chill off the room.

She wondered if it was worth trying to create a written schedule for the four of them who covered the bar. She tried to limit Rose's hours to days, not that there were many wild nights at Sullivan's that would be unsuitable for a girl of sixteen. But in general they all seemed to make it up as they went, and she trusted Mick and Jimmy to keep track of their own hours and request their pay accordingly. She had her doubts about Jimmy's count, but she hadn't wanted to start an argument. But she realized that if she didn't stand up for herself, Jimmy and maybe even Mick would trample all over her. She didn't mind putting in long hours herself — to set a good example — but she wasn't going to stand still and let anyone take advantage of her.

She checked the time, to find that it was later than she thought. Not a good day to visit with Bridget; she'd hoped to get in to Sullivan's early to do a bit of cleaning and check the inventory. Nominally it was Jimmy's job, but she wanted to count again, just in case. She showered and dressed, ate a quick breakfast, and arrived at Sullivan's by ten, before official opening time. Even with all the lights on, the place was kind of dim in this weather, but it certainly looked . . . authentic. Well, it *was* authentic. Sullivan's just oozed . . . what was the word? Ambience, that was it. She had ambience to spare.

She'd laid the fire, cleaned up the bar area, and was counting the contents of the till when she looked up to see a dark figure standing outside the front door. Checking her watch, she realized it was opening time, although there was only the one customer. But Maura wasn't going to turn anyone away. When she unlocked the door and pulled it open, she recognized the man: Tom O'Brien from the manor house. The man who didn't drink — or so said his wife, who was not with him.

The man appeared anything but menacing: his clothes were rumpled and damp, and he looked like he hadn't slept in days. Maura pulled the door open wider and stepped back. "Please, come in out of the wet. You're Tom O'Brien, right? We met the other day."

Tom walked through the door and stopped, as if confused. "Yer open, aren't yeh?"

"Of course I am. What can I get you?" Maura waited with some curiosity to see what a supposed nondrinker would order at ten thirty in the morning.

"A pint, if you will," he said.

"It'll just be a moment." Maura set about pulling the pint, wondering what had prompted Tom to come here now, of all times. Did he want to talk? Or did he want to get away from his wife, or the cloud hanging over the manor house?

Maura set the glass on a coaster in front

of Tom. "I haven't seen you in here before, have I?" she asked.

He shook his head. "I'm not much for the drink." Having said that, he downed half the glass in one long draw. Maybe he was trying to get drunk. "I wanted to hear a voice, friendly or no. Florence has gone cold on me, and I don't see much of Miss Eveline. With Seamus gone, there's no one left, not that he was much of one for the talking."

Why would his wife stop talking to him? Did she do this often, or was something troubling her? And why was he telling her? "Well, Tom O'Brien, you're welcome here anytime. And if you don't want to drink, the coffee's not bad." Maura figured she might as well talk to him now — she might never see him in Sullivan's again. "I was sorry to hear of the . . . troubles you've had up at the manor," she ventured.

He looked her in the eye, and Maura was struck by the pain that lurked in his gaze. "You mean Seamus's death, do you, now? A sad thing, that. The gardaí would have it that it was me who killed him, or my wife, or mebbe the two of us together, for they've nowhere else to look." He didn't turn away, as if challenging her to respond.

"Did you?" Maura responded, keeping her

gaze on him. "Kill him, I mean."

He gave a short bark of laughter. "Why would I? He was a good lad, as close to a son as we ever had a hope for. He was a fine worker and an honest man. When I saw him lying there that morning . . ." He had to take a moment to collect himself before going on, "It like to tore my guts out. He never deserved to die that way, layin' in his own blood."

"Who do *you* think did it?"

Tom looked away. "I don't know. God's truth. If I did, I'd tell the gardaí."

"I hear you fired a shot at someone last night."

"I did. Woulda hit the fella too, if the gun had been taken care of proper. Used to be I was a good shot."

"You actually saw the person?"

Tom dipped his head. "Like I told that young guard, I saw a man running away — only the back of him. But it weren't no dog, unless he stood on two feet." He swallowed the rest of his pint.

"Can I get you another?"

He shook his head. "What's the charge?"

"No charge."

"I don't take charity," he said dubiously.

"It's not charity. Call it a welcome."

"Then I thank you, Maura Donovan." He

turned and shuffled out into the rain.

Maura watched him go, feeling sad. She believed him: he seemed honestly heartbroken about Seamus's death, more so than anyone else she'd talked to. But if he didn't do it, who did?

She was no closer to an answer when Gillian arrived after three that afternoon. She looked as depressed as Tom had when she took a seat at the bar.

"No luck?" Maura asked.

"No. We went through every old book we'd collected, page by page. Nothing."

"Can I get you something?"

Gillian smiled. "You mean, do I want to drown my sorrows? No, a coffee'll do fine. After all, it's not as though I have a personal stake in this. I only agreed to help because Harry needs the money to keep Eveline at the manor."

Maura made her a cup of coffee and pushed it across the bar. "Have you talked to Althea today?"

"No, not yet. We did find one crumb, although it doesn't help us much. The account book for a couple of the years that might be relevant is missing."

"Missing as in somebody took it, or missing as in you can't find it?" Maura asked.

Gillian shrugged. "I have no way of knowing, although it's the only one of that period that we can't locate. Believe me, Harry and I looked. We went back up to the attic and checked every book. It could have been rebound because it was falling apart, or somebody could have pulled it out a hundred years ago to look at it and put it somewhere else. Problem is, we don't know where else to look. The coffee's good, by the way. Old Mick could never make a decent cup."

"Thanks. Jimmy's the one who brought in the machine, but I got it running. So now what?"

"Now I tell Althea that she'll have to run with what she has or give up."

"You think she'll give up?"

"I don't," Gillian said. "She's found the painting, after all, and I think it speaks for itself. Finding this bit of paper is important to her, but it's icing on the cake, no matter what she thinks. I don't know what it'll take to convince her that finding it is hopeless, at least in such a hurry. It would be easier if we had weeks or even months to do the looking."

"You'd better tell her that you didn't find anything, just to get it over with."

Gillian sighed. "I know. I'll be back." She found her mobile phone, then walked outside to make the call. She didn't look any happier when she came back. "She'll be here in ten, she says. You'll back me up, won't you? You know we tried."

Why did Gillian feel she had to apologize to Althea? She'd done her best. "Sure. Oh, there was one interesting thing this morning: Tom O'Brien stopped in."

"Tom from the manor? What did he want?"

"A drink and a friendly face, not necessarily in that order. He seemed really broken up about Seamus's death, and I don't think he was just putting on a show for me. There was no one else to see it. He seems to be the only one who actually cared for Seamus."

"If he didn't kill Seamus, does he have any idea who did?"

"No. He said more or less what everyone has been saying — a good lad, a hard worker, no enemies in the world. We're kind of short on suspects here, unless the gardaí are holding something back from us. If Tom didn't do it, and you were with Althea last night when Tom took a shot at the prowler, who's left?"

"Althea's accomplice, if she has one? Nate? We still aren't sure where he is. And there's always the useful 'person or persons unknown,' " Gillian finished glumly.

Maura started a few pints for some men in the corner who had raised their empty glasses to her. "You know, there are a lot of people around here, at least the ones who come into Sullivan's, who know about this big important painting up at the manor by now. Would they go after it? Or call in the press?"

Gillian laughed. "I can't see any of this lot organizing a heist or knowing what to do with the painting once they had their hands on it. But the reality is, most people around here would think it's our business and no one else's, so they wouldn't go talking to outsiders about it."

"You're not helping. Our suspect list is now down to a bunch of 'maybes.' " Then Maura brightened. "Hey, did you bring your paintings?"

"Oh, right — they're in the boot of my car. Let me fetch them. Although they won't look their best in this dark weather."

"Give 'em a chance — maybe they'll brighten up the place."

The pub was all but empty, so while Gillian unloaded her paintings, Maura wandered out from behind the bar to study the walls on either side of the fireplace. A couple of murky landscapes hung there, all but unreadable thanks to who knew how many years of wood, coal, and peat smoke, not to mention as many years of cigarette smoke before the government changed the rules on smoking in pubs. Maura gave about two seconds to wondering if they were old and valuable, but on closer inspection she decided they deserved to go in the trash. Or rubbish bin, as she was supposed to call it now.

"Looking at the art gallery, are yeh now?" Old Billy said, watching her with amusement.

"I am, Billy. Like I told you before, Gillian's going to hang some of her paintings here in their place, and maybe we could sell a few."

"Ah, Gillian love, what've you got for us?" he called out when she came in the door, carrying several framed paintings.

"Billy, I didn't see you there in the corner. How've you been?"

"I've no complaints. I was sad to say goodbye to Mick, and I worried a bit about whether I'd need to find a new pub, but this young lady here" — he nodded at Maura — "has done right by me."

"I couldn't throw you out, Billy," Maura said, smiling. "You're the one that keeps my customers coming in for your tales about

Old Ireland. And the longer the tales, the more they drink, and the happier I am. What did you bring, Gillian?"

"A couple of each — the pretty tourist pictures and the ones I show in the Dublin galleries. Take a look." Gillian stood them up in a row against the front face of the bar, then stepped back and waited for Maura's response.

When she'd seen the paintings in the light-filled space of the old creamery, Maura had liked Gillian's work, but since then she'd wondered if they would look out of place in her dark and shabby pub. But she was happily surprised: both styles looked good, and they definitely brightened up the place. The only question was, what style would work best in Sullivan's?

"Say something," Gillian prompted. "What do you think?"

"I think they look great — all of them. I'm just trying to decide which ones fit better here."

"Those." Althea's voice came from the doorway behind them. They turned to see her pointing to Gillian's "personal" works. "The others are pretty, but they're a dime a dozen. Those are intense, vivid, alive. Some people won't care for them, but the ones who like them will *really* like them, if you know what I mean."

"Actually, I do," Gillian said. "Thank you, Althea. Maura, what do you think?"

"You know, I agree with her. And thinking practically, the watercolors will get kind of lost in here — it's pretty dark most of the time. The others will make more of an impression, catch the eye, that kind of thing. You have any bigger ones?"

"Yes, at the studio. Why?"

"I'd put a big flashy one on either side of the chimney there, and then scatter some of the smaller ones around. People will notice the big ones, but maybe they'll buy the small ones."

"Maura, that's brilliant. I think you're getting the hang of this." Gillian turned to Billy, who had shuffled his slow way up behind them. "What do you think, Billy?"

"That one." He pointed to one of the bolder abstract pictures. "That's Ballinlough in the morning, isn't it?"

Gillian stared at him. "Spot on, Billy. How on earth did you know?"

"I used to fish there, when I was younger. You've caught the light just right."

Maura tilted her head and squinted her eyes but couldn't see whatever Billy saw. Still, the painting would look good in Billy's corner, and he might be inspired to spin more tales about it. He'd make an excellent salesman. "Gillian, go ahead and bring in a couple more and we'll decide where they'd look best."

"I'll do that. Thanks, Maura."

Althea interrupted. "Hey, this is all nice — but you called me, remember? Since you weren't screaming with glee, I assume you don't have good news."

Gillian sighed. "Let's sit in the corner there and I'll tell you."

A group of men came in the door, so Maura went back to the bar while Gillian and Althea settled around a table. As she served the men — strangers to her — she kept an eye on the women, neither of whom looked happy.

Rose came in at four. "How's it been?" she asked.

"Quiet." Maura surveyed the room. The latest arrivals had taken a table in the corner away from the fireplace; Billy was still settled in his favorite chair, with a half-filled pint in his hand, dozing; and Gillian and Althea were speaking in low, urgent voices in the corner. Maura hoped business would pick up in the next couple of hours. "Is Jimmy coming in?" she asked Rose.

"He may be in later. I left his supper for

him, and he said to call him if there's a rush here."

Luckily she paid Jimmy only for the hours he put in. "Did Mick say anything?"

"He'll be in at six, he told Da." She nodded at the paintings still arrayed against the bar. "They're Gillian's, aren't they? You're thinking of putting them up here? I like the bright ones. The others make me think of me gran."

Maura laughed. "I see what you mean. And we all think the bolder ones will work better. Gillian's going to bring in some bigger ones too."

She slid out from behind the bar and joined Gillian and Althea in the corner.

Althea looked depressed. "I don't know what to do now."

"Your museum isn't going to take your word for it that the little painting is related to the big painting?" Maura asked.

"Ha!" Althea said. "You know how long authentication takes? No, of course you don't. Nobody's going to commit to saying either painting is a Van Dyck without a hell of a lot of analysis. There are all sorts of tests they can run these days to make sure the canvas and the wood and the paint are all right for the period. And then there are the *other* experts who have to study the style and the brushwork and all that stuff. Short answer? Even if everybody is on the same page with it, it would take months, maybe even years, to decide. I don't have months — the exhibit opens in October."

"And having a document would jump over all this?" Gillian asked.

"Maybe. It would make my case a whole lot stronger, anyway. If I could convince the right people to look at the two paintings together, I think they'd see the connection immediately. But I have to get them to take me seriously first."

"What is it you want to do with the painting?" Maura asked.

"I told you, I'm pretty sure Dorothy Ryan would give permission to include her oil sketch in the show. Of course, it would help if we could show she owns the thing legally — that it wasn't stolen sometime in the past three hundred years. But if that's not a problem, I could tell her it would be worth a whole lot more money if it got that kind of exposure. I've talked to her, and I'd bet she'd be happy to sell it in a minute. Anyway, in the best of all possible worlds, I'd hang the two pictures together and get the story out there — great human interest angle. That is, if we knew the story . . ."
Now Althea looked depressed again.

"You mean, how the sketch ended up under a bed in New York?" Maura asked.

"Yes. How do we get from here to there? The big painting is here; the oil sketch is there. Why? How?"

Maura thought for a moment. "What do you know about the woman who owned it? Dorothy's great-aunt?"

"Not a whole lot. I think I told you everything I know the first time we met. I found her immigration record and a couple of local censuses, but that's all I had time for. There's a Social Security record for her death."

"Humor me," Maura said. "Run through it again, will you?"

Althea sighed. "A forty-something woman named Dorothy Ryan brings an old painting she's inherited to an open appraisal. Nate Reynolds, the appraiser, calls me, I look at the painting, I think, 'Wow.' I talk to Dorothy, but she knows next to squat. Her best guess is that her great-aunt Jane Deasy brought the painting with her when Jane joined her sister in New York in the 1940s but never told anybody about it. The great-aunt left all her meager belongings to Dorothy, one of those do-it-yourself wills that says 'I leave everything to' without any details. The painting was in a suitcase, and

Dorothy brought it home and stuck it in the attic. When she saw an ad in her local paper about the appraisal day, she figured what the heck and took it in."

Gillian picked up the thread. "Nate the appraiser and you agreed that her painting was a Van Dyck, and, knowing the great-aunt came from Ireland, and that Van Dyck had worked here, it fit."

"Exactly. But apparently nobody in Dorothy's family ever talked about where in Ireland they were from. The ship's records said only 'County Cork,' so I had to do a lot of legwork just to narrow down the possibilities in County Cork, and Leap here was my last stop. If there was a major finished painting for which the little painting was kind of a preliminary version, I had to look for someone who could have afforded a Van Dyck back in the day. And it was here!"

"But you still can't connect the woman who had it with the Townsend family?" Gillian asked.

"Nope."

Gillian thought for a moment. "It might be a good idea to find out if this Jane Deasy ever worked in Mycroft House. But how did she end up with the painting? If she stole it, then the great-niece Dorothy has no right

to it and it should come back to the Townsend family, I'd guess."

"Would there be a police report if it was
stolen?" Maura asked.

"Possibly, but maybe nobody missed it,"
Gillian suggested. "Based on what Harry
told me, they didn't even know the little
painting existed. But then, they didn't know
they had the big one, either. You've seen
that house — you think anybody's been
keeping track of anything there in the last
century? Especially if nobody thought it was
valuable?"

Althea smiled ruefully. "Good point."

"You need somebody who does research
into family history," Maura said suddenly.

"What?" Althea said.

"Somebody who can look at the history of
the Deasys — and the history of the woman,
right? I mean, if she worked there, shouldn't
there be employment records or something?
When did she leave? Was she ever accused
of stealing? There's got to be some trail. I
wouldn't know where to find it, but a
genealogist would."

"Harry and I can check the household account books for the twentieth century," Gillian said slowly, "although I don't know that
they recorded details like that. But we
should check. And Maura, you can ask Sean

if the gardaí have any records of a theft, or an accusation, going back that far."

"I could. You said her name was Jane Deasy?"

Althea fished in her purse and pulled out a small notebook. She leafed through it and said, "Yes, Jane Deasy. Spelled D-e-a-s-y, although I'm not sure I've been pronouncing it right."

"Or you might do well to talk to them as remembers the Deasy family hereabouts." Billy spoke up out of nowhere.

The three women turned to him in unison. "Do you, Billy?" Gillian asked.

"Bridget Nolan might."

Chapter 19

Althea looked between her two companions. "Who is Bridget Nolan?"

"A friend of Billy's, from way back," Maura said, then added, "And a neighbor of mine. And the grandmother of Mick Nolan, who works here."

Althea still looked confused. "Uh, okay. Why would she know anything about this Jane Deasy person?"

Gillian and Maura exchanged a glance. "Because," Maura began, "most people around here have lived here their whole lives, and they remember a lot of things." She turned to Billy. "You want to join us, Billy?"

He waved a dismissive hand. "I've said enough, and in truth, I don't know much more. I only know there was some trouble, a long time ago, and Jane went to the States to live with her sister. Bridget was closer to the family — you'd best talk with her."

"Okay. Can we go *now*?" Althea demanded.

Althea wasn't a very fast learner, Maura thought. "Althea, in case you haven't noticed, I have a business to run here. Plus, Bridget is in her eighties, and late afternoon is not her best time. Bridget's a friend, and I respect her privacy. In fact, I should go with you, so if you want to hear whatever Bridget has to say, you're going to have to wait until tomorrow morning."

Althea glared at Maura, then turned to Gillian. "What about you? Do you know her?"

Gillian glanced at Maura. "No, and I agree with what Maura says. You want something from Bridget Nolan, you're going to have to approach her politely, not go barging in making demands."

"Is that what you think I do?" Althea said, a bit more loudly than necessary.

"Yes," Gillian and Maura replied in unison.

"That's why you're barred from the manor, remember?" Gillian reminded her. "You got turned away at the front door, so you tried to sneak in the back door with Harry, so to speak, rather than waiting and doing it the right way. And look how well that turned out. You need to play by Irish rules, Althea. On an Irish schedule."

Althea threw up both hands. "All right, all right, I get it. But look at it from my side: the clock is ticking. If I don't find the paperwork here, the whole thing might fall apart and I'll be out of a job in a couple of months. I live in Manhattan, and I can't afford it without a job. I'd have to go back and live with my parents in Delaware!"

Maura swallowed a smile. "Althea, a lot of people around here are in the same boat, living with their family, because they don't have a choice. So don't expect us to feel sorry for you."

"Fine, whatever," Althea muttered. "So, when in the morning can we go see Bridget?"

Maura smiled at her. "Say, nine thirty, ten? Meet me at my house and we can walk over together."

"Where's your house?" Althea demanded.

"Uh . . ." Maura quailed at trying to explain to a New Yorker how to get to her house from Skibbereen.

Luckily Gillian stepped in. "I'll pick you up at your hotel in Skibbereen, Althea. The lanes can be a bit tricky if you don't know them well."

"All right, I'll be waiting," Althea replied. "Thank you, both of you."

Maybe Althea is learning something after all, Maura reflected. At least she'd said "thank you."

The evening rush, such as it was, began shortly after that, and Maura was kept busy for a while. Mick came in shortly after six, and in a quiet moment, Maura took him aside and asked, "Will Bridget mind if I bring Gillian and Althea to see her in the morning?"

"Sure, she'll be glad for the company, as long as you don't wear her out."

"Don't worry. I'll keep an eye on Althea, and Gillian and I can drag her out of there if she won't leave on her own."

"That I'd like to see. What's this about?"

"We're hoping she can tell us something about a family who used to live around here."

"And who might they be?"

"The Deasys?"

Mick shook his head. "Don't know the name."

"It has to do with that painting Althea is so hot to find, of course. The woman who had the smaller painting in America was named Jane Deasy, and Billy said that he remembered some story about the woman but he didn't know the details and said we should talk to Bridget."

274

"Ah," Mick said, as though Maura's explanation made sense to him. Which was good, because she wasn't sure what Billy thought Bridget might know. "When would all this have happened?"

"Nineteen-forty-something, I think. Bridget would have been, what, ten? Fifteen?"

"Even children listen. What's more, if there's a story to be told, people repeat it — you'll remember there was no telly then, so storytelling was all we had."

Maura looked hard at him to see if he was joking, and couldn't decide. Still, if Billy and Mick agreed that Bridget might know more, it was worth following up. "If you say so."

The next morning Gillian pulled up outside Maura's cottage with Althea. Maura had left her front door open so she could hear them arrive and came out to greet them. "Gillian, I remembered after you left that I hadn't told you where I lived."

"Ah, I knew you had Old Mick's place — those of us who grew up around here know each and every house."

Althea was looking around. "Jeez, you really are out in the country here. Are those cows?" She pointed to a field a few hundred feet away.

"Yeah, Althea, those are cows," Maura said with exaggerated patience. "This is a dairy farming area. In fact, Gillian lives in what used to be a creamery."

"A what?"

"Where they collected the farmers' milk, made butter and the like," Gillian said absently. "Have you talked to Bridget yet, Maura?"

"No. Though I probably should have warned her that she'd have some unexpected guests — she'll want to serve us tea."

"Not to worry," Gillian said, holding up a paper bag. "I picked up some fresh scones in Skib before I collected Althea." She turned to Althea. "Now, remember what I told you: let us introduce you and explain what we're doing here. Don't just jump in with your questions."

"Yeah, yeah, don't beat up on the old lady," Althea said impatiently.

"Althea," Maura snapped, "you'll be a guest in Bridget's home, and you want something from her, so let her take whatever time she wants, okay? Just keep your mouth shut and drink your tea."

"All right! Can we get on with this?"

Maura and Gillian exchanged a look, and Maura was relieved that it was the two of them against Althea. She valued Bridget's friendship, and she didn't want to spoil that by letting Althea trample all over her.

"Let's go." Maura led the way down the lane, stifling a laugh as she watched Althea try to make her way through the mud and the ruts in her fancy city shoes. Bridget's house was only a minute or two away — depending on your shoes — and they found her sitting out in front of her house enjoying the sun.

"Bridget," Maura called out as they approached, "I've brought you some company."

"How lovely, dear. Is that Gillian Callanan? I haven't seen you for quite some time. And who's this?" she asked, looking at Althea.

"This is Althea Melville. She's from New York, visiting here. It's her first trip to Ireland."

Bridget looked critically at Althea. "Welcome. Are you having a good visit?"

"Thank you, yes. It's a pleasure to meet you," Althea said politely, then shut up, to Maura's relief.

"Gillian's brought you some scones," Maura said. "Would you like me to make some tea to go with them?"

"That would be lovely, dear. You know

where everything is. So how's your mother keeping, Gillian?"

Maura left the women outside and went into Bridget's kitchen to make the tea. She put the kettle on to boil, then collected cups, the sugar bowl, and a pitcher of cream as well as plates for the scones, butter, and knives. When the water was hot she poured it over the tea leaves, then carried everything to the low table in the big room.

Back outside, she said, "All set, Bridget. Can I help you inside?"

Bridget waved off her offered hand. "I'm fine. It's a good day for me. Gillian and I were talking about some of the neighbors' children she knew, years ago." Bridget stood up slowly, then led the way into her home, and the others followed. "Please, sit down. Maura, would you pour?"

"Happy to, Bridget." It took a few minutes to serve tea to everyone, and Maura smiled inwardly: this was not a fast process, and Althea must be going nuts with the pace. She was doing a good job of holding it together, though, for which Maura was grateful.

When Maura finally took her seat, Bridget asked, "So, Althea, what brings you here? Do you have family in Cork?"

"No, it was something else." Althea looked

at Maura and Gillian for approval before plunging on. "You see, I work in a museum in New York, and I came here looking for an old painting, to put in a show. It turns out that it belongs to the Townsends."

Bridget's eyes were bright with curiosity. "Now, isn't that interesting? And have you seen your painting?"

"I found it, yes. But there's something else I wanted to ask you."

"And what would that be? Oh, please, help yourself to more tea. Maura, might you want to make another pot? Will we be a while?"

"Of course, Bridget," Maura said, ignoring Althea's imploring look.

When she returned with the refreshed teapot, Maura took her seat again and winked at Gillian, who signaled to Althea to pick up the thread. "Why don't you tell Bridget what you're looking for?"

"Thank you!" Althea recounted to Bridget the story and explained her need to prove that the small painting hadn't been stolen. "Billy at Maura's pub said that you might know something about the woman who had the painting when she . . . passed away not long ago. We wondered if she might have worked at the manor."

Bridget had been following Althea's story

closely, nodding from time to time, but now Maura thought she looked troubled.

"And would you know her name?" Bridget finally asked.

"Jane Deasy."

"Ah," Bridget said, then she fell silent.

Althea looked desperately between Maura and Gillian, asking for her next move. Maura gave a quick shake of her head, trying to tell Althea to wait.

Finally Bridget spoke. "We wondered what had happened to Jane. The Deasy family lived not far from here, closer to the village. None live here now — at best you might find a few stones in the Kilmacabea cemetery. I knew Jane from church, but we weren't close — she was a coupla years older than me. You're right that she went to work at the manor for a bit. And then she was gone . . ."

Althea looked ready to speak, but Maura placed a warning hand on her arm, then asked, "Do you know what happened?"

"She never said. Just left. She had a sister in New York, and it was said that she'd gone to join her, that her sister would find her a better job. It was a common enough story. Neither she nor her sister ever came back to visit. I suppose I never gave it much thought after a time. And you say she's just died?"

"A year or so ago," Althea said. "According to her great-niece Dorothy, the one who inherited the painting, Jane never married or had any children, so she left what little she had to Dorothy. The only important thing she left was that painting, and Dorothy had no idea what it was. I want to make sure Jane had a right to it and that it's really Dorothy's now."

"Yer thinking that Jane might have stolen it?" Bridget's gaze was less than friendly now, and Althea hurried to mollify her.

"I'm sorry, I don't mean to dirty Jane's memory, but if the painting is what I think it is, it's very valuable. She might have taken it thinking she could sell it in New York and nobody would think twice about it. The Townsends certainly don't seem to have missed it."

"But she never did sell it, yer telling me. She kept it always. So what're you askin'?"

"Whether she came by it rightfully. If not, the heir will have to return it — that's only fair. But if it truly was Jane's, there must be a story behind it."

Bridget's eyes had turned vague again as she searched her memories. "There was something, I know, but . . ." Then her expression sharpened. "If I'm right, it's not my story to tell. But Jane had a younger

281

sister who would know more."

"She's still alive? Where would I find her?" Althea asked eagerly.

"At the nunnery in Ballybeanrialta."

"There are still nunneries around?" Maura said, incredulous. "Oh, I'm sorry — was that rude? I just thought nobody did that kind of thing anymore."

"Fewer and fewer do," Bridget said sadly. "Many of the ones that hang on do so only because they're waiting . . ."

Maura mentally filled in the rest: waiting for the remaining aging sisters to die. "Can we visit the sister? I mean, outsiders are allowed in?"

Bridget laughed. "Of course they are — we're not in the Middle Ages here. In fact, they'd be glad fer the company. They have few visitors these days. I'm sure they'd welcome you."

Maura refused to look at Althea, who was no doubt itching to leave immediately to go interrogate some elderly nun.

"Do you know," Gillian said suddenly, "I believe I know the place — I've driven by it many a time, without thinking."

"As do so many these days," Bridget said. "It's Sister Benedicta you'll be wanting to speak with. She may be able to help. More tea?"

Despite the offer, Maura could tell that Bridget was tiring, so it was time to clear out. "Thank you, Bridget, but we should be on our way. It was kind of you to talk to us, and I'm sure Althea is grateful. Aren't you, Althea?"

"Of course. Thank you, Bridget," Althea said warmly. "I promise I'll let you know if I find out anything more. It was lovely to meet you."

"Good to see you, Bridget," Gillian echoed. "I'll give my mother your regards."

"Don't get up, Bridget," Maura said. "I'll see everyone out. And I'll stop in tomorrow?"

"God willing, I'll be here."

Maura and Gillian cleared up the tea things quickly, while Althea paced. Once outside, they walked quickly back to Maura's cottage. "I feel like every person I talk to just pawns me off to the next. Where the hell is this nunnery, now?" Althea demanded.

Gillian laughed. "Watch your language, Althea. It's not far, maybe half an hour. I assume you want to drive straight there?"

"Of course I do! Maybe this sister has the answer or knows something useful. And the way my luck has been running lately, she'll probably drop dead fifteen minutes before I get there. If you don't want to go, I'll go myself. If somebody will tell me where it is."

Gillian looked at Maura. "I'm willing to take you there, Althea. Maura, do you want to come?"

Maura was torn. She shouldn't leave Rose alone in the pub, in the unlikely event that a tour bus full of tourists broke down in front of Sullivan's. But maybe Jimmy could cover for her. She pulled out her cell phone. "Give me a minute."

Miraculously Jimmy answered and agreed to fill in. Maura promised that she'd be in no later than three. "Okay, I'm in. Let's go!"

"Right, then, ladies, we're off to the nunnery," Gillian said, laughing. "How often do we get to say that in this day and age?"

CHAPTER 20

Maura was relieved that Gillian was doing the driving, because she still got lost in the lanes, and there were pitifully few road signs to point the way anywhere, if she even recognized the names on them. This way she could enjoy the scenery, something she didn't have the chance to do when she was driving, since it still took concentration for her to drive on the left, and she was always more worried about running into hedgerows or stone walls or even cattle. They passed through more pretty country: small roads that wandered around, passing the occasional church or even an isolated roadside pub plus a lot of fields. There were patches of vivid yellow gorse, and the hedgerows were high and in full leaf.

Gillian's estimate proved correct, and they arrived at the nunnery after a half hour's drive. The nunnery turned out to be a rambling building behind a high wall in a midsized town, although in a part of town that had seen better days — maybe a century earlier. Gillian passed through a gate and pulled up in front of an L-shaped building that looked as though it had been built in the middle of the nineteenth century; there was a more modern school building visible beyond it, down a hill, its windows festooned with crayon drawings. The entrance was in the middle of the left-hand wing, and Gillian parked near it.

"Here we are," she proclaimed.

"I've never been inside a nunnery. Do we just walk in and ask for Sister Benedicta?" Althea said, sounding surprisingly uncertain.

"There must be some sort of reception desk," Maura guessed, although she knew no more than Althea. "Maybe we should have called ahead. Are the nuns allowed to have telephones?"

Gillian laughed. "Are the two of yeh afraid of some elderly ladies in long dresses?"

"I thought they gave up wearing habits a while ago," Althea said.

"The younger ones have done, but these here more likely stick to the old ways. They're the last of their kind. Come on."

Gillian waited until Althea and Maura had emerged from the car and then led the way into the building. There was in fact a reception desk of sorts, although it was unoccupied. The afternoon sunlight illuminated silent, empty rooms: there was no one in sight, but there was a bell on the desk, and Gillian rang it. After perhaps two minutes, someone finally appeared, moving slowly.

"May I help you?" the elderly nun, prim in her blue habit, inquired gently.

"Yes, I'm looking for a sister here," Gillian said — and a touch loudly, in case the nun was hard of hearing, Maura guessed. "Her name is Sister Benedicta?"

"Ah, yes, we do have a sister here by that name. And why is it you're after seeing her?" The nun's expression was only mildly curious as she eyed the three women in front of her.

"Well, we've actually come regarding her sister Jane, who moved to America a long time ago. Bridget Nolan in Knockskagh told us we'd find Sister Benedicta here."

"Ah, a family matter. I'm sure she'll be happy to see you. Follow me, if you will."

They all followed dutifully, and since the nun's pace was slow, Maura had time to study her surroundings. The building was clearly old, with a corridor along the side they had entered and rooms opening to the other side. The hallway was filled with light from the many large, tall windows. There were short flights of stairs in unexpected places, and it took some time for their elderly escort to negotiate those. And then there were unlikely turns and corners — apparently several buildings had been thrown together at some time long past. It was all quiet and immaculately clean; the patterned linoleum floor and the old oak woodwork gleamed with polish.

Sister Benedicta's room turned out to be on the next floor up, and its wide window overlooked a small and charming garden. Maura wasn't sure what she had expected, and she had wondered about the state of the sister's health, both physical and mental. As the four of them bumbled into the small room, Maura spotted a diminutive figure sitting in a comfortable armchair, a book in her hand. Her face was softly wrinkled, but her blue eyes were clear and observant, in spite of the reading glasses she had removed as they arrived.

The sister who had escorted them said, "Sister, you have visitors. Something about your sister Jane . . ."

Sister Benedicta responded crisply, "Thank you for showing them the way." It was clearly a dismissal, and the first nun smiled dubiously and all but backed out of the room. Sister Benedicta turned to them and asked, "And you are?"

Nobody seemed sure how to start. Maura wondered briefly if Althea was Catholic and was intimidated by nuns, but she decided to break the ice. "Sister, I'm Maura Donovan, and this is Althea Melville and Gillian Callanan. Althea's American. Well, so am I. But it was Althea who really wanted to talk to you . . ." She was babbling. Did nuns make her nervous? She'd never even been to a Catholic school, although she'd heard some bad stories about the ones friends had attended.

Sister Benedicta regarded the unlikely trio with something like amusement. "Well, two of you have come quite a way. I'm assuming you didn't come here just to look at a very old woman in a habit, now, did you?"

"No, but it's complicated," Maura said. "If you have the time to hear it."

Sister Benedicta settled back into her chair and motioned to the others to sit down, which produced some awkward shuffling because there was only one other chair in the room. Finally Althea took the chair, while Gillian and Maura perched on the neatly made single bed. "My dear," the sister resumed, "these days I welcome any diversion, especially from someone younger than I am. There are few of us left here, we're all much of an age, and we've all heard each other's stories too many times. So tell me, what brings you here?"

Althea took a deep breath. "First, I don't know if you're aware that your sister Jane died last year."

The nun stared at her, more with curiosity than with sorrow. "Heavenly days, I thought she'd died years ago. I haven't heard from her for, oh, close to fifty years now. Mary Margaret, my other sister in America, she used to write the odd letter, but I know she's been gone for quite a while. And she never mentioned anything about Jane, so I assumed they had lost touch. Poor Jane." She crossed herself and fell silent, reaching back into her memories, and nobody interrupted her.

Then she turned again to Althea. "And how does that bring you here? Certainly not just to tell me about that — you could have written a letter, you know. Don't tell me she's left a fortune."

Althea smiled briefly. "I suppose that may depend on your point of view," she said and launched into the now-familiar tale about Dorothy Ryan and Jane Deasy's painting. At the end of the tale Althea said, "I found out that Jane had come from Ireland, so I came over here to do some more research."

Surprisingly, Sister Benedicta appeared to have kept up with Althea's rather headlong explanation. "And you found yourself at Mycroft House."

"Yes," Althea said, startled. "How did you know?"

"Is Eveline Townsend still alive?" the sister asked, ignoring the question.

Althea glanced briefly at Maura before answering. "Yes, she is."

"I wondered . . . So, Jane kept the painting."

Her audience was momentarily stunned into silence. Then Althea managed to say, "You know about the painting?"

"Oh, yes. Jane told me about it. Richard Townsend gave it to her."

Maura could almost see wheels spinning in Althea's mind. "Richard Townsend? Who is that? Gillian, do you know?"

Gillian thought for a moment. "I think Richard was one of Harry's great-uncles, another of Eveline's brothers. Do I have that right, Sister?"

"You do. Richard died in World War Two, near the end. I don't know this young Harry, but it's a family name. Well, if you want the whole story, you'll have to take tea with me."

Althea said, "Yes! We'd love to," before Gillian and Maura could confer.

Sister Benedicta smiled. "How kind of you to humor an old woman. Stay where you are — you needn't do anything. One of the few pleasures of growing old is that you can ask others to do things for you. One of the young acolytes will bring it, if you'll be kind enough to pass the telephone to me."

As the nun requested tea and refreshments on the vintage black phone, Maura sat back on the bed, lost in amazement. Althea must be over the moon: Sister Benedicta had just casually confirmed that Jane Deasy's painting had come from Mycroft House, which confirmed its link to the large portrait there. And, according to Sister Benedicta, it had been given to her by a member of the Townsend family, although the legal status of that gift might be murky now.

The nun hung up the phone. "There, now. It won't be but a few minutes. I don't want to start on the story until I'm sure we won't be interrupted, so perhaps you can tell me a bit about yourself while we wait. Gillian, I'm guessing you're a local woman. Who are your people?"

Maura watched Althea swallow her obvious impatience as they passed the time in polite pleasantries until the tea arrived, when a very young novice in a simple habit arrived with a rolling cart arrayed with tea and bread, which she set down on a table under the window. Was the order still managing to recruit young nuns, in this day and age? Maura wondered. Sister Benedicta lifted the full pot carefully with both hands and poured a cup for each of them and one for herself. Then she waited until they had all helped themselves to soda bread and butter and jam, and were settled back in their seats, before she began her story.

"It's been a good many years since I've thought about all of this, you know. It was the 1940s, before I entered the nunnery — a difficult time, for our family, for our country and others. Yet we didn't complain — we worked hard, and we had each other. Until Mary Margaret left . . . She was the first to go. What do you know about our family, the Deasys?" Sister Benedicta asked.

Maura began, "Althea has worked it out that Mary Margaret went to America first, and that Jane joined her in the 1940s. Is that right?"

The sister nodded. "Well, the story goes back a bit before that. If you know anything about Ireland, especially in the first half of the century — my goodness, I mean the one before this, don't I? — you'll know life was hard. Families were large and the land was small — not enough to support everyone. You could get by on a farm if you worked hard and were careful; if you kept a cow for milk and butter; if you had your potato beds; and, if you were lucky, you had a pig. The money came from the sheep and cattle — selling wool, meat, milk. There wasn't much a girl could do to earn money in those days besides teach school, perhaps, but once she married and the babies started coming, that was the end of that."

She took a sip of her tea. "There were six of us children, the three girls first — Mary Margaret, Jane, and myself — then the three boys. That made it hard, since we girls weren't as much use on the farm, and Da had to wait for the boys to grow up. Many people went to America, where there was work, and the girls usually ended up in service in a city there, until they married. The wages were so much better there that they almost always managed to send something home, to help out. And since so many of us went, there were always friends and relatives who could help a young girl find a place, get her started. That's what Mary Margaret did. She was sixteen, the eldest, and our mother had a cousin in New York

City to look out for her, so off she went. It was hard on all of us, seeing her go. She wrote back to us, sometimes, and she always put a little something in the envelope. We so enjoyed reading her letters."

The old woman paused to work out her dates. "So it must have been about 1937 when she left — before the war — and she worked for a couple of years, and then she married a nice Irish boy, Joseph Ryan, a milkman she met through the back door — from Galway, I think he was, not from Cork. When they married, she stopped working, and their son Joseph was born in 1945. But I'm getting ahead of myself. Would you like some more tea?"

"Let me," Maura volunteered. Something about time in Ireland — no one ever seemed to rush. It must be driving Althea crazy.

Sister Benedicta resumed her story. "Where was I? Ah, yes. Well, Jane, bless her, was four years younger than Mary Margaret, and when she was sixteen, she went into service as well. Surely you can guess where."

"Mycroft House," Althea said.

"Yes," the sister said. "It was the nearest manor, and she was lucky to get a place. It was nice for us, because it meant that we could see her when she had a free day.

Once, when the Townsend family was away, she took some of us littler ones round the house. Oh, it was grand. So big and elegant and full of lovely things. It was all we could talk about for days after. Nearly drove Mam crazy. So . . . Jane was there about two years, working her way up — she was bright and the prettiest of us and a hard worker. I was two years younger than Jane, and I hadn't joined the sisters yet — that came later. I was thinking about looking for work myself and asked Jane could she get me a place at Mycroft House, but she put me off. I didn't push at first, but I asked her again and again, and finally she told me she was leaving, going to America, to Mary Margaret. I was that surprised — I hadn't known she was even in touch with her, and she hadn't said anything to Mam yet. And it made no sense. She liked the job, she liked the place, and she was making good money, for the time. But she'd changed — she'd always been cheerful, good-natured, but she'd become more quiet. So I asked her why. And Jane fussed and fretted and wouldn't answer me, but I was a determined girl, and I kept after her. And finally she told me she was going to have a baby."

CHAPTER 21

That simple statement met with stunned silence, even from Althea, who stared goggle-eyed at the elderly nun. Sister Benedicta returned her gaze calmly and finally smiled. "Yes, even in those days — you modern women, you think you've invented something new? Although it seems that more and more of you are skipping the marriage part these days and just having the babies. But in Ireland back then, it was a serious thing. As for Jane, I'd almost guessed it by then. I knew she was hiding something, and it had to be important. But she wasn't keeping company with anyone from the village — that's hard to keep secret in a small place. So it had to be someone at the house. She didn't want to tell who. But I kept asking and asking, and then I went up to the house to see her one day."

Sister Benedicta paused and looked at each of them in turn. "You know, it must be hard for your generation to understand what the world was like then. And in some ways, Ireland was still in an earlier time — and there was such a big difference between the rich people like the Townsends and people like us, poor farmers. Almost medieval, looking back at it now. I hear a lot of things have changed, and change is coming faster and faster. But not for me . . . Where was I?"

Althea said, surprisingly gently, "You went to see Jane at Mycroft House?"

"Ah, yes. Well, I knew she wasn't supposed to have visitors, except on her free days, which weren't very often, so I sneaked onto the grounds and I was going to come in by the kitchen at the back. But I came upon Jane before I got there — and she was with Richard Townsend. And after that, I made her tell me what was going on, although I guessed a good bit of it." She cocked her head at them. "Tell me, you know this young Harry? What kind of a man is he?"

Gillian looked at the others and answered, "I know him fairly well — and I think I know what you're asking. He's good-looking and knows it. Smart enough, and he's look-ing out for his great-aunt Eveline, which is sweet of him."

"And I'm guessing that he can lay on the

charm thick as Irish butter."

Gillian laughed. "That's a good way of putting it — and yes, he does."

"The Townsend men were always like that. Oh, not that they were bad sorts, really. And Richard was a decent man. He wasn't much older than Jane, maybe twenty, and had spent some time at university, but he was home for the summer, getting ready to leave to join an English regiment. He was the third son, if I recall — his eldest brother was already married, and there was another one after him, before Richard. And Jane was lovely, fresh and sunny. I suppose you'd have to say they fell in love. Certainly they believed they were in love. I think Richard did love her — he wasn't just having a bit of summer fun before he went off to war. When I saw them together, they sort of glowed. But there was nothing they could do. Richard had no money of his own, and his family would not have welcomed his marriage to their maid. Fair they might have been, and good employers, but there they would have drawn the line."

Sister Benedicta sighed. "So I saw them together when I came looking for Jane. I remember I envied them — I was sixteen myself. Ah, well, that was a long time ago. And seeing how things turned out, maybe I was wrong to envy them."

"What happened?" Maura asked quietly, although by now she thought she could guess.

"Well, Jane decided she had to leave, and she wrote to Mary Margaret. Again — you young things don't know what it was like to have a baby with no father about, in those days. Not that it didn't happen, but it wasn't easy for the girl. And if she'd stayed, it might have made trouble for Richard with his family. So she decided she had to go, and she told him. He didn't want her to go, and what was worse, he couldn't help her, because he had no money to give her. And that's where the painting came in. Seeing as he couldn't give her money, he thought she could take the little painting with her and sell it in America — it would be small enough to carry, and he said it would be worth more there, and easier to sell. Have you seen the painting?"

"Yes, I have — it's lovely," Althea said.

"And it's the image of Richard Townsend. Jane slipped me up to her room and showed it to me, just before she left, when I worried about how she'd get on in New York."

"Jane's Richard?" Gillian said. "Well, the family breeds true, because it's a grand likeness of Harry as well."

300

"And here you all are, because of it, it seems. So, Jane left her post and took off for America. She'd saved up for passage, and Mary Margaret sent a bit as well. Off she went, not two months after she first decided. I don't know how she managed it, with the war on in the Atlantic — whether Richard could find a way for her or whether she went by way of Canada. And then Mary Margaret wrote that she'd had a baby, young Joseph. First time she'd made any mention of expecting a child." Sister Benedicta paused and looked at them, as if daring them to comment.

Maura looked squarely at the sister, since Althea seemed to have lost her tongue at this latest revelation or was busy working out the details in her own mind. "You're saying that Mary Margaret claimed Jane's child as her own?"

"I am," Sister Benedicta said. "And they lived by that story. Mary Margaret never had another child, you know — and we never asked why. But I know that she and Jane, they drifted apart. Maybe it was too hard on Jane, watching the boy grow up, looking so much like her Richard — I saw the photos Mary Margaret used to send. Or maybe Mary Margaret held it over her — she always had a mean streak. I never had a letter from Jane after she left. I guess she didn't want me asking any more questions." She lapsed into silence.

Althea spoke carefully. "I know a bit more, but it's kind of sad, I guess. Jane never sold the painting. She kept it, in an old suitcase, probably the one she came to America with. She never married, and she worked all her life. You're saying that Joseph Ryan was her son. Well, Joseph married, and he had a daughter, Dorothy, the one who inherited the painting. The only time she remembered seeing Jane was at her grandmother's — Mary Margaret's — funeral. So you're saying that Dorothy's real grandmother was living right there in the same city, and she never knew it? Jane left the painting to her without ever explaining anything, and it was too late to ask Mary Margaret."

"Would that painting be worth much?" the nun asked.

Althea shrugged. "Quite a bit now, probably. But I think Dorothy needs to hear the story first, before she decides what to do with the painting. Don't you?"

That's new, Maura thought with surprise. Although Althea probably had an endgame in mind — like bringing this information to Dorothy might make Dorothy more willing to do what Althea wanted.

Sister Benedicta was looking at some spot beyond them all, or maybe she was looking into her own memories. "I don't know," she said slowly. "It was so long ago. Does it matter to anyone now?"

Would Althea want to go over all the details? Maura worried. Some old nun's tale about the gift probably wouldn't carry much weight at the museum. At the very least Althea would want Sister Benedicta to make some kind of legal statement, and Maura hated the idea of putting the old nun through something like that. Maybe social conventions had changed, but what had happened in the 1940s had been distressing then, and the sister had kept her own sister's secret for a very long time. Would she want it made public? Maura needed to talk to Althea about all this, even if it meant dragging her bodily out of the room, before she started browbeating Sister Benedicta.

But then Maura realized there was another angle that could help. "You know, Sister, Dorothy never knew her grandmother, but you're a relative too, and you knew Jane. Wouldn't you like to be able to meet her?"

The nun was silent for a few long moments. Then she said, "Perhaps you should tell her the story and let her make the choice. God willing, I'll still be here. Most

303

of our family lives past eighty, easy — and two of my brothers are still alive, although not around here any longer. She has more family than she knows." She sat up a bit straighter in her chair. "Well, now, that's what I know. I hadn't thought about all that for years. How strange to think that the story goes on and has brought you here after all these years. I hope I've been able to help you."

Althea was out of her seat before Maura or Gillian could answer. She grasped Sister Benedicta's papery hands between her own. "You have, believe me. I never thought I'd be lucky enough to get this kind of information. Thank you!" Her statement left Maura wondering if maybe Althea was learning something from Ireland.

"You're welcome. And thank you for coming to me with this story. It may sadden me, but I'm glad to know what happened."

They left Sister Benedicta sitting in her chair, staring out the window. Remembering? Althea was barely out of earshot of the room when she started burbling, "Can you believe it? What an angle! Star-crossed lovers, a farewell gift, a woman who refused to part with it — kind of O. Henry, you know? Shoot, I wish I'd recorded it. I'll have to come back . . ."

"Leave Sister Benedicta be," Gillian said. "She's not young, and she's told us all she knows. Telling it officially, if that's what you need, she may not be willing to do. If you want proof that might stand up in court, maybe Harry can confirm what she's told us. Or Eveline. I wonder how much she knew . . ."

Thwarted in her first idea, Althea seized on Gillian's last. "Eveline! Of course, we have to talk with her. Do you think she'll talk to me now?"

"No! Althea, she didn't want to see you after she learned you were carrying on with her beloved Harry and running around the halls bare-bottomed. Why in heaven's name do you think she's going to share anything about her brother's dalliance with the maid?"

Althea would not be stopped. "Then can you talk to Eveline? Please? I know you're more tactful than I am. You can bring up brother Richard, say how much Harry looks like him, and see what she comes up with. Maybe she's not as dotty as you think. Wait — does she even know about the painting? What it might be worth?"

"I can't say," Gillian said. "Harry hasn't wanted to bother her about things like the state of her finances, but she has little or no money left, so he's been carrying the costs. It's not clear whether or not he has the right to sell the painting now, in any case — he'd have to check the terms of his grandfather's will and how he left things for Eveline. So I'm betting that he hasn't spoken to her about it and he's waiting to see how things fall out. It's not as simple as you'd like."

Gillian fell silent for the trip back to Leap until she pulled over in front of Sullivan's. "You should get to work, right, Maura?"

"I should," Maura agreed reluctantly. In spite of herself she was getting caught up in the story of Jane and Richard and whatever had happened some seventy years earlier. Had Old Billy known something, or guessed? Was that why he had sent them to talk to Bridget Nolan? She was amazed once again at how long memories were in Ireland, even for something as vague as a rumor of some family trouble. Of course, if the Townsends were the local lords, so to speak, all of their activities would have been closely watched.

"Come on in," she finally said. "I'll see how busy it is, and you two can work out what to do next. Do you want to bring Harry into it?"

"I think we must," Gillian said. "Althea, let's talk."

Inside Maura counted heads: the pub was moderately busy, for a Wednesday afternoon.

"Ah, there you are, at long last. Decided to grace us with your presence?" Jimmy Sweeney said.

"I told you I'd be in late, Jimmy. Doesn't look like you're overworked. Anything going on that I need to know about?"

"It's all well in hand," Jimmy said. "You go chat with your girlfriends there."

Maura debated about saying something about his tone but decided she didn't want to get into it right now. It would keep, though it soured her mood. Maura stalked over to the table where Althea and Gillian were sitting. "Can I get you anything?"

Gillian looked past Maura at Jimmy. "Problems?" she said in a low voice.

"No. Just Jimmy being Jimmy. Drinks?"

"Coffee for me," Gillian said. "Althea?"

"Yeah, sure, fine, whatever. Can we get moving here?"

Maura left Gillian to clamp down on Althea's impatience while she went to prepare the coffees. Rose emerged from the back room. "Ah, Maura, there you are," she said. "All's well?"

At least Rose meant her question kindly, unlike her father. "Just fine, Rose. We visited a nunnery."

"Really, now? They're still around?"

"They are. I'll tell you about it later. Although I'm not sure how much later — we've still got a couple of things to work out. Sean hasn't stopped by, has he?"

"Officer Sean? And why would he do that?" Rose dimpled.

"I wondered if he'd come up with anything new about Seamus Daly's death. That's all."

"No sign of the man," Rose said cheerfully. "Maybe you should call him and ask. About the murder, I mean."

"Right," Maura muttered. She collected the coffees and joined Althea and Gillian at their table. "What've you got?"

"Much as I hate to say it," Gillian began, "I think we do need to bring Harry in now."

"Hey, I've said I'm sorry," Althea protested. "I'm not going to crawl all over him. He's yours if you want him."

"You're too kind," Gillian drawled, and it took Althea a moment to realize that she was being sarcastic.

"Quit with the catfight, okay?" Maura said. "You can work that out later. Rose wondered if we should talk to Sean too, and I think she's right. I already told him that we found the painting at the manor, and now we can add the story about Jane and Richard Townsend."

"And that connects to the gardener's murder how?" Althea asked.

"Dunno, but at least we've got a few facts. Let's give them to Sean and let him figure it out. Okay? We're not hiding anything, unless an 'oops' baby seventy years ago matters to anyone now."

"It might matter to Eveline," Gillian said softly.

"Then let Harry decide what to tell her or not tell her — we sure don't have to. Call him," Maura said.

"And you call Sean," Gillian shot back.

"Meet here? ASAP?"

"Where else?"

CHAPTER 22

Sean arrived first, in uniform and all business, and Maura went to meet him at the door, avoiding Rose's amused look. "Thanks for coming," Maura said.

"You told me it had to do with Seamus Daly's death?"

"It does. It's not exactly evidence, but it could help explain some of what is going on. Do you have anything new?"

Sean took a step back onto the sidewalk, and Maura followed him. "I shouldn't be telling you this, and don't spread it to those two." He looked toward the corner inside where Gillian and Althea were sitting. "The fewer who know, the better off we'll be."

So why is he telling me? Maura wondered. "All right. What've you got?"

"We've had the results of the postmortem. Seamus Daly was killed by a blow to the head, but it didn't come from the shovel."

That was unexpected. "So what was he

hit with?" Maura asked.

"Something heavy, more square than flat, which rules out the shovel."

Maura thought for a moment. "Does that mean he wasn't killed out on the lawn either?"

"The postmortem wouldn't tell us that, but I wondered that there was so little blood where he was found, outside."

"So the shovel was used to make it look like he was killed outside of the house?"

"Could be," Sean said.

This was definitely disturbing. "Now what do you do? If he wasn't hit outside, then you have to look inside the house? Or what if he wasn't even killed there, but somewhere else altogether?"

Sean seemed amused by her response. "Let's not get ahead of ourselves here. Seamus seldom left the grounds, so it's good odds that he was killed there, inside or out. It does mean that we have to take a harder look at other parts of the place."

"You've got crime scene guys for that?"

"Yeah, but they'd be coming from Dublin, and we can't just call them in to look 'everywhere,' not without a bit more to tell them."

"It's been nearly a week, Sean. And wouldn't the O'Briens have noticed a pool of blood that first day?" And hadn't Tom O'Brien said something to her about seeing Seamus lying in his own blood? But, she recalled, he hadn't said where.

"Look, Maura, I've already said more than I should. I'll have to talk to the O'Briens again, or maybe my sergeant will. Sure, if Seamus was killed inside the house, there could be more evidence to be found, for all that it's been a few days. But you know there aren't many people who could have done it. One of them would be Gillian's friend Harry."

"But Harry was in Dublin that night!" Maura protested.

"Was he? He said he didn't come down till the garda told him about the death, but we've talked to his mates there, and they're having a bit of trouble remembering which night was which. Let's say it's not a hundred percent sure. And don't spread this around."

"You mean, don't tell Gillian? If you say not to, I won't. We've got some things to tell you — and Harry's on his way too — but there's nothing there that we can't say in front of everyone. You can figure out how much of it you want to take to your meeting at the station."

Sean looked past her, up the street. "Townsend," he said neutrally.

Harry Townsend was striding purposefully toward the pub. "Officer . . . Murphy, is it? Gillian inside?" The last was directed toward Maura.

"She is. So's Althea." Maura watched with pleasure as he flinched, although he tried to hide it.

"The two of them? Together?"

"Yup. Let's go on in." Maura led Harry and Sean into the pub, and they spent a minute collecting extra chairs. Harry smiled briefly at Gillian and exchanged curt hellos with Althea, but apart from that he wisely kept his mouth shut. *Well,* Maura reflected to herself, *you made your own bed . . .*

When everyone was settled, and had waited until Rose delivered drinks, with a wink for Maura, Maura said, "Sean, Harry, we've found some interesting stuff that might have something to do with what's going on at the manor. Harry, you may know some of this, or maybe not. I'm sure you can fill in some of the blanks, anyway. Gillian, you want to start?"

"Sean," Gillian began, "we should start by telling you that we've found the Van Dyck painting that Althea came here looking for."

"On Sunday," Sean said, pulling out a notebook and flipping to a page. "Maura told me Monday night. Then I was called away when a gunshot was heard at the manor."

Gillian straightened up in her chair. "Well, then, to move on . . . After we found the painting, Althea told us that we should look for some proof that it really was a Van Dyck. We agreed to do that, and Harry and I looked through the estate records at the manor for anything that might show the purchase of the original painting. We finished up yesterday but found nothing. I came over here to cry on Maura's shoulder. And I guess Old Billy —"

Sean interrupted. "That would be Billy Sheahan?"

"Yes. I'm sure Althea told you that what brought her here to Ireland was the smaller painting found in New Jersey. We knew that the painting had belonged to a woman named Jane Deasy, and Billy overheard and suggested we should talk to Bridget Nolan."

"Mick's gran?" Sean said, scribbling quickly.

"Bang on. So Maura took us over to see Bridget this morning, and Bridget said that we should talk with Jane Deasy's sister, who's a nun with the Brigidine Sisters over at Ballybeanrialta."

Sean was beginning to look confused, and Maura didn't blame him. What had begun

314

with the murder of a gardener had somehow led to a nunnery.

"And . . ." Gillian paused a moment for dramatic effect. "Sister Benedicta told us that when Jane emigrated to America back in the 1940s, she was pregnant with Richard Townsend's child."

Now Harry looked shocked. "Wait — Richard? Aunt Evie's brother? The one who died in the war?"

"The same," Gillian said triumphantly. Althea sat quietly, looking smug.

Harry's brow furrowed with his effort to understand. "Let me get this straight. Say Van Dyck painted that big portrait of the first Richard Townsend that's hanging in the library. And say we accept that he also painted the little one that made its way to America. How did Jane get it? Did Great-uncle Richard give it to Jane? Or did she steal it and run?"

"Apparently the first one." Althea finally spoke. "According to Jane's sister the sister, Richard had no money of his own, but he thought that Jane could sell the sketch to support herself and the child. But it seems Jane couldn't bear to part with it — she kept the painting but gave the baby, a boy, to her older sister to pass off as her own. The woman who brought the painting to the auctioneer's open house is his daughter, and therefore Jane's granddaughter."

"Can you prove any of this?" Sean asked.

"Not yet, but it fits, doesn't it?" Althea retorted. "We know Jane worked at the manor and was pregnant when she left, and we know the painting was among her things when she died. We just have to connect the dots."

"And how does that lead us to the murder of Seamus Daly?" Sean asked.

Maura cheered silently for Sean: he'd managed to follow their patchy logic and now he'd asked the right question.

Althea's face fell. "We don't know. We know the big painting is worth a lot, and so's the little one — more if we connect the two. But we can't prove who owns the little one — all we've got is Sister Benedicta's story that Richard gave it to Jane. She couldn't have sold it anyway, not legally, without any papers. Harry, would your great-uncle Richard have given her some proof of ownership?"

Harry stared incredulously at Althea. "How should I know? He died long before I was born, and nobody in the family ever mentioned it. Hell, nobody talked about the art at all — mostly they went on about hunting and how to pay the second mortgage or which piece of land to sell off next. If the sketch was stolen, maybe somebody in the family reported it to the gardaí. Sean, would you be able to find out?"

Sean scribbled yet another note. "If there's a record."

"Harry, if the family didn't want all the shameful details to come out, they might have done nothing," Gillian said.

"Good point," Harry admitted. "Don't dirty the family name and all that."

"Harry, would your aunt Eveline know something?" Maura asked before Althea could.

"We've never been close enough to talk about things like that, what with the difference in our ages and my not being around much. I think I remember that someone said she was close to Richard, amongst all her family members, even though she was a few years younger than he was. You know, dashing big brother in uniform and all that. I've never been one to stir up old trouble with her. Besides, she's a sweetheart, but she does seem a bit out of it these days and tends to ramble on. Of course, I'm away a lot, always trying to pay that blasted mortgage — that's why I'm so grateful to the O'Briens for keeping an eye on her."

"Harry," Gillian said, "her mind's still

fairly sharp. I know she tires easily, and her arthritis makes it hard for her to get around. But it's hardly fair to her to shut her up in that big old house, with only the O'Briens to talk to."

"She likes to garden, when she feels up to it," Harry volunteered. "She'd take a chair out back and supervise Seamus."

"How well did she know Seamus Daly, then?" Sean asked.

"She knew him as a servant," Harry said. "I don't mean to be crass, but she was of a generation that treated their hired help differently than we would. Well, except maybe Great-uncle Richard, it seems. I wouldn't say they were close."

Maura had been mulling over what Gillian had said, and realized that she — and Sean? — might have been assuming things about Eveline and her state of mind that weren't true. "Harry," she said, breaking in, "what's if she's not half as fuzzy minded as you seem to think? Would that change the picture here?"

Sean shot a glance at her, then leafed through his notes. "When I first spoke with the O'Briens, they told me that Eveline Townsend wouldn't be of much use if I asked her to account for events at the house . . ." Sean looked up, his jaw set.

"Perhaps I was a bit too quick to accept what I was told."

"Surely you're not insinuating that my elderly great-aunt had anything to do with Seamus's death!" Harry protested.

"She could have seen or heard something that could apply," Sean responded firmly. "I'd like to speak with her."

"She did seem sharp enough when we had tea with her," Maura said. "Maybe that took a lot of effort, or she stuck to what she was comfortable with, but she seemed to be all there. And if we're looking to understand how Jane and the two paintings fit with Seamus's death, and if her mind's stuck in the past, she might remember what happened with Jane better than what happened last week."

"Good point, Maura," Gillian said. "Harry, I didn't think she's gone downhill much since the last time I saw her — what, last year? Maybe the O'Briens are keeping her packed away in cotton wool to make things easier for themselves. They don't have to take her anywhere, and they don't have to worry about entertaining guests, that kind of thing."

"Oh, for God's sake," Harry said impatiently. "The parts of the house she spends time in are spotless; she's well fed; she's clean; she's healthy, or as healthy as anyone of her age can be. Do you know how hard it is these days to find that kind of help?"

"I didn't say the O'Briens were taking advantage of her, but how often does she see anyone else? Surely the woman's lonely." Gillian pressed on, "You just said 'the parts of the house she spends time in' — obviously there are parts of the manor where she never goes, like the library where the painting is."

"Are you accusing me of neglect, Gillian?" Harry demanded. "Or of letting the O'Briens keep her locked away for their own convenience? They're decent people. They've been working in that house for years."

"And how many raises have they had in that time?" Maura shot back. "Maybe they're putting together a retirement fund — did you ever think of that?"

"What for all that's holy would they do with a million-dollar painting?" Harry all but yelled at her.

"You can sell anything on the Internet, or so I hear," Maura replied, raising her voice to match his.

Harry stared at her for a moment, then broke out laughing. "Can you imagine either of the O'Briens using the Internet?"

Gillian smiled, then said, "Is there even a computer in the house, Harry?"

"Not that I know about," he replied.

"What if it was Seamus who was hunting for the painting?" Before anyone could protest, Gillian added, "No, I'm not pretending that Seamus knew anything about old art, but he could have been persuaded to look by someone else. After all, Seamus had the access, didn't he?"

"But how would he have known what he was looking for?" Harry asked. "He was a nice fellow, but we all know he was a few sandwiches short of a picnic."

"Maybe someone showed him a photo of something similar," Gillian countered. "You know, like the one we had."

Everyone turned to look at Althea, who held up her hands. "Hey, not me. I wasn't going to go spreading any photos around until I knew I had the right place. And I never even met Seamus, remember?"

"You arrived in Leap before his death, and you went to the manor," Sean reminded her.

"But why would I kill him if he hadn't finished his job and found the picture?" Althea protested. "It had to be someone else. It's your job to find him."

"What about whoever Tom O'Brien shot at on Monday night?" Maura asked. "If Tom

321

wasn't shooting at a dog or a fox, and he says it wasn't."

Sean turned to look at her. "You've spoken with him?"

"He came into the pub yesterday, so I asked him about it. He said it was definitely a man, not a dog."

Sean wasn't happy about this last revelation. "Look, you lot, I'm getting a bit put out that you keep giving me bits of information when you think you're ready. Let's be straight about it: Is any one of you suggesting that Eveline Townsend killed Seamus Daly? Or has knowledge of his death?"

His question was met with silence, even from Harry, who looked bewildered at the turn of the conversation.

"What about the O'Briens?" Sean demanded. "Does any of you have reason to believe that they know something they haven't said?" He glanced quickly at Maura, but she had nothing to add.

More silence.

Sean continued, "Maura here has told me that no one had visited the library at the manor or the painting until you three this past week. Is that correct?"

When Gillian and Harry turned to Maura, she said, "I told him about the dust."

Sean ignored Maura's interruption. "Does

any of you have reason to believe that Eveline Townsend knows anything about that painting?"

"I couldn't say," Harry said. "I haven't discussed it with her. She may think it's just another old canvas hanging on the wall, if she thinks of it at all. I mean, for her it's just part of the decor, as it always has been."

"But, Harry, she *may* know something about the sketch that's now in New York, right?" Maura said. "Shouldn't we find out? Ask her?"

Sean Murphy shut his notebook with a crisp snap. "I'm sorry, Maura, but I still can't see my way to connecting this old painting and the death of Seamus Daly. I thank you for the information you've provided, but I need to get back to the station now. I'll have to remind the superintendent that no one has spoken directly to Eveline Townsend and that it is my opinion that someone should, officially."

"Sean, would you get into any trouble if we went ahead and talked to Eveline about the paintings?" Maura asked.

"Only if she turns out to be a murderer," he said, and Maura wasn't sure if he was joking. "I'll see myself out."

"Who's 'we'?" Althea demanded when he was gone.

"You want to talk to Eveline with the rest of us?" Harry asked, looking pained.

"If I promise to be nice? If I apologize six ways from Sunday for embarrassing her and making a fool of myself? Please?" Althea pleaded. "Look, either she knows about the painting or she doesn't, and so far nobody's asked her. Right?"

"I guess that's true," Gillian said.

"And you can ask about the painting without asking about Seamus's death, right? So we're not messing with the police investigation."

"I'm less sure of that," Harry said, looking troubled. "We have no proof that the two are connected, but the reality of it is, Mycroft House was a very peaceful place until you came poking your nose in last week, Althea."

Chapter 23

Rose cleared the empty coffee cups from the table, leaving Maura, Althea, Gillian, and Harry sitting there in a funk. Customers were beginning to drift into the pub, Maura noted. Soon she'd have to get back to work. "What now?" she asked.

Harry shook his head. "I'm still trying to make sense of all this. Seamus Daly is dead, and nobody knows why. It may or may not have something to do with a painting that could be worth millions that's been hanging in the library for three hundred years collecting dust. And you three seem to think Aunt Eveline might know something that would help sort all this out."

"That's about it," Althea said. Her mood seemed to have improved. "Can we go talk to her now?"

"No," Harry said firmly. "Not now. I want to think this through. I want to have a word first with the O'Briens and with Aunt Evie.

You can talk with her in the morning." Harry looked straight at Althea. "Don't nag. You'll get your chance, but not yet."

"How much will you tell her?" Gillian asked.

Harry turned to Gillian. "I haven't decided. I've come to realize that I'm not sure myself what her mental state is. You may be right to think that seeing more people would be a good thing for her. Maybe I've just taken the easiest path, leaving her to the O'Briens' care, but that may not be what's best for her. Thank you."

"For what?" Gillian asked, surprised.

"For making me see it. I could have been around more, but I do have a job to keep. God knows, if this painting is worth what you say it is, it would make a world of difference, but I'm not counting the euros just yet."

"What about the little painting that started all this?" asked Maura. "If it was stolen in the forties, are you going to want it back? It's going to be worth something too."

Harry was shaking his head. "I don't know. The woman who has it now, she did nothing wrong, if Jane's sister is to be believed — and would a nun lie? But the woman in America doesn't know any of this — what we've found out — does she,

Althea? What do you think her expectations are?"

Althea shook her head. "As of this minute, Dorothy has no expectations of anything. Nate and I were both careful not to commit to anything, and she was so boggled by what she was hearing that I doubt she took in much of it anyway. I certainly never told her that I was going to Ireland. I don't know what Nate told her. But you do realize, if what Sister Benedicta said is true, that makes Dorothy a cousin of some sort to you, Harry, so it's still in the family."

Harry stood up abruptly. "I've got to get out of here — I'm going home. I'll speak to Aunt Evie and if she's willing, we can all meet with her in the morning — say, ten? Does that suit all of you?"

Althea looked frustrated at yet more delays. Gillian said, "Call my mobile and let us know."

"You want me there?" Maura asked.

"Of course we do," Gillian said before Harry could respond. "You know as much about all this as any of us."

"In the morning, then." And Harry turned and left. Gillian watched him go, and once again Maura wondered just what their relationship was — or what Gillian wanted it to be.

"Shall we meet here, Maura?" Gillian said. "Althea, I can pick you up, or you can meet us here and we'll go together."

"Still want to keep an eye on me, huh?" Althea said. "I'll meet you here, just before ten o'clock." She stood up quickly. "I'll see you tomorrow."

After Althea left, Maura turned to Gillian. "Where do you think she's going?"

Gillian sighed. "Who knows? Chasing after Harry? Meeting with her accomplice to get their stories straight? Looking for thugs to help her steal the painting tonight? Or maybe she's just going to go stew at her hotel."

"You really think she's working with somebody? Like Nate, maybe? It would make sense — she gets the glory of discovering the painting, and when the exhibit is over, Nate sells it at the auction house for big bucks. Everybody wins."

"You'd think so, wouldn't you?" Gillian agreed. "But as you may have noticed, Althea doesn't play well with others. She likes to be in control. She wanted to be the one to find the thing, which is why she kept the trip to Ireland a secret from Nate rather than sharing the work. And the credit."

"I know what you mean," Maura said, laughing.

Gillian turned in her chair to face Maura. "You know, Maura, Althea may not think so, but this discovery is as much your doing as hers. More, even. I doubt she'd have gotten this far without all your help."

"It's Old Billy who has pointed us in the right direction. I can't believe people around here remember things that happened that long ago."

"But from what I've seen, you've made Old Billy a friend. There are those who would've thrown him out as a nuisance."

"I wouldn't do that. He's a part of the place."

"You haven't changed much here. Are you not planning to stay on?"

"I haven't decided. It's not like I had any plans when I got here, but I'm not in any hurry to leave. I still don't know if I can keep the business going, so I figured I'd better see what the summer season was like. I mean, I own the building and the license, but I've still got to pay salaries, even if they are pathetic. I kind of feel like I owe Jimmy and Rose something, and I know jobs around here are hard to find."

"And Mick?"

"To tell the truth, I don't know why he stays around, except for his grannie. Couldn't he be doing something else, something better than tending bar part-time? Actually, I'd like to stick around long enough to see Rose find something she wants to do, beyond looking after her father. I want her to have some choices, at least. What about you? From what you've said, you shuttle between here and Dublin. Is that working for you?"

"Ah, Maura, you're very American. You think I should have a career plan laid out?"

"Ha! Hardly. I mean, I sure don't, and even if I had, running a pub in Ireland wasn't on the list. I'm just going with the flow and seeing what happens. But that's me. You've got talent — Althea sees it, and she should know. You want to do anything more with it?"

"Maura, I'm happy enough, and I get by — when my work doesn't sell in Dublin, I pick up a little extra waiting tables or the like. Summers, this is home to me. It suits me. Shall we see about hanging those pictures now?"

Gillian had clearly shut the door on that discussion.

"Sure, let's," Maura said. "Then we can see what the customers think."

Well, at least she'd have new pictures on the walls. The bar itself she hadn't really touched, because the whole area — behind, above, all sides — was layered with mementos from past visitors from all over. Maybe it wasn't very clean or tidy, but it sure was interesting. She wondered if there was anybody around who could identify who all the people in the pictures were. Somehow that wouldn't surprise her.

Maura and Gillian spent a happy half hour shuttling pictures around the room, drawing comments from the patrons. In the end everyone was satisfied with the layout — and Gillian had sold another painting — but then they faced the problem of driving nails into the old walls, which took another half hour to work out. They were still at it when Mick came in a bit after six.

He stopped in the doorway to take a critical look. "Looks grand," he said. "Livens up the old place, doesn't it?" He came around the bar, where Maura was working the taps, and she saw Gillian slip out the door with a wave.

"You missed the party earlier," Maura told Mick. "We had Harry and Althea here too, and Sean."

"You've been spending a lot of time with that lot, haven't yeh, Maura?" he asked quietly.

"Why?" Maura shot back, suddenly defensive. "You think I'm not pulling my weight here at Sullivan's?"

"Nothing like that. But Harry's never been so fond of this place, nor has Gillian. Is there something more going on? Care to fill me in?"

Maura wasn't sure how much Mick had overheard over the past few days, but she suspected it was quite a bit, and they hadn't exactly been trying to keep things quiet. Still, she wasn't in the mood to explain the whole mess. "I'm not sure who would have been fond of the place, under Old Mick. I doubt Dublin Harry would have felt exactly at home here."

Mick looked at her quizzically for a long moment but didn't press. "Point taken." He distributed a few of the pints that Maura had poured to waiting customers, then came back and picked up the conversation. "He thinks he's too good for the likes of us," he said.

"What, you mean all that class stuff again?" Maura asked.

"Just a bit. Not so much with the younger crowd, but some of the older ones remember when it mattered. The Townsends have been lording it over Leap for centuries."

"Well, now they're down on their luck and hanging on by their fingernails. But now that I've spent some time with him, I don't think that's Harry's attitude — it's just that his head is somewhere else, like Dublin. He doesn't live here, and when he's here, it's only for his aunt Eveline, right? How's that different from the relationship between you and Bridget?"

Mick shrugged, concentrating on washing more glasses. Finally he said, "Maybe it's not, but the old ways die hard. Take the priests, like. They don't hold half the power they once did, but they still command respect. The old ones, anyway — hardly anyone signs up these days. It's the end of an era."

"Who the heck *would* want to become a priest these days?" Maura demanded. "They've sure gotten lousy press for a few years now, here and back in Boston. They got away with a lot, for a long time. Why was it nobody said anything when all the bad stuff was going on?"

"Because priests used to have the power. Now we've all seen that they're human and far from perfect."

Sister Benedicta had been a nun through those days, when priests could do no wrong — of if they did, no one talked about it. What had she known? That was a question Maura didn't plan to ask. "Too many secrets," she muttered and turned her attention to her job.

The following morning Maura walked over to Bridget Nolan's cottage earlier than usual and didn't find her outside yet, so she rapped on the door then waited patiently while Bridget, uttering encouraging comments about her progress along the way, made her slow way to open it. When the door opened, Maura said, "I'm not too early, am I?"

"Of course not, unless you were wanting a bit of bread, for it's still in the oven. Come in, come in. What did you make of your visit to the nunnery?"

"It was kind of odd, being there. It was so quiet and so empty. Not a lot of new nuns coming along anymore."

"That may be. Did you speak with Sister Benedicta?"

"We did, all of us. You were right, of course, that there was something going on with Jane at the manor. Did you know about it?"

"About the baby? I did, although it was none of my business, and I didn't speak of it to anyone else. But people knew, even if they kept silent."

"Why didn't you just tell us and save us all a trip?"

"That kind of story shouldn't come from someone who wasn't part of the family. And I thought Sister Benedicta would be glad of the visit. They're easily forgotten these days, the nuns."

"I know what you're saying. I didn't mean to complain. The whole place was kind of cool, and sad at the same time. So Jane Deasy got pregnant and had to leave the village?"

"She could have stayed, but there were those around here who would have looked down on her, her and the little one. Now, I'm told, things are very different."

"In some ways." Maura thought of the girls she'd gone to high school with, more than one of whom had a toddler at home by the time she got her diploma. It wasn't always easy for them, but it happened a lot.

"What will you do now?" Bridget's question interrupted Maura's thoughts.

"We'll go talk to Miss Eveline, see what she knew back then. At least, that was the plan yesterday."

"Would it not be better to leave things be?" Bridget said gently.

"To spare Eveline's feelings? Maybe. But we really want to work out the story of those two paintings, and I've got to think that Seamus Daly's death may be connected somehow, even if the gardaí don't. The only way to figure out what happened, I think, is to know who knew what when. Everyone says Seamus was kind of . . . slow, wasn't he?"

"He was," Bridget said with a touch of sadness. "He could handle no more than telling Tom O'Brien to order more seeds. Although I will say, he was eager to please. If you asked him to do something for you, he'd try his best."

"Which still wouldn't include stealing a large painting, I'll bet."

"*Buíochas le Dia,* no. He was always a good lad and he worked hard — gave no trouble to anyone. Have you heard anything about his funeral? His people are gone now, and there's only the O'Briens to see to it."

"I haven't heard anything. I'm not even sure the gardaí have released his body yet."

"Speaking of the gardaí, how're you and young Sean getting on?"

"Fine," Maura replied guardedly. They'd been on exactly one date, or maybe not even a whole date, and it was a little early to decide how things were going with them.

"I've not seen him at work, but I've heard that he's very thorough. And careful. He doesn't like to jump to conclusions." Bridget hesitated, which was unusual for her.

"Maura, please don't take my interest amiss. Your gran is gone, and you've no mother to talk to. Seems as though it's fallen to me to see you settled."

So Bridget really was playing matchmaker, wasn't she? "Bridget, I appreciate what you're trying to do, but right now I'm as settled as I've ever been in my life — I have a steady job and a house. If you're trying to marry me off, well, I'm not ready for that. Not that Sean's not a nice guy, so if I decide I'm ready to look I'll keep him on my list." Maura checked her watch. "Shoot, I'd better get going — I told Gillian and Althea I'd meet them at Sullivan's at ten."

"You go on your way, dear."

"And I promise we'll be careful with Eveline, even if we have to sit on Althea to keep her quiet."

"I wish you luck. On your way, now."

CHAPTER 24

Driving toward Leap, Maura reviewed what they now knew and wondered what they could say to Eveline Townsend. First of all, did Eveline know that the big painting at Mycroft House was by an important artist? Second, since they hadn't found any proof of its purchase by the Townsend family, they needed to find out if Eveline had any ideas about that, if it existed at all and where to look for it. Third, Sister Benedicta had independently confirmed that the little painting that had started the whole mess had in fact come from Mycroft House and claimed it had been a gift from Richard Townsend, long deceased, to pregnant housemaid Jane Deasy. Of course, someone might ask whether Richard Townsend had had the right to give it away, but at least he'd done what he'd thought was the responsible thing, helping Jane out by giving her the painting, not realizing she'd be too sentimental to sell it. Had Eveline known anything about that? Harry said he thought she'd been close to her brother, so it was worth asking about. Maura tried to picture Jane, alone in her bleak room in a strange city, taking the painting out and gazing on the face that looked so much like the man she had loved.

Had anyone ever told Jane that Richard had died in the war? Had she assumed that when she didn't hear from him? Or had she figured he'd just brushed her off? Jane had cut herself off from her past and her family back in Ireland, but she hadn't made much of a new life for herself in New York. Yet, as Sister Benedicta had pointed out, they were all here now because of that brief summer love affair so long ago.

How were they going to tie up all the loose ends? Heck, what *were* the loose ends? Would the Townsends agree to lend or sell the painting? Who did the little painting really belong to now?

And where did Seamus Daly's death fit in? It had to be connected somehow. It seemed just too big a coincidence to think that Seamus had been killed by a random prowler. Besides, given Sean's latest news that Seamus *hadn't* been killed with the shovel, there were only a few possibilities:

One, Seamus Daly hadn't died on the lawn where he was found, so he had been killed by someone in the house and dumped on the lawn. That someone could have been a member of the household, but that was a pretty short list: Eveline and the O'Briens. But why would any of them have wanted to kill Seamus? He was harmless, and he was a good worker. So it still could be some unknown outsider.

Two, Seamus had come face-to-face with an intruder who was looking for the painting in the house, and the intruder had killed him and dragged him outside to draw attention away from the house and what might be in it. Say Seamus had interrupted someone in the house who was looking for the painting. Seamus had the right to be in the house, although maybe not in the middle of the night. Maybe an intruder wouldn't have expected to run into him, thinking all the residents were safely tucked into bed at that late hour. Had Seamus confronted this person and been killed for it? And the killer had tried to draw attention away from the house by moving his body. But the intruder hadn't gotten near the painting, if the years of undisturbed dust meant anything. Had he come back for a second try? That would mean he was probably the same person Tom O'Brien had fired at.

Three, someone unknown — an outsider? — had killed Seamus somewhere else altogether, then dumped his body on the lawn, thinking it would look like an ordinary crime — except that crime wasn't ordinary here in County Cork. At least that solution would mean it had nothing to do with the painting, but why would anyone kill Seamus, who hardly ever left the grounds of the manor?

Maura pulled up and parked outside Sullivan's. Gillian was already there, leaning against her car. She waved in greeting.

"Where's Althea?" Maura called out as she approached.

"I don't know. I tried her mobile but she didn't answer."

"Maybe she went straight to the manor," Maura suggested.

"I don't think so. She knows better than that now."

"Have you heard from Harry?"

"I talked to him after he spoke to Eveline last night, and she's agreed to meet with us. Despite what Harry seems to think, she's not all that fragile." Gillian looked down the road to where Mycroft House lay, concealed behind thickly leafed trees. "I really don't know where he stands on all of this. I won't pretty it up — Harry's weak, and he doesn't like confrontations. And I'm not sure he's had a genuine conversation with Eveline in years. He treats her like a piece of china that has to be handled carefully, not as a person."

"What's your take on her?"

"You mean, is she senile? I don't think so. Are her memories intact? Possibly. That's why we want to talk with her, isn't it?"

Maura looked up to see a police car pull up behind hers, with Sean Murphy at the wheel. "Good morning, Sean," she called out. "What brings you here?"

Sean's expression was somber. "Maura, we might do well to take this inside, if you don't mind?"

Confused, Maura fished her keys out of her bag and opened the door of Sullivan's. It was still early, and no one else was in yet. Sean let them pass, then closed the door behind him.

"What's wrong?" Maura said.

Sean swallowed. "Your friend Althea Melville's at the garda station in Skibbereen."

"Why?"

"She's worried she might have killed a man, an American. Might we sit?"

"What?" Gillian gasped.

Althea's really put her foot in it now, was Maura's first thought. Was it Nate? She waved toward the table in the front corner, and they all pulled out chairs and sat. "What's the man's name?"

"She wasn't sure."

Not sure? That didn't make sense. "Sean, why are you telling us?" Maura asked.

"Because of Seamus Daly's death and what you say has been going on at the manor. Now you've got me thinking that this is tied together somehow."

Finally! "How can we help?" Maura asked.

"Let me start by telling you how Althea described the man to us. In his forties, clean shaven, short hair, fairly muscular. Ordinary clothes. She heard him speak so she knew he was American, but she claims she'd never seen him before. Have you seen anyone of that description in Sullivan's lately?"

Maura suppressed the urge to laugh. She'd seen plenty of American men over the past few weeks, especially the week since Althea had arrived. Of course, not all had come in alone — could she eliminate the guys who had appeared with a girlfriend or family in tow? "There have been a few Americans, and a lot of them kind of fit that description. Wait — one guy about that age I do remember because he spent a good bit

343

of time looking at Gillian — Rose noticed."

Sean smiled. "Sure and there are plenty of men who enjoy looking at Gillian."

"It's no big thing," Gillian said, ignoring his compliment. "I didn't notice anything out of the ordinary, and nobody tried to strike up a conversation with me. But, Maura — Althea was sitting at the table too. You're sure it was me he was looking at?"

"Actually, no. I guess it could have been either one of you."

"Would you remember when that might have been, Maura?" Sean asked.

Maura shook her head. "No, sorry. Maybe I can ask Rose when she comes in. Hang on — you said Althea was just *worried* she'd killed this guy. Is there a body?"

"None that we've found, but he went into the river in Skibbereen, and he could be anywhere downstream by now."

Maura tried to figure out which question she wanted to ask first — apart from why Althea had chosen this moment to grow a conscience and turn herself in, when she was so close to getting what she wanted. "Why did Althea think she'd killed him? And how'd he end up in the river?"

"Perhaps I need to make myself more clear. Althea wasn't alone — she was with a man named Nate Reynolds."

"What?" Maura and Gillian said in unison.

Sean looked startled by their response. "Do you know the man?"

Gillian spoke first, her words coming in a rush. "We know *of* him, but we've never seen him. So he and Althea were together when this other man went over the wall? Did she explain why Nate was there? What time was this?"

"I'll try to answer your questions one at a time, and I'm sure you'll be thinking of more. Althea told us that this Nate person was nearby, to her surprise, and he called her on her mobile and asked to meet with her. He came to her hotel, and they took a walk along the river, to keep their meeting private. This was close to midnight, and it was dark. Then she said that this other man appeared and confronted them both. She says there was an . . . altercation, and all three of them took part. Somehow the newcomer went over the edge of the wall there and into the river. They looked for him, but it was dark and they could find no sign of him."

"Why didn't she go straight to the garda station right then?" Maura demanded.

"She claims this Nate Reynolds begged her to wait while he sorted this through. He went back to where he was staying. She went back to her hotel, but by morning she decided to do the right thing and came to us and told us the story."

Kind of late for the guy in the river, Maura thought, *but maybe better late than never.*

"Have you found Nate Reynolds?" Gillian asked.

"We've sent a man over to Clonakilty to look for him."

"Sean, what are you asking us?" Maura asked carefully.

"I wondered if you might know something more about this Nate Reynolds. But" — he hesitated — "Althea kept saying something like, 'I'm going to miss the meeting.' What might you know about that?"

Maura and Gillian exchanged a glance. "After we talked to you last," Gillian began, "we decided to meet with Eveline Townsend this morning, since you said we could. All of us, and Harry as well. It was important to Althea — we had some questions that only Eveline can answer. Althea wouldn't want to miss it. Although what it has to do with this man in the river I can't say."

"Did Althea know anyone else around here?" Sean said.

"Apart from us and Harry Townsend? And Nate, I guess? Not really, though she's spoken to others in town," Maura answered. "Like Billy Sheahan."

"Sean," Gillian said, "did Althea explain about Nate Reynolds?"

"What should I know?"

Gillian took a deep breath. "Nate's the appraiser from New Jersey who first found the oil sketch and who called in Althea to look at it."

"Did she not know he was in Ireland now?" Sean asked.

"She says she didn't," Maura answered, "but it's possible he's been hunting for the same painting as Althea, so it's not surprising he's here."

"Is this Nate a friend of hers?"

"More like a competitor at the moment," Maura said. "They were kind of racing each other to find the Van Dyck. That's why we all wondered whether he was around here somewhere."

"And would you know what he looks like?"

"We've never seen him, nor a picture of him," Gillian said. "You might find a photo on the website for his auction house."

Sean made another note in his notebook. "Is there anything else you can tell me?"

"I think that's all we know, Sean," Maura said. "Is it all right if we go ahead and talk with Eveline? Unless your people need to talk with her first."

"That interview depends on Detective Hurley, but as far as I know, you're free to see Eveline Townsend as you planned. I'll be needing to get back to the station."

"What do you do now? About the guy in the river, I mean?" Maura asked.

"We'll be looking for a body downstream, for a start. Maybe Nate Reynolds can put a name to him, when we find him. We'll see what his story is and if he knew the man. Given all that's gone before, I don't think this was a simple assault on a pair of careless tourists. We don't see much of that here, although if he's an American . . ." Sean smiled to soften the criticism.

"Yeah, yeah, we're all thugs back in the States," Maura countered.

Sean stood up. "Thank you for your help."

"No problem," Maura said. "Let us know what you find out, will you?"

"I will, when I can."

Gillian and Maura fell silent, watching Sean leave, get into his car, and make a U-turn to go back toward Skibbereen.

"Well," Maura began, "I didn't see that coming. So Althea finally decided that she'd lost control of things and agreed to talk to Nate?"

"Perhaps. Although I'd have been less surprised if it was Nate went into the river," Gillian said. "Maybe she only wanted to know what he knew."

"And this American in the river is probably connected somehow. Think he was following Nate?"

Gillian shrugged. "The odds are good, don't you think? Unless Althea has been lying and he's actually her mysterious accomplice."

"Then why would she have gone to the gardaí? In any case, I just can't believe that we've had a murder and a prowler at the manor and now an attack on Althea and they're not all part of the same story. From what I've seen, Ireland doesn't work like that. And this is all about that damn painting? Harry hasn't been doing anything on the side, like smuggling drugs, to make ends meet, has he?" Maura asked.

Gillian laughed. "I'm afraid Harry isn't the type. Maybe a bet on the horses here and there, but nothing illegal."

"What should we do now?"

"You mean about talking to Eveline? I guess we go ahead — we know what the questions are, do we not? I don't know what the gardaí plan to do with Althea, but why wait? If the painting is really a Van Dyck, and if it's worth a lot, that could make a difference to Harry and Eveline. They'd probably want to know regardless."

Maura looked up to see Rose, who seemed surprised to see anyone else in the pub. "Was it not my day to open?" she asked.

"Yes, it is, Rose. We were going to meet Althea here and then go over to the manor. But then Sean Murphy came by to tell us that she was involved in . . . an attack in Skibbereen."

"Is she all right? Do the gardaí know what happened?"

"As far as we know she's all right, and the gardaí are looking into it. But Althea claims the attacker went into the river, and he hasn't been found."

"Oh, my! Let's hope they find him. Where'll you be?"

"With Harry Townsend and his aunt Eveline this morning, minus Althea. If the gardaí turn her loose and she happens to stop here, tell her that's where we are. Oh, one other thing — do you remember that solo American man at the bar, the one who kept checking us out? You said something to me about it."

"Sure. He came in alone, and he had a pint, took his time with it. He kept looking toward you three in the corner, but he never made a move." Rose's expression changed. "Yer thinkin' now that he might have been looking at Althea? And would he be the man who attacked her? I'm sorry I can't remember more."

"Thanks, Rose — you remembered more than I did. I guess we'll head out now."

"Don't worry yerself — we'll be fine here. Gillian, what should I do if someone asks after yer paintings? Are they for sale?"

"They are. I put some stickers with prices on the backs, but let me know if anyone shows an interest — you can call my mobile. Thanks, Rose."

"See you later, Rose," Maura called out as they went out the door.

CHAPTER 25

Harry was waiting for them at the front entrance to the manor, and Maura was reminded of her first visit. Even with what she'd learned about him since, he still looked like he belonged there. He waited until Gillian had turned off the engine, then opened the driver's door for her while Maura clambered out on her own.

"Have you heard?" Maura asked him.

"About what?"

"Althea was" — Gillian seemed to struggle to find the right words — "involved in a scuffle in Skibbereen last night, and there might be another death — an American. And as it happens, she was with Nate Reynolds at the time."

"Nate Reynolds? The man from the auction house?" Harry sputtered.

"The same. Sean Murphy told us the bare details, but it's still not certain that Althea knew Nate was in Ireland, and now there's this other thing. Althea says she didn't know the man, but somehow he ended up in the river and hasn't been found, and the gardaí are off looking for Nate."

"What's that to do with us now?" Harry asked.

Gillian answered, "It's troubling, don't you think, coming on the heels of the rest of it? But Sean said there was no reason we shouldn't talk to Eveline about the painting."

Harry didn't look very concerned. "Shall we go in?" He turned and led the way into the cool, dark interior, where his painted ancestors still loomed over visitors. "Aunt Eveline will meet us in the small sitting room. I asked Mrs. O'Brien to provide refreshments."

"Not to be confused with the large sitting room or one of your thirty-seven public rooms?" Gillian laughed. "Harry, you sound like someone out of a Noël Coward comedy. That's grand. Is she expecting us now?"

"Indeed." Harry led them down the hall and opened a door toward the back of the building. He stood aside to let them enter, then followed. Eveline was settled on a brocade-covered settee at the far end of the room. There was a fire burning in the fireplace to her left, and the low table in front of her groaned under the weight of an immense silver tray, silver teapot, silver creamer and sugar bowl, spoons, tongs, porcelain cups and saucers, napkins, and a three-level silver thing Maura couldn't name heaped with sliced cake and scones. Maura immediately felt terrified that she would drop, break, or spill something. The whole room looked like a stage set, and Maura wondered if she'd wandered into a PBS episode of something or other.

Gillian took the lead. "Eveline, how lovely to see you again, and so soon."

"Gillian, my dear, I'm always delighted to see you, and welcome again to your friend Maura. Please, make yourselves comfortable. Now, may I offer you some tea? As you may recall, Mrs. O'Brien makes the most delightful scones."

It took another five minutes to get everyone settled in a chair, equipped with tea and a delicate plate with scones and butter. Clearly Eveline was in no hurry to move the conversation forward, although maybe Harry hadn't told her what they were looking for. Maybe she was reliving the golden days of her past, acting as lady of the manor. Or maybe she was putting off for as long as possible a discussion she could guess would be unpleasant.

Finally there were no more excuses for stalling. "It was Harry who suggested this little gathering," Eveline began. "I gather it has something to do with poor Seamus?"

"In part. Were you close to Seamus, Eveline?" Gillian asked gently.

Eveline took a moment, apparently weighing her answer. "Some years ago the O'Briens came to me, as they live under my roof, and asked if they could take him in. Seamus had no family left, and he . . . wasn't qualified for most employment. I told Tom that we needed a gardener — I was getting on in years and could no longer keep up with the heavier work, so I agreed to take him on in that role. Seamus was a very conscientious young man and a good worker. If I identified a plant as one that should be protected, he never forgot. I suppose one might say that he was a friend. He was certainly more than a mere employee. Does that answer your question, Gillian?"

Maura noticed that Harry looked a bit startled at Eveline's statement. Had he really assumed that Eveline and Seamus never even talked?

"Yes, thank you," Gillian said. "I'm sorry to ask, but have you any idea why he might have been killed?"

"None. He seldom left the grounds here,

and he had no friends, or even acquaintances, in town, to the best of my knowledge. He seemed content, and he loved his work. I can't imagine why he met such a violent end. But I assume someone will be obliged to find out — is that right, Harry?"

Harry ducked his head. "Yes. I've spoken to the gardaí in Skibbereen, but I told them you had little to add."

"Kind of you, dear, but not altogether necessary. I miss Seamus, and I'll speak to the guards if I must. But no mind. What moved you to request this gathering? Please, Maura, Gillian, enjoy your tea. And Mrs. O'Brien's shortbread is not to be missed."

"Aunt Evie," Harry began, "when I suggested we all get together, I had a purpose in mind. The woman you . . . encountered in the hallway last week . . . do you recall her?"

"The one with no clothes on?" Aunt Eveline responded, her mouth twitching as she hid a smile.

Harry looked surprised at Eveline's response. "Yes, that one. Well, she never had a chance to explain to you what she was doing here, beyond . . . visiting me, that is."

"And you believe I need to know this reason?"

"Yes. You see . . ." And Harry proceeded

to lay out the story that Althea had spun for them about the appearance of the small painting in New Jersey and her hurried search for its origins and the grand painting she hoped still existed somewhere in Ireland. "And as it turns out, she was right — the painting is right here and has been for centuries. It's that one of the first Richard Townsend, in the library? Althea also needed to know how the smaller painting ended up in America and whether the woman who owned it came by it legally."

Eveline gave a small, sad smile. "I've been waiting for someone to ask me about that for a very long time."

There was a shared moment of stunned silence. Finally Harry asked, "Whatever do you mean?"

Eveline regarded each of them in turn. "Shall I tell you the story?"

"Please," Gillian said.

Eveline settled herself more comfortably on the settee and began.

"Your parents were all born well after the war, and I can't say how much you know of it. Here in Ireland we stayed neutral throughout the Emergency, so it hardly touched us, save that it was difficult to get some things. But my brother Richard took it into his head that it would be the honorable thing to enlist and to fight with the English. He and our father had some major rows about it, but Richard was determined. I hated the idea, but I could understand, in a way — as third son, he had few prospects here, and he did always have a romantic imagination. We were several years apart, but he would talk to me about a lot of things. Including Jane Deasy."

"You knew about them?" Gillian exclaimed.

"I did. He told me, but you had only to see them together to know. Of course, the rest of the family would have been horrified, but I knew Jane — she was close in age to me — and she was a good girl. Uneducated, unpolished, but sweet and kind and hardworking. When Richard realized that I knew, I think he was relieved. He so wanted someone he could talk to about her, and he couldn't tell the others."

"Did you know when she left that she was . . . ?" Gillian hesitated.

"Pregnant? Yes. I might have been young, but I wasn't blind or ignorant. I saw them together that summer. I don't think the rest of the family noticed much — but I was always lurking about the house and the grounds. I didn't have many friends, and there wasn't a lot to do here. They looked so happy, at least at first."

"And then?" Gillian asked.

"Then they weren't happy anymore, and I came on them one day, and Jane was crying, and he was holding her, and when he saw me, he looked so angry that I just turned and ran. I had never seen him look like that. He came to my room later that night to explain. He said Jane was pregnant and that he loved her, but our parents would never approve, and if they ran away together he had no way of supporting himself, much less Jane and a child. And he hated himself for being so dependent, but he couldn't think what to do. And then she left."

"That was when she went to America?" Maura said.

"I suppose. All I know is that one day Jane was gone, and my mother was angry because she had to find a replacement quickly — we were expecting houseguests that weekend and she was suddenly short a maid. She thought it was very inconsiderate of Jane to just give notice like that."

"So how did the painting come into it?" Maura asked.

"I'd always loved the little painting because it looked so much like Richard and he was my favorite brother. I guess I knew about the big painting too, but there were a lot of those in the house, and they were all so dark and stuffy! The little one was tucked away in a dark corner — Richard would salute it when he passed it. Then one day it wasn't there, so I asked Richard about it, because I knew that he liked it. He took me aside to tell me that he had given the painting to Jane, because he had nothing else to give her, and that he hoped she would be able to sell it and get enough money to take care of herself and the baby in America. And he told me that I couldn't tell anyone, that it would be our secret and he trusted me to keep my word. And I promised that I would never tell, and I didn't, not even after he died in the war. There didn't seem to be any point."

"But what about the baby?" Maura protested.

"There wasn't much I could do. I didn't know where to find Jane, and she never contacted us. She knew that our parents wouldn't have understood. To them Jane would have been just a farm girl, no doubt looking for a settlement, or at least that's how they would have seen it."

"Richard thought Jane could sell the painting?" Gillian asked.

"Oh, he was sure she could, once she got to New York. After all, it was by an important artist."

Harry spoke for the first time, surprised. "He said that? He knew?"

"Oh, yes," Eveline said quickly. "He took an art course at university, and when he was home, he looked it up in the estate records. The artist was Van something — I've forgotten now."

Gillian said, "Van Dyck?"

Eveline shrugged. "Perhaps. The name meant nothing to me then, but Richard had asked me to look after the record of it, and it was the least I could do."

"But we looked through the books, up in the attic, and we didn't find anything about that painting," Gillian said.

"Oh, but the book wasn't upstairs — Richard kept the book in his room, after he'd looked up the painting and knew what it was. He was afraid it would get shuffled off to the attic, and no one would ever find it again."

Maura and Gillian exchanged a look: so Althea's proof did exist, and she wasn't even here to hear it. "And what happened to the book?" Gillian asked.

"When Richard went to war, he gave it to me to keep. I've always kept it in my room. I promised Richard I'd look after it. I can show it to you later."

"Wait, I'm still confused," Maura said. "How did Richard think Jane was supposed to sell the painting in New York, without any kind of proof that she owned it? Like you said, she was a farm girl. Wouldn't anyone have taken one look at her and at the painting and called the cops?"

"I think perhaps I can guess," Harry said thoughtfully. "You have to remember, photocopying hadn't been invented yet. Even if there were a photostat of the original, Richard wouldn't have wanted to tip his hand to your parents by bringing in a solicitor or something like that. He couldn't exactly give her the original book, since you still have it upstairs. I have no idea how Jane managed to carry the painting on the ship, but the book as well? Not likely."

"Richard did have a will," Eveline said, "not that there was much to leave. It may well be that he left instructions for Jane with the same solicitor and he'd told her to contact him when she was ready to sell her painting."

"How very sad," Gillian said. "Eveline, Jane lived a long life — she died only last year. And she always kept the painting. Perhaps because it reminded her of Richard, so I guess she really did love him. It was the only thing of his that she had left."

"Not the child?" Eveline said softly.

"We understand that Jane gave the baby to her married sister in New York to raise as her own. It was a son, and it was his daughter who inherited the little painting when Jane died. That's how Althea came to be here — she saw the painting and knew it was special, so she came to Ireland to find the big painting."

"So it's all come right in the end," Eveline said, closing her eyes briefly. "I don't mean to be rude, but I'm rather tired now. Perhaps we could talk more another time."

Gillian was quickly on her feet. "Of course we can. I'm sorry if this has been difficult for you, but we thought it was important. I'm so glad you explained to us —"

Gillian was cut off by the abrupt arrival of Florence O'Brien. "Excuse me, but there's a coupla gardaí here says they have to talk with you straightaway and won't take no for an answer."

Eveline straightened her back. "Then by all means, see them in. And please refresh the teapot, if you will."

Mrs. O'Brien gave her an incredulous look but did as she was asked.

CHAPTER 26

A moment later a flustered Mrs. O'Brien ushered in a motley group. Maura was quick to recognize Detective Chief Superintendent Patrick Hurley, head of the Skibbereen gardaí. She'd spent some time in his company not long after she'd arrived in Ireland, when a thug had been giving her trouble for reasons she didn't understand. But she would have remembered him anyway, because he was a good-looking fifty-something man who gave the impression of both calm and authority. To her surprise, he was followed by Althea and a man Maura didn't recognize, with Sean Murphy bringing up the rear. Althea looked frazzled, which was not surprising under the circumstances. The man looked even worse, not to mention slightly feverish. He was younger than Althea but not by much, and his clothes, while rumpled and torn, were of good quality. Maura guessed this might be the mysterious Nate Reynolds. If so, the Skibbereen gardaí had worked fast.

Detective Hurley scanned the room before speaking. He smiled briefly when he saw Maura, but when he spoke it was to Eveline Townsend. "Miss Townsend, I'm Patrick Hurley, detective chief superintendent of the Skibbereen gardaí, and this is my officer Sean Murphy. I apologize for intruding like this, but we've just gotten these two together, and I thought it would save time if we heard their stories, all of us together. I'm guessing there are some things you need to hear. Perhaps we should begin with introductions all around?"

Harry stepped forward quickly. "Harry Townsend," he said, extending his hand. "Sir," he added belatedly. "And as you've already determined, this is my great-aunt, Eveline Townsend."

"It's a pleasure to meet you, Miss Townsend," Detective Hurley said. "I believe you live here at Mycroft House?"

Eveline dipped her head graciously. "I do, and I have done my entire life, although I can't recall having entertained a garda before now. How should I address you?"

" 'Detective Hurley' will do fine, ma'am." He turned to Harry. "Mr. Townsend, do you live here as well?"

Maura knew he already knew the answer to that question. Maybe he was just testing the waters to see how Harry would respond.

Harry looked squarely at the detective. "No, I live in Dublin most of the time. I came down when I learned about Seamus Daly's death, to support my great-aunt. The O'Briens — I believe you met Mrs. O'Brien at the door — live in. Florence looks after the house, and her husband, Tom, takes care of the grounds. Seamus Daly worked for him, as a gardener. As I told your sergeant at the station."

"And this is?" The detective turned to Gillian.

Gillian stood and held out her hand as well. "I'm Gillian Callanan. I also live mainly in Dublin, but I spend my summers here — I'm a painter. I grew up in the area, and I've known Harry most of my life."

Detective Hurley shook her hand. "I've seen some of your work in the gallery at Skibbereen — impressive."

Gillian looked at him with surprise. "Thank you," she said and sat down again.

Finally he turned to Maura. "And Maura Donovan. You'll have to tell me how you come to be involved in all this, but that can wait. I understand you all know Althea Melville." He inclined his head in her direction.

"And this gentleman" — he gestured toward the man — "is Nathan Reynolds."

Gotcha! Maura thought happily. "I guess he's not in the States."

The detective glanced at her briefly before adding, "From what we've learned, Mr. Reynolds has been in the country for several days."

Eveline broke in. "Gentlemen, it sounds as though this may take some time. Won't you please sit down? Harry, would you please find our new guests some chairs?"

"What? Oh, right." While Harry collected side chairs from the corners of the room and arrayed them in front of Eveline's settee, so that they were all facing each other in a rough circle, Eveline acknowledged the rest of her guests. "Althea, it's nice to see you again, or should I say, it's nice to see less of you?" Eveline's eyes twinkled, and Maura stifled a laugh: Eveline had a sense of humor. She was really beginning to like the old lady.

"About that, Miss Townsend, I'm really, really sorry," Althea said. "I never meant to offend you."

Eveline looked at her levelly. "My dear, when you reach my age you will have seen everything at least once. You startled me, nothing more. I gather, though, that it was

Florence who was the more upset."

Althea managed a smile. "I'm so glad you aren't angry with me." She looked around her. "May I sit down? It's been a rather stressful night."

"I don't think I can stand up much longer," Nate said in a faint voice.

"Please, everyone make yourselves comfortable," Detective Hurley said. "This is not a formal interrogation. We are here merely to obtain information. Neither of you is under arrest at this time. We thought we might move more quickly if we did this together."

"I see." Eveline nodded. "Well, then, we definitely need more tea. Harry, please go tell Mrs. O'Brien to bring more cakes as well."

Harry left quickly, and Maura could swear that Patrick Hurley was trying hard not to smile. She felt the same way: the scene unfolding in front of her hardly matched what she knew about Boston police procedures, not that she'd ever experienced them firsthand. But she was pretty sure that Boston police officers did not take tea and scones in the drawing room when they were investigating a murder. Harry reappeared quickly. "She'll be here directly."

"Thank you, dear," Eveline said, unruffled. "Now, Detective, what would you like to know?"

Detective Hurley cleared his throat. "If I may sum up briefly, Althea Melville arrived in Leap a week ago, on Thursday last, and Seamus Daly died that same night. I understand that she admitted to having visited Mycroft House earlier that evening. Miss Townsend, do you know what sparked her interest in this house?" Detective Hurley surveyed the crowd.

Eveline spoke quickly, with no sign of fatigue. "Detective Hurley, I encountered Miss Melville in the house very early Saturday morning, I believe it was. We did not speak to one another, so I was unaware of her interest in the house until the others here explained it to me just before you arrived."

Maura spoke up. "I was the first person Althea talked to in Leap, when she came into the pub for a cup of coffee. She told me she was looking for an old established family house, the kind that might have an important portrait. I told her if she wanted to know about the families around here, she should talk to Old Billy, who was at Sullivan's at the time."

"That would be William Sheahan?" the detective asked.

"That's him. Billy told Althea about Mycroft House, and I guess she headed over there after we ate dinner together, although she didn't tell us she was going to. And she got turned away by Florence O'Brien, she told us later. Then Sean — Garda Murphy — came to Sullivan's the next morning to tell us about the murder."

Harry spoke up. "I drove down from Dublin as soon as I heard about poor Seamus from the O'Briens, and I stopped in at Sullivan's, then came to the house to see Aunt Evie, and then I went to Skibbereen to talk to the guards. I met Althea at the pub. That's also when I met Maura."

"And I assumed Harry would be coming down, so I stopped by Sullivan's as well," Gillian said. "Then Harry and Althea left together."

"Althea came back to the manor as my guest, and she encountered Aunt Evie and Mrs. O'Brien in the morning, as Aunt Evie said," Harry volunteered.

"Under less-than-ideal conditions," Althea added, contrite.

"I thought maybe Gillian could help Althea find the painting," Maura said, "so I got them together Saturday. Then Harry, Gillian, and I went to Mycroft House the next day, Sunday, and we had tea with Eveline in the garden, and then we found the painting."

"Miss Melville did not accompany you to look for the painting?" the detective asked.

"That was at my request," Harry said. "After our encounter with Aunt Evie in the hallway, I thought Althea might not be a welcome visitor, so I told her to stay away." He glanced at Eveline, who was contemplating the nondescript landscape painting hanging over the fireplace, although Maura wondered if she saw a hint of a smile on her face.

"I said I was sorry," Althea muttered to no one in particular.

Detective Hurley ignored her comment. "And did she stay away?"

"As far as I know," Maura said. "Gillian and I went back to the pub and told Althea we'd found the painting, and of course she was excited. And then she asked us to do something *else* for her."

"And that would be?" When Althea started to interrupt, he stopped her with a gesture. "You've given me your version of events, Miss Melville. I'd like to hear what the others have to say."

Maura continued, "She told us that finding the painting was great, but what she needed was some proof of what it was, more than just her guess. She wanted to put it in a show she was working on in New York, but she knew they wouldn't use it based on only her word. She hoped that there was some record here at the manor, and she asked us to look for it. We went back to the house, to look through the records in the attic, but we didn't find it. Oh, and I told Sean that from what I'd seen in the room where the picture was, nobody had been in the room where the painting is for a really long time."

Detective Hurley glanced briefly at Sean Murphy. "As I understand it, on Monday night Garda Murphy responded to a report that gunshots were heard at Mycroft House."

"That's correct, sir," Sean said. "I came to the house and learned that Thomas O'Brien had fired an unlicensed shotgun at someone or something. It was dark, so he wasn't sure what it was. I thought I'd seen blood on the grass, and when I looked more closely by daylight the next morning, I found it again, but I could not ascertain whether it was human or animal. I reprimanded O'Brien about the status of the weapon."

Detective Hurley glanced at Nate Reynolds, who was shifting uncomfortably in his chair, and Maura wondered if he was the one who'd been on the receiving end of Tom O'Brien's blast. "What happened next?" Hurley asked the group.

Maura walked him through how they had come to find Sister Benedicta, then faltered, not wanting to embarrass Eveline with Jane Deasy's story.

"That's all right, dear," Eveline said kindly. "It's ancient history now. Detective, while she was employed here Jane Deasy became pregnant with my brother Richard's child, and she decided to go to her sister in New York to have the baby. Richard had no money of his own to give her, so instead he gave her the small portrait, thinking she could sell it when she arrived in New York."

"Only she never sold it." Althea jumped in quickly. "Which is how it came to be in the possession of Dorothy Ryan, who took it to an event hosted by Nate's auction house, and that's how I saw it and knew exactly what it was. Which turned out to be right," she finished triumphantly.

"Thank you all. Now —" the detective began, but the rattle of a wheeled tray interrupted the discussion. Mrs. O'Brien appeared, pushing a laden tea tray, and everyone fell silent as she swapped the first teapot for a fresh one and added clean cups to the table for the newcomers. Most important to Maura, she filled up the Pretty Silver Thing with more scones and other goodies. Then she looked around the group. "Will there be anything else?"

"Thank you, Florence," Eveline said. "I think we're all set for now." After Mrs. O'Brien had left, and her footsteps could no longer be heard in the hallway, and after teacups had been refilled, Eveline turned back to Detective Hurley. "Now I expect you will explain the presence of Miss Melville and this other man?"

CHAPTER 27

"I will," Detective Hurley replied. "As I said, this man is Nathan Reynolds, an employee of the auction house which hosted the appraisal event that brought out the oil sketch. If I may summarize, Mr. Reynolds suspected he had found something special at that open house, and he called in Miss Melville to confirm his opinion, which she did. And that led both of them to travel to Ireland, unbeknownst to each other. Mr. Reynolds arrived a couple of days after Miss Melville, but they both claim they did not see each other until late last night."

"But it's true!" Althea protested. "I didn't know. I thought Nate was back in New Jersey, until he called me last night and asked to meet me."

Detective Hurley sent her a sharp look that silenced her. "Miss Melville, we've already heard the outlines of your story. Right now I believe we need to hear what

Mr. Reynolds has to say."

"Wait — how did you find him?" Maura interrupted. "Did he turn himself in?"

The detective didn't appear troubled by her intrusion. "I'll let Garda Murphy tell it, since it was his work that tracked Mr. Reynolds down."

Sean looked to be blushing, but his voice was steady. "When I found the blood on the lawn at the manor, I rang round to the local clinics to ask if they'd seen anyone come in with any kind of gunshot wound. None had at that time, but I asked them to keep their eyes open. Well, this morning, early, there was a call from the clinic in Rosscarbery, saying they'd had a request from the conference center there to look at a man who was bleeding but wouldn't explain why. Being anxious to serve their guests, they insisted that he seek medical attention. He did and was found to have several shotgun pellets embedded in his . . . lower body. They were a couple of days old, but his wounds had been torn open again by some exertion on his part, and they were on the road to being infected as well. Sorry, Miss Townsend — this isn't proper conversation to be having over tea," Sean said apologetically.

"Young man, don't trouble yourself. I'm as eager as you are to get to the bottom of whatever is going on. Please continue," Eveline said firmly.

"Well, then, the clinic called me, and I went over and found our Mr. Reynolds. When I learned he was American I put two and two together and guessed he was Miss Melville's colleague, so I brought him to Skibbereen — after he'd been patched up, of course."

"Is he under arrest?" Maura asked.

"Uh, not exactly," Sean said. "Right now, we've no more than a suspicion and some coincidences, so we've asked Mr. Reynolds to assist the gardaí with our inquiries, as we put it. Mr. Reynolds understands the difference, do you not?"

To Maura's eye, Nate Reynolds looked numb — had he taken painkillers for what Maura guessed was buckshot in his butt? Or was being suspected of murder in a foreign country too much for him to handle? "Yeah, yeah, you told me," he said glumly. "Twice. And until you arrest me, I can leave at any time, right?"

"That is correct," Detective Hurley answered.

"So why should I tell you anything?"

"Because we're hoping that you can help us clear up what happened to Seamus Daly, and possibly to the man Miss Melville

377

thinks may have died in the river late last night," Detective Hurley said. "You were with her late last night when the assault occurred?" He glanced at Sean. "Garda Murphy, would you keep the record of this discussion?"

Sean pulled a small pad from a pocket and prepared to take notes.

Once again Althea interrupted. "Nate, just tell them, will you? They already know a lot of it."

Nate rubbed his hands over his face, which sported a day's worth of stubble. "Okay, okay — I just want this to be over."

"Mr. Reynolds," Detective Hurley said. "From the beginning, if you don't mind."

Nate shifted uncomfortably in his chair once again. "It all began with that damn painting."

Nate had their full attention, whether he noticed it or not. Maura thought he was too focused on his own misery, mental and physical, to care. "You want the long version or the short one?" he asked the detective.

"We're in no hurry," Detective Hurley replied. *Not much like Boston,* Maura thought yet again.

"Okay, let me start at the beginning. Back home I work for an auction house in New

Jersey, and I go out scouting for auction items, usually estate sales — you know, like when somebody dies and the relatives want to unload the contents of the house. Once in a while we put out a call for people to bring in things they think might be valuable, and we set up in a big space and take a look. You might not believe it, but a lot of people show up, especially these days when money's tight. Of course, a lot of what they bring in isn't worth much at all, but there are those rare occasions when we see something special."

He paused for a swallow of tea. "So at one of those, in the middle of the afternoon, this ordinary-looking woman named Dorothy Ryan comes in and unwraps this painting and I nearly pass out, it was that good. That's the kind of thing we all hope for, but not many people find things like that. But I wanted to be sure before I made a big thing of it, so I called Althea to double-check. I've known her for years — she's got a good eye, and sometimes she points people toward our auction house. I knew she was working on a portrait exhibit, so I asked if she'd come by and take a look at the painting. She and I met with Dorothy the next day, and Althea's reaction was about the same as mine — basically, 'Wow.' But we agreed that the painting was only a sketch. When we asked Dorothy about where she thought her painting came from, she didn't have a clue. All she could tell us was that the person she'd inherited it from, her great-aunt Jane Deasy, had come from Ireland as a young woman, but nobody in the family talked about Ireland at all. So that was all we had. I told Dorothy that our auction house would be delighted to help her sell the painting she had. She didn't say anything at the time, but I figured out that Althea was betting that there was a finished portrait to go with the sketch. I mean, it made sense. And I knew that if she could find it, it would be really big news in the art history world. But that was later. When we were all together, I think Dorothy would have gone along with selling it right away — she's not an oil painting kind of woman, and I think she needs the money. But then Althea told her that it would be worth more if it had a solid provenance."

"Is that correct, Miss Melville?" Detective Hurley asked.

"Please, call me Althea. I hate this 'Miss Melville' thing. Okay, yeah, Nate is correct as far as it goes. But I never told him that I was going to Ireland — that idea didn't even occur to me until later that night, after I'd done a little poking around on the Internet. And he didn't tell me he was going to do the same thing." Althea sat back, crossed her arms, and glared at Nate.

"Well, I didn't plan to either!" Nate shot back. "After you left, I figured I'd talk to Dorothy Ryan and convince her that selling through us quickly was in her best interests."

"Jerk," Althea muttered. "And you're wrong. Putting the two paintings together would increase the value *substantially.* You should know that."

"But I didn't know there was another painting!" Nate protested. "Not then."

"So we know that Althea moved quickly and came to Ireland," Detective Hurley said, putting the discussion back on track. "When did you decide to follow?"

"I didn't follow her, not exactly. I don't know what I would have done, but Dorothy went home and blabbed to her dad, Joseph Ryan, all about the wonderful things she'd found out about that old painting and how much money it might be worth. So the next day, Dad comes looking for me. He asks me if what Dorothy said was right, and when I say yes, he says something like, 'I'll be damned — it was true.' Turns out his mother, or rather, the woman he grew up believing was his mother, had died a while back, and after she was gone, his so-called father thought he deserved the truth, that Joseph was really Jane's son, but Mary Margaret Deasy had refused to tell Joseph or let her husband do it. Joseph didn't know what to make of the story, and he had no idea where to find Jane or even if he wanted to, so in the end he did nothing. Then Dorothy told him about the painting and he realized that the story was true. He didn't have a lot of details, but did have the name of the place: Leap. Which has only one manor house, so it was easy to find. I figured it was worth a shot, and I hopped on a plane. That's how I got here so fast."

Harry snorted. "I hope they're not looking for money, because they're going to be disappointed — we have none. Look, I'm happy to let Dorothy keep the painting and sell it if she wishes, so Nate and Althea can settle that between them."

"So let me be sure I have this right," the detective said to Nate. "You wanted Dorothy to sell the painting she has — through your company — as quickly as possible, and then suddenly you decided that Althea was looking for its mate, and you came chasing after her? Why the urgency?"

"Selling the painting as a 'maybe' Van Dyck would definitely bring in money,"

Nate said, "but putting it up for sale with authentication would bring in a whole lot more, and finding the finished portrait would up the value again. I know Althea didn't care about seeing it sold — she was thinking about her precious exhibition, and if she could find the second one she'd be on top of the world. Of course, the little sketch would sell well later, after the exhibition closed, but that would be months later . . ." Nate stopped, realizing that his own argument didn't make sense.

"You wanted the money now," Maura said flatly. "Why so fast, if you could make a lot more if you waited?"

Nate looked more and more uncomfortable. "Well, it's true that I need the money. I'll admit that some of the bigger items I've brought to the auction house didn't bring as much as I'd hoped. And the auction business is struggling right now, as you might guess, although I believe it's on the way to recovering."

He was still dodging around something, Maura thought. "Okay, you wanted money now instead of later," she said. "You didn't want to wait, what, six months, a year, to make a whole lot more? Why? You've got a kid who needs surgery? A mother who can't afford her nursing home? A huge drug habit?"

Nate just looked at her miserably. And then something clicked for Maura. "You're from New Jersey. Atlantic City. You're a gambler, and you owe somebody, big time."

"Is that what this is about, Nate? How stupid are you?" Althea burst out. She turned to the rest of the group. "Would you believe we actually met at a conference in Atlantic City? It never occurred to me that he might be a gambler. And then he turns around and double-crosses me and goes behind my back to try to sell this thing" — she faced Nate again — "just to pay off your bookie or whatever?"

"Loan shark," Nate muttered, looking at his feet.

Sean Murphy watched the exchange, bewildered, and Maura took pity on him. "Nate got in over his head with his gambling problem, and now somebody wants their money, fast. This woman Dorothy dropped in like a gift from heaven, and of course he wants to sell the painting as fast as he can, to settle up with whoever it is he owes. How'm I doing, Nate?"

Nate shut his eyes. "About ninety percent right. Yes, I kind of got in over my head, and, yes, that sale would put things right for me. When Joe Ryan told me where to look in Ireland, I figured I could get here before Althea and cut a deal with the owner. Assuming, of course, that the painting existed."

"I never told you I was coming to Ireland!" Althea all but shrieked. "And I would have shared with you."

Nate shrugged. "I figured you'd do what I'd do, and I was right, because here you are. And I couldn't wait — I'm in for too much now."

"Yet Althea beat you to it," the detective said. "You knew that she was close to finding the painting?"

"Hard not to, once I got here. Everybody around here talks. God, how they talk! Lots of people in pubs around here were going on about this American lady's treasure hunt. I worked it out that she was using Sullivan's as her home base, so I stayed away from there. I figured the most important thing was to find out if the painting really was here in the manor, and if it was, I had to talk to the owner before she did."

"Could you not have approached the house directly?"

"I knew that Althea had tried and had the door shut in her face," Nate replied.

"Oh, dear," Eveline said. "The O'Briens

are quite protective. I fear they let few people in. I must have a word with them." Harry rolled his eyes.

Detective Hurley's eyes had grown cold. "Mr. Reynolds, you're telling us a nice tale, but it doesn't ring true. You say you were hard on the heels of Althea?"

"Yes."

"She arrived in Leap on the Thursday and first approached the house that same evening and failed to gain entry. Later that night a man was killed at the manor. Where were you that night?"

"Last Thursday?" Nate made a good show of trying to think. "I've been staying at that hotel in Rosscarbery where your officer found me. I think that's the night I checked in. You can check with them."

"Why that place in particular?"

"There's not a lot to choose from around here, is there?"

"There's a nice hotel in Skibbereen," the detective said.

"Yeah, but that's where Althea was staying, and I didn't want to run into her."

"But Althea didn't know she was going to stay there until I sent her there, Thursday night," Maura said suddenly. "How would you know she was there?"

"I followed her from the pub that night."

Althea apparently couldn't think of any-thing to say to that, so she settled for glar-ing at Nate.

"And yet you somehow managed to avoid being observed," the detective said, "which I'm sure you've noticed can be difficult in small towns such as this. You saw Althea go to Mycroft House, and you were close enough to observe the reception she re-ceived there. You saw her leave. But you didn't leave, did you? You believed the painting was in that house, so you thought you'd find out for yourself. You waited until it was full dark, and then you tried to gain access to the house, to look for yourself. You waited until all the lights went out, but you hadn't counted on meeting the gardener in the dark."

"I don't have to answer that, do I?" Nate said.

"We're just discussing hypothetical situa-tions here," Detective Hurley said, unper-turbed. "The doctor at the Rosscarbery clinic extracted several shotgun pellets from your backside. Tom O'Brien, the caretaker here, admits to having fired a shotgun at what he thought was a prowler on Monday night, and Garda Murphy found blood at the scene. I find it unlikely that the pellets retrieved from you came from anywhere other than Tom O'Brien's shotgun."

"But that was Monday! Okay, okay, that was me trying to get into the house on Monday, to find the painting, but I didn't kill the guy on the Thursday before!"

"Then let's return to that Thursday night, if we may?"

Nate's chin came up defiantly. "If you have a question, ask it."

"Seamus Daly was found dead on the lawn at Mycroft House on Friday morning, by Tom O'Brien."

"On the lawn?" Nate looked first incredulous, then relieved. "Then he didn't . . ."

"What, Mr. Reynolds? Who didn't do what?"

At first it looked as though Nate was going to refuse to answer, but finally his shoulders slumped and he said, "I guess I'm going to have to tell the truth."

CHAPTER 28

Detective Hurley gave a nearly imperceptible sigh. "Mr. Reynolds, I think you'll need to explain. And try to be thorough this time, will you?"

"Fine. I'm *not* going to take the blame for the gardener's murder." Nate Reynolds sat up straighter. "All right, I *was* at the house Thursday night, late, but I wasn't alone, and I didn't go inside."

"Who was with you? Was it Althea?"

"No. It was some goon named Ray who works for that loan shark and who insisted on tagging along from New Jersey so I wouldn't skip out on what I owed. His parents were Irish, so I guess he thought it would be funny to be here with me, kind of like a working vacation. Althea didn't know either of us was here."

"So it was your . . . shall we say, watchdog, who went inside the manor house on Thursday?"

"Yeah. And it was his idea. He wanted to be sure the painting was real and I wasn't just handing him a line about it. He figured I was too much of a klutz to break in and find it myself — which is true — so he decided to do it. We waited until about three o'clock and thought everybody would be asleep. The windows on this manor are a joke — no locks or anything. I told him what to look for. Ray went in through a window, but he came out about five minutes later and said we were leaving, no explanation. I heard about the murder the next day. But the reports said the guy was found on the lawn, and he sure wasn't on the lawn when Ray and I left the place."

Detective Hurley did not comment immediately, and Maura could understand why. If Ray had run into Seamus inside the house and killed him, then how had Seamus ended up on the lawn with the bloody shovel? Who had moved him outside and placed the shovel nearby? And why?

Detective Hurley turned away from Nate Reynolds and addressed Eveline. "Miss Townsend, how long have the O'Briens worked at Mycroft House?"

Eveline glanced at Harry. "Oh, it must be ten years now. I couldn't manage this place by myself. And Harry wanted to know that there was someone here to look after me. Sweet of him."

"Is that correct, Mr. Townsend?"

"More or less," Harry said. "I worried about Aunt Evie, rattling around alone in this drafty old barn of a place, but she didn't want to leave it, and she had every right to stay. So I found the O'Briens. I couldn't afford to pay them much, but I offered them a place to stay in the manor. Overall it's worked out well."

"Are you happy here with the O'Briens, Miss Townsend?"

"I have no complaints. I know this old building has its problems, but Tom has managed to keep it going, although there are rooms we no longer use. And Florence is an excellent cook and has very high standards for cleaning."

"And Seamus? How did he fit in?"

"Seamus had nowhere else to go. As you know, he was a bit touched, but a hard worker and a good person. If Seamus came upon someone and confronted him, he'd have only been looking out for the household."

"I don't doubt it. I suspect he surprised an intruder and unfortunately paid the price."

"But he was killed by a shovel, on the

lawn!" Nate protested.

"The blow from the shovel was not the fatal one. It was intended to conceal the real cause. Harry, I'd like to have a word with the O'Briens. Can you fetch them for me?"

"The both of them?" Harry stood up reluctantly. "Why?"

"They may know more than they've said," the detective replied, giving nothing away.

A tense silence fell after Harry left to round up the O'Briens. Althea refused even to look at Nate, and Maura wondered if she was mentally orchestrating her campaign to trumpet her discovery of the lost painting, although it now appeared to be slipping away rapidly. Maybe she could take comfort in the fact that Nate wasn't going to get either painting anytime soon.

Gillian leaned toward Eveline. "Are you all right? Would you like more tea?"

Eveline gave her a sweet smile. "I'm quite fine, my dear, and thank you for asking. To tell the truth, I haven't had so much excitement in years. I regret that it came about through the death of poor Seamus, though. Do you know what happened to him, Detective?"

"I think I do, Miss Townsend, but let's not get ahead of ourselves."

Harry returned quickly, shepherding Florence and Tom O'Brien before him. Maura thought they looked nervous, but maybe they weren't used to dealing with the head of the Skibbereen gardaí. Or did they have something to hide? The drawing room was becoming crowded now. "Shall I find some more chairs?" Harry said, looking at Detective Hurley.

"If you don't mind," he replied.

With a barely suppressed sigh, Harry went out into the hall and retrieved two side chairs. There was more shifting and bumping while everyone adjusted their positions to accommodate the two newcomers. When they were all more or less settled, Detective Hurley began, "How long have you been employed at Mycroft House, Mr. O'Brien?"

"I worked here as a boy," Tom O'Brien said. "There was more staff then. I married Florence some twenty years ago, and we've been here ten, give or take."

"Harry — we've watched him grow up," Florence said. "His parents died in that awful accident, right after he left university. When he left to find work in Dublin, he wanted someone to look after Eveline, keep the house up, and the like. It suited us all."

"And Seamus?"

"Our families came from the same townland," Tom said. "We knew Seamus was slow, but he was a good worker, so when his mother died, we took him on. Eveline didn't mind, and we've loads of space here that no one's using."

"Was he happy here?"

"Oh, yes. He loved the place. He loved being useful too."

"So if he saw an intruder, would he have tried to stop him?"

Florence and Tom exchanged a look. "I'd say so, yes," Tom said, answering for the both of them.

Detective Hurley said, "How would you describe him?"

"Short of six foot, maybe. Strong, stoutly built. What're you getting at?"

"I wondered how physically strong he was. I would assume he was in good shape, if he did the heavy work in the gardens." Detective Hurley gave Nate a long look. "I'm guessing that Nate's companion found his way into the house, but Seamus saw him sneaking in and followed him. Perhaps you can tell me what Seamus was doing, wandering around the grounds in the small hours of the night?"

Tom shrugged. "He was a restless sleeper. Might be that he heard your man Reynolds here or his mate bumbling about."

"Thank you," the detective said. "In any event, the man was startled — he probably thought no one was about, and then suddenly he was confronted by a strong young man in the dark. No doubt this Ray lashed out at him with whatever came to hand. Something that was already in the room. Where did you find Seamus, Tom?"

Tom's mouth opened and closed, like a beached fish. Then he looked at his wife, who put a hand over her mouth. "In the dining room," Tom said reluctantly.

"Good God, man!" Harry exclaimed.

The detective ignored Harry's interruption. "You'll have to show my men where, when we're finished here. When did this occur?"

"I come down early, the Thursday — it's hard to sleep in summer, with the sun up so early and there's so much to be done around the place. The dining room door to the hall was open, which it never is, so I looked in and there Seamus was, laying on the floor, a great pool of blood around his head. I touched him, but he was gone. There was nothing to be done for him."

"Was there a weapon?"

"A small bronze statue, Indian or Chinese, I think it was. It's always been on the mantel in that room, along with a lot of other bits and bobs. It was lying on the floor next to Seamus."

"What did you do then?"

"I said a few words over Seamus, then I went and got Florence."

"So it was you who moved the body?"

"Yes. I thought . . ." He looked up at Eveline. "I'm sorry, but I know you've been wandering about the place nights. I thought you'd come upon a figure in the dark, not knowing it was Seamus, and hit him."

"Good gracious, Tom!" Eveline exclaimed. "I'm horrified you'd think me capable of such a thing." She turned to Detective Hurley. "It's true that I don't sleep well at my age, and I've been known to roam about at night, but I'm always fully awake. Sometimes I'll sit in one room or another and remember them as they were, when the house was so much livelier."

"Including the dining room?"

"Not as much; it's rather dreary, I find, and there are no comfortable chairs in there. If you're asking, Detective, no, I did not fatally assault Seamus Daly with the bronze Buddha. I hope you believe me." Suddenly tearing up, Eveline fished into the pocket of her dress and retrieved a spotless linen handkerchief and dried her eyes. "Poor Seamus. He didn't deserve what happened to him — he was only trying to help, I'm sure."

"I do believe you, Miss Townsend. I think the final analysis will show that you're not tall enough to have struck him at the angle at which he was hit. So, O'Brien, you incorrectly believed your employer had just killed the gardener and then wandered back to her bed, without realizing what she'd done, improbable as it sounds. I assume you moved Seamus's body in order to divert attention from this house?"

"I did that. I hoped that if the poor boy was found outside, your lot might think it was someone from outside who killed him."

And, Maura thought to herself, *maybe you didn't want to lose the cushy niche you and your wife had found here.* Murder could mess things up, she knew.

"It was *my* plan, Detective," Florence said. "Tom came to me, near to tears, and told me what he'd found. I knew there was no bringing Seamus back, and I didn't want Eveline here to be accused of all sorts of awful things, nor Tom and me, I guess. I knew it wasn't Tom who did it, because he was with me, and he didn't come out of our rooms until first light. So I thought it best to . . . well, I guess you'd say, muddle things up a bit. As Tom said, we thought that if he moved Seamus outside, it might look as though he had been surprised by an outsider. So I told Tom to take him out and put him on the lawn — it was still early enough that there was no one about — and try to hide the blow that killed him." As she said that, Tom paled and shut his eyes. "And while he was doing that, I set about cleaning up all the . . . blood."

"And the murder weapon?"

"I pitched that into the harbor," Tom said. "Will it be trouble for us?"

Detective Hurley sat back in his chair and sighed. "I can't say just yet. Certainly you've interfered with our investigation, concealed evidence, and all the rest. I agree with Miss Townsend, though — it is hard to envision her as a killer, so your conclusion may have been a bit hasty."

He turned back to Nate. "But you, and your colleague Ray, returned to the manor on Monday, in spite of Seamus's death?"

"Yeah. Ray had heard that nobody in Ireland carried guns, even the police, so he thought we'd be safe enough. Figures I'd be the one to get shot — he wasn't even scratched."

"Why didn't he go alone?"

"Because he didn't trust me. He thought I'd cut and run for the airport, which I

398

might in fact have tried to do, so he dragged me along."

Detective Hurley studied Nate. "So, Mr. Reynolds, you claim that Seamus Daly's death can be laid at the feet of this Ray person, who hit him over the head with a statuette after he broke in that Thursday night, or rather, very early Friday morning. You yourself were never in the house, and you had no knowledge of what Ray did while he was in there, nor did he tell you when he emerged. However, in addition, you say you accompanied him on a *second* trip here, after you'd learned of Seamus's death, at which time you were wounded by Tom O'Brien. Tell me, if you will: where is Ray now?"

"Let me guess — he's the guy in the river," Althea volunteered.

Nate looked at her. "Yes. I'm sorry, Althea. I didn't know he'd followed me."

Althea took a deep breath and surveyed her audience. "Detective, first let me apologize for not telling you the whole truth from the beginning. I was upset, as you can guess. And I wasn't sure that this Ray person was really dead, or at least I hoped he wasn't. If he is, we didn't mean to kill him."

Detective Hurley gave a small, dignified sigh. "Perhaps you'd better fill in the details now." He glanced at Sean, who was still scribbling fast.

Althea sat up straighter in her chair and faced the detective. "It was an accident, I swear. Last night, after I got back to the hotel and ate dinner, Nate called me on my cell. Believe me, I really didn't know he was anywhere around here. He said he was in Ireland, not far away, and we had to meet, but he was afraid to come to the hotel in Skibbereen, said somebody might see us. So Nate suggested we meet by the river outside the hotel. I was pretty upset with him, but I agreed to meet him because I really wanted to hear his story and he refused to come to the hotel. I think it was about eleven, maybe later. There's a dark stretch of road between that rotary thing and the hotel, and there was nobody around. I went out the back of the hotel and followed the river until I saw Nate. I was surprised at how light it was, even that late, so I felt safe enough. When I saw Nate, we sat down on the wall there and Nate explained to me about what had been going on. He was really freaked out by the gardener's death and all the attention it was getting, and how he was pretty sure this Ray guy was involved, even though the details about the body didn't match up. Nate said he was afraid Ray would just kill him and go home, because Nate was the only person who could connect him to the murder at the manor."

Althea sighed and shut her eyes for a moment. "Nate told me everything he'd done and wanted to know if we could work together somehow to get away from Ray *and* get the painting, under whatever terms I wanted. He was desperate."

"Mr. Reynolds, you told Althea about your financial difficulties?" the detective asked.

"I told her the whole story. But then Ray showed up, out of nowhere! I thought I'd been careful, but he must have guessed where I was headed and followed — I don't know how, since I'd taken the rental car. Anyway, there he was. He'd gotten close enough to hear that we were going to double-cross him if we could, so he came at me. He didn't count on Althea, though, and we were all struggling and somehow he went over the wall, into the river. I know I heard a splash, but by then it was too dark to see anything down by the water. We didn't hear anything after that — he didn't call out or anything."

"So you just left? Did it not occur to you to get help?" Detective Hurley asked, clearly exasperated.

"He'd just tried to kill us!" Nate protested.

Detective Hurley sighed again, this time more loudly. He also raised one hand to keep Althea from speaking, which she clearly wanted to do. "What did you do next?"

"I went back to the car and drove to the hotel at Rosscarbery," Nate said. "I was exhausted. And, as you know, I was bleeding again."

Detective Hurley asked, "About that hotel — isn't it rather expensive for you?"

"Damn right it is. But if I went anyplace else around here — hotel, bed-and-breakfast, or whatever — I'd stick out like a sore thumb, and Ray more than me. The Rosscarbery place was the biggest I could find, and it looked like they had plenty of people passing through, so I figured I wouldn't be noticed. Besides, I didn't plan to stay long — find the painting and go home, in and out. That was the plan originally. Ray kind of sneaked in — he wasn't registered, but he was staying in the room. So this morning, practically at dawn, I stumbled in, and the snarky night clerk at the hotel got all hot and bothered about the blood on my jeans and insisted on tracking down a doctor and wouldn't take no for an answer. And I just couldn't fight anymore. I guess I had a fever too, some kind of infection. The doctor they found patched me up and gave me some sort of prescription for antibiotics."

"He didn't ask any questions about how you acquired a number of buckshot pellets?"

"No, he did not. Or if he did, I ignored him."

Detective Hurley glanced at Sean Murphy, and Sean said quickly, "He called the guards, though, which is how we found you."

Detective Hurley turned his attention to a nervous-looking Althea. "And you, Althea? Where did you go?"

Althea had lost all her cockiness and looked pale and small. "After all that had happened, and a couple of nights without enough sleep, and seeing that man, Ray . . . fall in, I had no idea what to do. I pulled myself together and went back to my room at the hotel, but I couldn't sleep. After a couple of hours I went out and just walked around for a while. There was a café that was open early, so I went in and got some coffee and tried to figure out what to do next. I mean, I knew I hadn't had anything to do with Seamus Daly's death, but I was kind of unclear what had happened to Ray and who was responsible for it, so in the end I finally just walked up the street to the police station and said I needed to talk with someone. And you all took it from there."

"Thank you, Althea. You did the right thing," the detective said gravely.

"I sure hope so. What happens now?"

Detective Hurley looked at her, not unkindly. "That is not an easy question to answer. This case has been rather unusual. I need to review some things before I know whether to charge you with any crimes, or which ones. You'll both be coming back to the station with me, and I'll determine whether we will file any charges."

He suddenly sat up straighter, then pulled a cell phone from his pocket. When he read the screen, he stood up and said, "Excuse me for a moment," then walked into the hall and shut the door behind him.

Harry said suddenly, "Good God, who would have thought that dusty old painting would have caused so much trouble? Aunt Evie, how're you doing?"

Eveline shook her head slowly. "I'm all right, dear. What a terrible thing. One man dead, another missing, all for some dry old canvas and paint. Nobody's even looked at that painting for years."

Detective Hurley appeared in the room

again, and Maura thought he looked something like excited. "Your missing man has been found — alive."

CHAPTER 29

He had the attention of the room. "Ray's not dead?" Nate said incredulously.

"Oh, thank God," Althea said. "Where was he? And where is he now?"

"And what has he said?" Nate demanded.

The detective held up a hand. "Apparently after he fell into the river following your confrontation, he did indeed hit his head, but he didn't lose consciousness immediately. He drifted downstream a ways and fetched up on a sandbar near Abbeystrowry and passed out, and a motorist saw him and called the station. He was taken to the clinic, where they found his identification in his pocket."

"Will he be all right?" Althea asked anxiously.

"Apart from a knot on his head, he seems to have come through remarkably well. A few bumps and bruises, but otherwise in satisfactory condition. Shall I have him brought in?"

"No!" Nate said vehemently at the same time that Althea said, "Yes!"

The detective took stock of his audience. "I think it might be wise if I heard what he had to say first. He'll be here shortly — one of my men is bringing him over."

"Sir?" Tom O'Brien stood up and faced Patrick Hurley. "Are we in any trouble, the missus and me?"

The detective gave him a long and searching look. "Mr. O'Brien, you do realize that you tampered with a crime scene and disposed of the murder weapon. Those are serious offenses," the detective replied.

Tom dipped his head, not meeting Detective Hurley's eyes. Florence looked scared.

"You acted to protect Miss Townsend, even if your motives were misguided. And I don't see the two of you turning to a life of crime."

Tom looked up then, puzzled for a moment, then said, "No, sir, not likely."

"Then you're free to get on with your jobs. And either dispose of that shotgun properly or see to it that you register it."

"Thank you, sir." He glanced briefly at Florence. "I'll go to the front and wait for your man — the locks can be tricky." He exited as fast as he could.

"Detective?" Eveline said softly. "I fear all this excitement has been rather wearing. If you don't mind, I think I might like to lie down for a bit." When Harry looked concerned, she added quickly, "Don't worry, I'm just tired, and perhaps a bit sad, nothing more. But I see nothing to be gained from my meeting this man who may have killed Seamus."

"Thank you for taking the time to speak with us, Miss Townsend," Detective Hurley said gravely. "I apologize for any inconvenience we may have caused you."

"It was my pleasure, Detective. I hope you'll call on me again, when this whole awful episode is closed. Florence, would you mind seeing me to my room now?"

"Of course." Florence O'Brien helped Eveline out of her chair, and they made their slow way to the door and disappeared.

Detective Hurley watched her departure. "A charming woman."

"She is that," Harry said, with something like wonder. "How long before your man arrives?"

"A few minutes, perhaps. Why?"

"You haven't seen the painting, have you?"

The detective turned to him. "So the painting is here, in this house, after all?"

"It is, Detective," Gillian answered for

408

Harry. "Would you like to see it?"

Althea bounded to her feet. "Hey, I haven't seen it yet, and neither has Nate. Can we? See it now, I mean?"

"I suppose there's no harm in it," the detective said.

"I'll take you to it," Harry said, and he led the small procession to the library and opened the door. Althea went in first, and Detective Hurley let Nate precede him, then Gillian and Maura, before following. They all clustered in the center of the room, looking up at the massive painting.

"Meet my great-great-whatever," Harry said with a touch of pride. "Good-looking devil, isn't he?"

"Oh, my God, oh, my God," Althea whispered. "He's freaking gorgeous!" She took a few steps closer. "Surprisingly good condition, considering. Nate? What do you think?"

Nate was still standing and staring, his expression a mix of excitement and wistfulness, and he didn't answer.

"Are yeh happy now, Althea?" Gillian said quietly.

Althea tore her gaze away from the painting to look at Gillian. "Yes, and I have you to thank. And Maura. I know I'm a pain in the ass, but look at it — isn't this worth it?"

Maura looked at the painting again and wondered what it was about this piece of canvas and paint that had somehow led to Seamus Daly's death. It didn't seem right. But they'd finally made Althea happy, and she'd actually thanked them. That was progress.

The detective did not hurry in his inspection of the painting, but finally he said, "Thank you," as well, to Harry, and added, "We should get back now."

When they returned to the drawing room, a garda was keeping a close eye on a scruffy man of medium height whose clothes had clearly been soaked then dried. Tom O'Brien was watching both of them, but he stepped back when Detective Hurley entered the room, followed by Maura, Gillian, Nate, and Althea, with Sean Murphy bringing up the rear.

"Ray Finneran?" the detective asked the newcomer.

"Yeah, that's right. What is it you want from me? Those two there" — he pointed to Nate and Althea — "they almost killed me last night. Have you arrested them?"

"We are still gathering information," Detective Hurley said, giving nothing away. "Do I hear Irish in your accent?"

"I'm from New York. My parents came

from around here, long time ago. I'm just visiting."

"How did you come to be at that particular place last night, in Skibbereen?"

"I was taking a walk. No law against that here, is there?" Ray said belligerently.

"No, there is not. Are you staying in Skibbereen, Mr. Finneran?"

For the first time, Ray looked unsure. Apparently he hadn't prepared for that question. "I hadn't made up my mind."

"So you were not sharing a room in Rosscarbery with Mr. Reynolds here? And no one there will recognize you?"

Ray didn't answer quickly. "I might have done." He didn't elaborate.

"How did you get to Skibbereen, then, Mr. Finneran?"

"I drove." Maura thought that Ray Finneran was sweating now, even though the room was cool.

"And where is your car?"

Definitely sweating, Maura decided.

"It's parked in town."

"Can you tell us where?" the detective went on relentlessly.

"I . . . uh . . . well . . ." Ray stumbled.

"Let me save you the trouble. My men report that they have recovered a car reported stolen from the hotel in Rosscarbery.

411

Will we find your fingerprints in it?"

"I want a lawyer," Ray snarled.

"Very well. You are entitled to representation, of course. Let's move this discussion to the garda station, shall we? Althea, Nate, I would appreciate it if you would accompany us there."

Like they had a choice, Maura thought.

"Uh, okay," Althea said tentatively. Nate just shrugged.

"Garda Murphy, take Miss Melville and Mr. Reynolds with you. I'll see to Mr. Finneran." He turned to the others. "Thank you for your assistance. I'm sure we'll be speaking again."

When they were all gone, Maura said, "Well, that was interesting. I wonder what happens next."

"I know what you mean," Gillian said. "Harry, what about the painting?"

"What?" Harry said, looking confused.

"The painting, Harry," Gillian repeated. "What do you think you'll do with it now?"

"Blast if I know," Harry said. "I suppose after all this, I'd be happy to be rid of it, but I'll have to talk to Eveline about it. After all that's happened, she may be ready to part with it. Do I have to decide right now?"

"Of course you don't, although you might want to think about getting an alarm system or something, to protect it. But if Althea's not facing any legal charges, I bet you'll be hearing from her again."

Harry rubbed his hands over his face. "You're probably right. Then if Althea's not guilty of anything, legally at least, I'll consider what she proposes. I'm not sure Nate will get off as easily, but there'll be other ways to sell it, if that's what Eveline and I decide to do. Will you help me with that part of it, Gilly?"

"Of course."

"You two can figure that out," Maura said. "Right now I've got to get to work . . . After all this excitement, it's bound to be a busy night. You two want to come over?" she asked Harry and Gillian.

"I for one could use a drink," Harry said. "We'll be along in a bit, right, Gillian?"

"We will," she replied.

Maura hadn't realized how much time had passed while they'd been more or less locked in the drawing room at Mycroft House, finally untangling Seamus Daly's death and maybe the history of the two paintings. It was midafternoon now, and Maura was emotionally exhausted. And that was only from watching the process unfold. She couldn't imagine how the others felt.

Jimmy Sweeney greeted her when she

came into Sullivan's. "Well, look who's here. The lady's finally decided to show her face."

Maura stalked around the bar and stuffed her bag beneath it. "Put a sock in it, Jimmy. I've been over at Mycroft House with the gardaí, sorting out Seamus Daly's death."

"Oh-ho! Now you've a second job? They're using consultants such as yourself, since the government can't afford to pay the gardaí?"

"What's the right term? 'Assisting the guards in their inquiries'? Either way, it should be a busy night here. I'm sure everyone will want to know what really happened. Hey, Rose," Maura said in greeting as Rose emerged from the back room.

"Ah, there you are, Maura. Is everything all right?"

"As right as it can be, with a dead body in the mix. Don't worry — we worked it out. Busy day?"

"Middling."

"Well, expect a busy night. Depends on how fast the word gets out, but it moves pretty fast around here, although I still haven't figured out how. And don't tell me 'mobile phone'!"

"Would it be telepathy, then?" Rose suggested, smiling.

"Maybe. I'm going to go say hello to Old

Billy there. Does he need another pint yet?"

"No, he says he's grand for now. I think he's waiting for a tourist to offer to buy him one so we won't have to."

"Smart man, Billy." Maura crossed the room to Billy's "throne" near the fireplace. "Hey, Billy. Thanks for the hint."

Billy smiled. "What hint would that be?"

"Telling me we should talk to Bridget Nolan about Jane Deasy."

"And what did she tell you?"

"She said that Jane's sister was still alive, in a nunnery, so we talked to her yesterday, and she pointed us back to Mycroft House. And Eveline Townsend filled in the blanks for us today."

"About poor Jane?" Billy said softly.

"And the baby, yes. I think I understand why you didn't just come out and tell me."

"Ah, that kind of thing is women's business. So you worked it out in the end?"

"Almost. The child — a boy — was raised by Jane's sister in New York, and it was his daughter who inherited the painting and kind of started this whole thing." And indirectly led to Seamus Daly's death, not that that was Dorothy Ryan's fault. "Anyway, thank you. You led us to find Seamus's killer."

"Glad to be of help," Billy said, and he

asked no more questions.

As Maura made her way back to the bar, stopping to greet a couple of people she recognized, she marveled once again at the invisible network that seemed to link everyone around here. How did it happen that Old Billy should happen to overhear a conversation at Sullivan's and know enough to send them to the person who held a critical piece of information, which then led them back to where it all began? Maura wondered if she'd ever understand how Ireland worked.

Gillian and Harry came in more than an hour later, as the evening crowd was beginning to build. Rose saw them before Maura and called out, "Gillian, we've just sold another one of the paintings!"

Gillian came over to the bar. "Have you, now?"

"Yes, and at the full price. The woman said she'd be back in the morning. Are there more?"

"There are. I'll bring some by in the morning and I can meet her then. Thanks, Rose. Harry, can you snag that table in the corner? It looks like those people are leaving."

"Consider it done."

As Harry left on his mission, Maura

leaned toward Gillian. "Is Eveline all right?"

"Just tired, as she said. Harry talked to her for a bit. I'll fill you in when we get settled."

"Okay. Pints, or you need something stronger?"

"This calls for whiskey, I think."

"I'll bring it over."

Mick came in not long after and stopped to speak to Maura. "It's all sorted out now?"

"More or less. Believe it or not, it looks like it was a thug from New Jersey who killed Seamus, or at least that's the story of the moment. And now he's at the garda station, as are Althea and Nate, although I'm not sure how many of them are under arrest." At Mick's bewildered look, Maura laughed. "It's complicated — I'll tell you when things aren't quite so busy."

"I can see that we need to talk." He was interrupted by a trio of men who wanted drinks, and he turned away. "What can I get for yeh?"

Maura poured three glasses of Paddy whiskey and carried them over to the table Harry had grabbed. "Here you go," she said, setting down the glasses and taking a seat herself. "Have I missed anything? Harry, is Eveline really all right?"

"She is, no thanks to us." Harry took a

long swallow of his drink and stared into what remained. "I realize now that I haven't been fair to her. Sure, her practical needs are met — the O'Briens are good and loyal people, and they'd be hard to replace. I hope Hurley's right and they won't be in any sort of trouble. But I'd sort of put Eveline on a shelf, in my mind. You know, 'old lady: taken care of; done.' It never occurred to me that she would feel shunted aside. Lonely, as you put it, Gillian. I wasn't paying attention — I just went about my life in Dublin."

"Harry, you have to work to keep the place going," Gillian said. "There are few jobs around here."

Harry looked at her with a brief smile. "Ah, love, you're making excuses for me. But, do you know, if I can sell that cursed painting, things would be a lot easier all around."

"Do you think you can just sell off your ancestor like that?" Maura asked.

Harry smiled. "Nobody ever liked the thing, and nobody's looked at it for years. From all I've ever heard, the old boy was a bit of a . . . what shall I say? A cad? A whacker? Come on, help me out here."

"Bounder? Rake?" Gillian suggested.

"Pond scum," Maura added.

"Any of the above will do. Bottom line, I wouldn't miss him or his painting, nor would Aunt Evie. If there's some museum or collector out there who's willing to come up with a few million euros, they're welcome to him. As I said earlier, I'll give Althea a shot at handling it, but I'd like Gillian here to keep her honest, so we get a fair price for it."

"I'm happy to help, Harry," Gillian said.

"Thanks. I appreciate it." A look passed between them, and Maura wondered if maybe the whole mess had opened Harry's eyes to what — or who — was right in front of him.

"What about Dorothy Ryan?" Maura said.

"Ah, right. Can we track her down?" Harry asked.

"No doubt Althea or Nate will know how to find her. But what do you want to do?"

"As far as I'm concerned, the small painting belongs to Dorothy, to do with as she pleases," Harry said. "If it comes to legal proof, I'm sure it exists, according to what Aunt Evie told us, and I'll be glad to pass it on to her."

"If Dorothy chooses to sell, I'd guess Althea's right — it would fetch more if it's linked to the painting here," Gillian commented. "But somebody has to explain it to her."

"You're kind of forgetting the other side of all this," Maura said. "She's a Townsend, even if she doesn't have the name."

"Maura, there's no estate or title to claim," Harry protested.

"That's not what I meant," Maura replied. "It's not about claims or money. She's family. Dorothy grew up thinking Mary Margaret Deasy was her grandmother. She barely knew her real grandmother, Jane, and only as some great-aunt she never saw. Her father was an only child. So no matter how you look at it, she hasn't got many relatives, on that side, at least. But Eveline is her great-aunt, same as she is yours. And you're some kind of cousin. So like I said, she's family, and she should at least have the chance to know that and maybe to meet you. And Eveline, before it's too late. And Sister Benedicta."

Gillian smiled her approval. Harry looked a bit stunned. "I never thought about that. Do you think Aunt Evie would like to meet her?"

"Of course, Harry," Gillian said. "The only grandchild of her favorite brother, and Joseph, who's his son? Let's see if we can make it happen, or at least get in touch with

Dorothy and offer her the chance. I can follow up on that too, if you like."

"Please," Harry said gratefully.

Maura took a look around the room. More and more people were coming in, and the noise level had definitely gone up. Rose had to get home, which meant Maura had better take over. She stood up. "Hey, guys, I'd better get to work. Let me know if I can help with anything." Not that she knew the first thing about high-end art auctions, but maybe she could offer Dorothy some advice, as one American to another, about how to deal with Ireland and unexpected relatives — now, *that* she did know a little about.

Maura was busy when Harry and Gillian slipped out not much later; Gillian waved on the way out the door. Nate and Althea hadn't shown up: maybe the gardaí had decided to hold them. Though Maura had a feeling she hadn't seen the last of Althea.

Sean Murphy came in an hour later, when the pub was full to overflowing. He waded through the crowd to the bar.

"Sean! You off duty now?" Maura had to yell to be heard.

"I am. I'll have a pint."

"Coming up," Maura replied and started filling yet another glass. "Everything wrapped up?"

"Let's say the process has begun. Ray is after telling us that he's a tourist here to visit relatives, but no one believes that. I think we've plenty of evidence against him to make a case. At least we know what happened to Seamus now."

"You believe Nate's story? Is Althea in the clear?"

"Most likely. And you can trust Detective Hurley to be fair."

"That's good. It's been kind of a crazy week, hasn't it? I mean, Althea just arrived here a week ago, and look at all that's happened." She topped off the pint and slid it across the bar to Sean. "I can't hear myself think — do you want to go outside?"

"Can't and take this," Sean yelled, holding up his glass. "Against the law."

"How about in back?" Maura led the way to the large, empty back room, where it was much quieter.

Sean appeared fascinated by the space. "I never knew this room was here. You've a bar back here as well?"

Maura surveyed the mess of jumbled tables and chairs and discarded equipment. "I really don't know the history of the place. I've been kind of waiting to see what business is like during the busy season before I decide if I need to use this part. And if I do,

I won't be able to get it cleaned up until fall."

"Looks like there's been music here, if not lately." Sean nodded toward what looked like a mishmash of drums and bulky amplifiers stashed on the balcony that ran around the upper part of the room.

"Could be. I can ask around, and I'll talk with Billy — I'm sure he'd know the whole story. So tell me, why haven't you arrested Ray?"

"It's about getting the warrant. It's not like in the States, from what I hear. We take a suspect into custody, and we can hold him for a time, but we have to request the warrant for the arrest itself directly from Dublin, and we have to present convincing evidence for it before they'll issue it."

"You mean, put the whole case together before you can get it? No wonder it's not easy. You think you have enough?"

"We do for Raymond Finneran. Is it the others yet worried about?"

"Not so much Nate, but maybe Althea. Althea may be annoying, but she didn't plan to kill anyone. According to her story, Ray attacked Nate, and she was only trying to help. Nate doesn't sound like the smartest guy, but he's not responsible for what Ray might have done. Well, maybe for his being here at all, but he couldn't have known what would happen."

"Maura Donovan, are you tellin' me yer stickin' up for Althea now?" Sean took a swig from his pint.

"Well, maybe. Kind of. She didn't ask for any of this."

"Do you know, Maura Donovan, you were a great help in our investigation. You watched and listened. If you hadn't put Althea together with Old Billy, Althea might have just given up and gone home."

Which might have been a better outcome for everyone, Maura thought. "I think she was pretty determined — she might have worked it out on her own."

"Not if no one would've talked to her. And you listened to Billy when he told you to talk with Bridget Nolan. There are some would've blown him off."

"I like Old Billy. He has a sharp memory, no matter what he looks like. Although I have noticed he puts on kind of an act for tourists, but it gets him plenty of free drinks."

"I'm not surprised. What I'm trying to say is, Detective Hurley sends his thanks. And I thank you as well. You've done me a good turn, helping me out with this. It looks good on the record, that I've had a hand in solving another murder."

Maura could feel herself blushing. "Well, thank you, I guess."

They both fell into an awkward silence, and for a wild moment Maura wondered if Sean was thinking of kissing her — and realized that maybe she wanted him to. Before either of them could decide, Mick ducked his head in the doorway.

"Maura, can you lend a hand out here? The word's out about the murders, and it's mad busy."

"I'd better go," Maura told Sean. "I've got a business to run."

"I'll be seeing you later, then," Sean said.

CHAPTER 30

It turned out to be one of the busiest nights Maura had seen at Sullivan's. The solution of Seamus Daly's murder combined with a juicy story about the local nobs had everyone buzzing — and buying pints. Maura was glad she knew a lot of what had happened behind the scenes, but she restricted herself to correcting errors rather than spreading gossip — there was enough of that floating around the pub without her adding to it.

Billy Sheahan stuck around for a couple of hours early in the evening, but Maura wasn't worried that he'd say too much. He was more discreet than most people gave him credit for. Gillian and Harry had left together, and Harry'd had an arm over Gillian's shoulder — had they gone home together? Maybe this past week had shaken Harry up a bit, made him look at things in a new light, but whether he would stay with Gillian was another question. Maura was pretty sure that Eveline would like that, though.

Mick was shooing the last patrons out the door at closing time when Maura saw Althea come in, looking drained. Long gone was the New York fashionista she'd been only a week earlier. Mick arched an eyebrow at Maura, and Maura mouthed, "It's okay." Mick took one last look around the room, then went out, closing the door behind him. His day was over.

Althea approached the bar tentatively. "Am I welcome here?"

"Sure. You want something to drink?"

"Isn't it past closing time? I don't want to risk breaking any more Irish laws than I already have."

"I can offer a drink to a friend, if I like."

"Thank you. For the 'friend' part, I mean. I'll take a Jameson's, if you have it. Will you have one with me?"

Maura found two clean glasses and poured. She slid them across the bar, then came around to sit on the stool next to Althea's. "So the guards didn't hold you?"

"No. It took me this long to talk my way out of there, but you were right. That detective is a fair man, and a thorough one. I'm glad he believed me in the end. I'm not a criminal, just stupid."

Maura didn't contradict her. She sipped her whiskey — not her favorite drink, but she had to admit this one was smooth. "And Nate?"

"That's a little more complicated. The police aren't very happy with him, mostly because he concealed a lot of things, and there were consequences. They may keep him around for a while."

"Do you believe he had anything to do with Seamus's death?"

Althea shook her head. "Not beyond bringing that Jersey goon here. Nate's an idiot, but I'm glad Ray isn't dead — that would have been a real mess. And I wouldn't want to think I'd killed someone, even by accident."

They sat in silence for a minute or two. Finally Althea said, "Maura, I'm really here to apologize. You've been great about trying to help me, and all I've done is complain and make demands. You and Gillian both — you tried to tell me to dial it back, and I didn't want to hear it."

"You had a lot at stake," Maura said carefully.

"Sure, I thought finding that painting was important, but I've realized I was only thinking of myself. I never stopped to think that looking for it and finding it would

428

involve so many other people's lives. I never thought anyone would die because of it."

Maura sneaked a glance at her. Were those tears in Althea's eyes? "What are you going to do now?"

"I . . . don't know. I mean, I — no, *we* found the painting and it's everything I hoped it would be, and it's a terrific story, but . . ."

"What?"

"I don't feel right using that for my own ends. Not after all that's happened."

"You go public with the story, and it's worth more. You told me that," Maura pointed out.

"I know. But . . . I guess it's not as important to me to get it into that exhibit and to have my moment of glory as it was when I started. I can still work to get the word out, so that Eveline and Harry will benefit. Somebody in the world — and I'd like to hope it's a museum rather than a private collector who'll hide it away for another century — will get an incredible painting. But I don't want to profit from something that caused someone's death."

"Why, Althea, I do believe you've grown a conscience!" Maura said, smiling.

Althea looked at her then and returned the smile. "Ya think?" They clinked glasses.

Then Althea went on, "You know, I should spend more time talking with you. I mean, you've got to have a story, right? You can't have had an easy life, growing up in South Boston, losing your family, not a lot of opportunities. And here you are, where you never expected to be, and it looks to me like you're doing just fine. How did that happen?"

"Ireland happened. I think you've seen some of that. Time seems slower here. People are willing to help you, if you'll give them a chance. I've got deep roots here, ones I never knew I had. I'm still trying to figure out how and where I fit, but it's a good place to be."

"Maybe I should stick around a while longer, or come back after the exhibit opens. I wonder if Harry would let me inventory his collection of paintings. At least then he'd know what he's got. Maybe I could bring Dorothy and her father over and introduce them to the rest of the family. And I could still help Gillian place some of her paintings where they'll get more attention. She really does have talent."

"All good ideas, but it's up to you. I've got enough on my hands here without trying to manage *your* life."

"You couldn't do worse than I have

lately!" Althea laughed. "Anyway, I just wanted to thank you for everything. I guess I'd better get back to the hotel — I'm exhausted."

"Slán abhaile," Maura said. When Althea looked blankly at her she said, "That means 'safe home' in Irish."

"Ah. Well, thanks again."

Maura watched her go, to make sure she got safely to her car. She did and drove off, leaving Maura alone in Sullivan's.

Chalk up one more victory for Ireland, Maura thought. Funny how the place changed people.

ABOUT THE AUTHOR

Sheila Connolly is the *New York Times* bestselling, Anthony and Agatha award–nominated author of the Orchard Mysteries, the Museum Mysteries, and the County Cork Mysteries. She has taught art history, structured and marketed municipal bonds for major cities, worked as a staff member on two statewide political campaigns, and served as a fundraiser for several nonprofit organizations. She also managed her own consulting company, providing genealogical research services. In addition to genealogy. Sheila loves restoring old houses, visiting cemeteries, and traveling. Now a full-time writer, she thinks writing mysteries is a lot more fun than any of her previous occupations.

She is married and has one daughter and two cats. Visit her online at sheilaconnolly .com.